KARI HOTAKAINEN was born breakthrough came in 1997 Finlandia Prize, which he late... written children's plays, radio dramas, newspaper columns a... television scripts.

OWEN F. WITESMAN's translations from Finnish include Juhani Aho's classic *The Railroad*, Petri Tamminen's *Hiding Places*, Anita Konkka's *A Fool's Paradise* (co-translator) and several forthcoming crime novels and thrillers.

"A beautifully crafted tale of bereavement, intimate human suffering and the curious specks of reparation that death can bring . . . This is a stunning book"   SARAH PEACH, *Time Out*

"Funny and extremely dark . . . he paints a very dystopian picture of present-day Finland . . . Full of an intriguing weirdness, scenes that have haunted me"   HARRIET GILBERT, *BBC World Book Club*

"Kari Hotakainen . . . quietly but effectively, the marketisation and marginalisation of Finnish life . . . in a novel packed with sophisticated ideas which should, like a rare delicacy, be savoured slowly"   SCARLETT MCCGWIRE, *Tribune*

"Hotakainen intimately and humorously depicts a family with a strong matriach at its centre . . . Salme's gentle homespun philosophy . . . lingers beautifully after this quaint and quirky book is closed"   CLAIRE LOOBY, *Irish Times*

"This is an extremely clever book, which is also deeply witty. Splendid!"   *Image Magazine*

"Dammit MacLehose are so good. They've just published another cracker of a story . . . The thing that makes this book so good is the perfect balance Hotakainen strikes between humour and gravitas. I devoured it and found it quite unexpectedly moving. I know it's one I will return to" *The Lady Loves Books*

"A remarkable and affecting work of fiction" *Complete Review*

"Exactly what I usually look for: a book that examines the darkness at the heart of the human condition . . . A beautiful package that won't disappoint on any level" *Reader Dad*

"This is a book that, though set in Finland, can ring true to everyone in this modern world" *Winston's Dad*

"In its satire of society, in holding up a mirror to the absurdities and things taken for granted in contemporary life, I felt *The Human Part* was one of the more succesful books I have read" *Iris on Books*

"This book was instantly engaging and I fell in love with Salme, the elderly woman, and the way she wasn't afraid to put her viewpoint across . . . [it] did a fantastic job of explaining the complex mixture of emotions that exist within a family and how life changes as everyone grows up" *Farm Lane Books*

"Told in a beautiful, terse style with a few laugh-out-loud moments to alleviate what is, essentially, a bleak story of human frailty and failure. The book is also especially withering about what Hotakainen clearly sees as the absurdity of parts of modern corporate culture" FRANK PATRICK MORGAN, *The National*

THE HUMAN PART

Kari Hotakainen

Translated from the Finnish by
Owen F. Witesman

MACLEHOSE PRESS
QUERCUS · LONDON

First published in the Finnish language as *Ihmisen osa*
by Siltala Publishing, Helsinki, 2009
First published in Great Britain in 2012 by MacLehose Press
This paperback edition published in 2013 by

MacLehose Press
an imprint of Quercus
55 Baker Street
7th Floor, South Block
London W1U 8EW

This work has been published with the financial assistance of

FILI
FINNISH LITERATURE EXCHANGE

ISBN (MMP) 978 0 85705 106 6
ISBN (Ebook) 978 0 857383 56 3

10 9 8 7 6 5 4 3 2 1

Designed and typeset in Collis by Libanus Press, Marlborough
Printed and bound in Great Britain by Clays Ltd, St Ives plc

TRANSLATOR'S ACKNOWLEDGEMENT

The translator would like to thank Soila Lehtonen, Anne Colin du Terrail, Vladimír Piskor and the author for their help and assistance.

THE FIRST PART

THE SELLER

My name is Salme Sinikka Malmikunnas, and everything that I say will be printed word for word in this book. The author promised me this. In alarm, he even suggested that my words be printed *in italics*, which apparently emphasizes the importance of words. When I saw what he meant by *italics*, I immediately said that I didn't want it. I'm already bent over enough without calling any more attention to it. I admit that I gave the author a little bit of a tongue-lashing over this, so he promised me heaven and earth. I might have been a little over-excited, since it was the first time I had seen or met a person like him.

First of all, and in partial defence of myself, I should say that I do not like made-up books or the people who write them. It has always irritated me that they are taken seriously, that people get so immersed in them and listen so carefully to the people who write them. I am now referring to the novels and other things on the shelves labelled "fiction" or "translated fiction". It irritated me even more when Paavo and I found out that people go all the way to other countries to find these made-up stories and that people who have studied languages transfer these obvious lies over into our language.

I will not speak evil of non-fiction though, because that includes books whose very titles inspire confidence: *The Birth of the Solar System. The History of Finland. Birds, Past and Present. Mammals (Colour Illustrated).*

And of course the encyclopedia.

We have that book too, and it has been a delight. We haven't had to wonder if it's true or if it might be some amateur's clumsy fantasy or delusion. No matter what page you turn to, the mysteries of human life are revealed. Where do the starlings fly? What is the difference between a chimpanzee and an orangutan? How large and powerful a country was Sweden in bygone days, and from where do its prosperity, good humour and communal spirit come? Sometimes we forget about it, living right here next door, but you can check in the encyclopedia.

But no book tells what will happen next Tuesday or when Paavo and I go dark upstairs once and for all. What happens when the lights go out? In your head, I mean. Does some gateway open up, and what does it open on to? Since no-one knows, we have all these alternative theories, the religions I mean. Just to be safe, I believe in all of the gods that they recommend in books, in magazines, and on television. Or, of course, not in the ones that you worship with a tuft of feathers on your head and rings in your nose. Paavo doesn't believe in any gods. He doesn't believe in anything he hasn't seen. He didn't even believe in Onni Suuronen before he saw him. I had to take him to another county by bus to see Onni riding his motorcycle like a bat out of hell around that wooden track. "He does exist," Paavo kept repeating to himself on the return trip. "But show me Our Lord Jesus Christ and God the Father. Show me. You can't," Paavo said over and over. I said, as I have a million times in my life, "Not so loud. People will hear."

You are wondering how I could have met an author – me, who does not respect authors of made-up books. It was a complete coincidence. Life has thrown all sorts of things in front of me, even though I haven't gone looking for anything. It happened that my eldest, my daughter Helena, invited me to visit the capital. Usually I don't go anywhere, but I agreed to this invitation because of a certain very sad thing.

It was October when I came to the capital.

The name of the station was Pasila.

Helena lived right nearby but said first thing on the platform that we couldn't go to her house because there she would be reminded of it immediately. Helena suggested that we go to the book fair to start with. I wasn't at all eager when I found out that, in addition to books, the people who write them would also be there. Helena pleaded, and I couldn't stand to hurt my daughter's feelings. Let me interject here that Paavo had stayed home, because he was temporarily mute.

They had built an enormous hall for their exhibitionism. There were at least three entrances. We went in through the biggest one and paid a total of twenty-four euros for two people. I thought that it would include at least lunch and coffee, but Helena said we didn't get any food for that price, but that there was all the more nourishment for the soul.

The place was black with people.

It was an anthill.

Noise came from every direction.

Big platforms had been set up everywhere and on the platforms podiums to which the authors were led.

We stopped in front of one of the platforms. Above it was written in big letters "Katri Vala". I don't know that person, but soon some queen-bee-looking woman approached the podium and began oozing flattery, bumbling and buzzing around, practically rubbing up against the author sitting behind her on a chair. Doting and warbling. She sang his praises and blew him kisses. It was good she didn't sit down on his lap. And in conclusion she reminded everyone about the discount they would get on the book at such-and-such a stand and on which stool this poor unfortunate soul would be sitting, happy to write his name in this unique work.

It was as good as a play, and after watching and listening to it without coffee and buns for an hour or two, I started longing for truth from the very bottom of my heart. Not that I've never lied in my life, but at least I haven't put those lies between the covers of a book.

I talked Helena into going for coffee at a sort of little booth in the main hallway. I didn't dare express my opinions to my daughter, even though I wanted to. Helena wanted to smoke. We were directed out through a large door, behind the building.

And there I saw him, the author, although I didn't immediately recognize him as such with these eyes. He was just some man, sitting on a grit box, smoking a cigarette, glancing around nervously. I couldn't guess his age because nowadays everyone is younger than I am. He looked like a maintenance man, and that's probably why I started chatting him up. He answered my questions uncertainly, and I quickly realized that this was no maintenance man. They are energetic – this one was skittish.

Helena didn't say anything. She was embarrassed by my talkativeness. Children are always ashamed of something in their parents. There's no use being offended by it.

I said to the man that there wasn't any need to play at being any smarter than he was. I could see he wasn't a maintenance worker, but that didn't matter. We could talk all we wanted since we were at a fair for lies, after all. Helena gave me the evil eye, but I stayed positive.

The man was a quiet sort, but that didn't bother me, the wife of a mute. I said to him that if I were to write a book, I would start with non-fiction and write everything just as it is, not how it should be. I could write a book about crocheting or rug weaving or baking Boston cake any old day, but I don't feel like it. And good books like that have already been written anyway. For example, *Cooking for Every Home* is the sort of book that there's no reason to write all over again. I got it from my grandma and everything in it still holds true. I've bought a copy for each of my children, and they've never wanted for soups and roasts.

The man nodded. He was clearly a listener. Or he didn't have anything to add. Helena was already trying to hustle me inside. Her cigarette was down to a stub. I found myself saying to Helena that she should go ahead, that I would catch up soon. Helena looked at me for a long time, gauging whether I was serious. I gave her a look that told her everything was O.K. I felt like talking to a complete stranger. It would give me a little vacation from Helena's big thing.

When I was left alone there with the man, I had to introduce myself – I couldn't be there otherwise. With a name, a person is at least connected to something. I gave the man mine, and he gave me his, which I've already forgotten. I said I was a retired yarn dealer. He was encouraged by this, and announced that he was an author. He followed this immediately by saying that he didn't have anything to do at the fair this time, because he hadn't published a new book.

I wondered why he had bothered to show up then. He said he had been given a free ticket. I asked if it wasn't a little difficult to be at his workplace when he was unemployed. He didn't reply.

It occurred to me to say what I thought about authors and made-up stories, but it didn't feel necessary anymore. I asked when his next book would be coming – surely he was working on it. The author didn't reply. He just quickly lit another cigarette. He held it with his thumb and forefinger, which told me he was not a regular smoker.

We observed a moment of silence. I had become used to that with Paavo, but silence with a stranger is different, loud almost.

I was already making to leave when he asked what sort of life I had lived. It isn't proper to ask things like that of strangers, but somehow it didn't feel intrusive just then. I said I had lived so much that I hadn't had time to brush my teeth properly. I told him all sorts of things about this and that, jumping from one thing to another – I may have even used a couple of swear words – I just let it come at a sort of low boil, but I didn't go into detail.

He wanted to know more.

I said that I wasn't going to go telling any more just like that. I wasn't going to make that mistake a second time. Once, sitting on a bench at the hospital waiting for Paavo's test results, I told a stranger about my life. My burden was lightened, but in the wrong way. I was overcome by the feeling that something of my own life had remained with that other person.

Then the author made his proposal.

If I would tell him about my life, he would give me five thousand euros.

I had to sit down.

I was a little afraid.

Helena was somewhere in the crowd, and I didn't have a mobile phone – I had left it with Paavo. I had never been offered five thousand euros for anything. The author said that I could think it over for an hour, perhaps with my daughter. I asked what on earth the author would do with my life. He said he didn't have any life of his own and that he wanted to write one more book.

I was more afraid. I felt like saying, "Come on, everyone has their own life."

I stood up. I didn't dare stay sitting down to think about something so outlandish. The display designer Alfred Supinen always said that a person should think about difficult things standing up, and that for the most difficult things you should go out walking.

I thought the author was clearly insane, but there was no point in going and telling that to an insane person. They don't have the same understanding of human nature as the rest of us, who know full well that we go insane now and then. A truly insane person lives inside his insanity like a pearl inside an oyster.

I said I wasn't going to start selling my life, the only thing I truly owned, and that the author would be best off writing what he knew the most about – his own life. He claimed that there wasn't anything to write about, that nothing had ever happened to him. I pressed him about how he had managed to write up until then if he didn't have anything to tell and nothing had happened. The author claimed that it was perfectly reasonable to write ten books out of nothing, but no more than that.

It wasn't my fault if he didn't have anything to write, I thought – there wasn't any sense in dumping it on me.

The author said that I could get all sorts of things in this world for five thousand euros, and my own life in hardcover into the bargain.

After that I had to say that I hated made-up books, and the worst thing would be for someone to make up my life all over again for some book. He practically flew into raptures over this, saying that was exactly what he had planned to do. He needed a good life as a foundation, and on top of it he would invent more, and the final result would be an even better life than what the one on the bottom had been originally.

To hell with that! Putting my life on the bottom, as if it were worse than the made-up one. And paying me five thousand euros for this disgrace. Suddenly if felt like a very small sum.

The author thought I was taking everything the wrong way now. My life wouldn't be lost – it would be there underneath, a little like the soil under a beautiful planting. Truth and fiction would inter-twine and together be more than they would have been separately.

His explanation just confused this old woman even more.

So that I would not become completely confused, I started think-ing about the money. It's a good thing to think about. It gives you a scale. People speak far too much evil of money. Sometimes it's the only thing that clearly delineates people's intentions.

I ordered the author to be quiet while I thought.

I counted in my mind all the good things I could get with that much money. The first things that occurred to me were new curtains, fixing up our old car, garden furniture, a winter fur coat, and perhaps a spa vacation. I didn't beat myself up over all of the things that would bring me pleasure that came to mind before the most important thing, the thing that was weighing on my heart.

Suddenly everything was completely clear. I knew exactly what I would do with the money.

At the same time I decided that I wouldn't tell Helena or Paavo anything about this.

As a former button merchant, I knew the value of money and understood that this was a seller's market. There was only one life for sale here behind this building, so I decided to raise the price. I said it would cost him seven thousand euros. I calculated that with that much I could get all the good I wouldn't have any possibility of getting otherwise.

The author became uneasy, saying he had already sold everything he owned to get the five thousand together. He raised his hands at his sides, claiming there was nowhere he could get two thousand euros more from. I knew from experience that a person could dig that kind of money from the frozen ground with his bare hands if he really wanted something badly enough. I remembered how Helena had squatted in a strawberry field for three sweltering weeks with a sore back to get to go see some filthy-looking singer at a hippie festival in Turku.

I told the author the price was determined by what I had seen and experienced and that for the price mentioned he would get a marketable, truthful life, the authenticity of which nobody would have any reason to doubt. I found myself falling into the pattern of speech of my old life, as if I were selling yarn, needles and buttons.

I was ashamed to raise the price, but I didn't regret it, because the more I thought about my life, the more precious it felt. It was a result of my age and everything that had happened recently.

As a twenty-something just graduated from business school, I would have sold my life for a few hundred.

The author said I was taking advantage of his desperate situation by raising the price. I reminded him of our roles. He wanted to buy something that I wasn't selling. I also emphasized that I didn't know a single thing about his situation in life, but I told him there were bigger emergencies in this world than one author's lack of inspiration. I also said that if the price felt too high, he could feel free to visit another shop. This time our price was firm – there wasn't any wiggle room.

The author went quiet. As a former saleswoman, I recognized what was happening. The customer was playing for time. He knew he was going to buy, but was resisting finally giving in. He hated the salesperson, who had set a firm price for a product he had to have. He had to buy, but had to not buy. He had to want, but had to resist. In a situation like this, the salesperson's job is to help the shy customer over the stream with dry feet. I didn't have time.

The author said he was going to accept the price, but that he needed extra time for the two thousand. I didn't want to wait for the money for long, so I asked him a very personal question. "Have you really and truly sold all of your property? Isn't there something left sitting in a corner that you could bear to give up? An old chest of drawers or a lumpy glass vase designed by some celebrity?"

The author denied owning anything anymore that he could give up for two thousand euros, but he thought his publisher might give him an advance on the upcoming book if the content seemed promising.

I agreed to the delay, and we made an oral agreement for the payment of the five thousand. I put out my hand. His handshake was firm. Just as I had extracted my hand, Helena walked up.

I felt guilty, as if I'd just committed a sin, even though I had made an agreement that would end up benefiting Helena. Helena asked why on earth I had stayed outside for more than half an hour. She had had time to start thinking all sorts of horrible things. I felt like saying I've just made a big sale, all for your good, but I just said my how time had flown chatting with this craftsman about the stairway renovation we've talked about so many times at home. I shot a glance at the author to tell him not a word now about the agreement we just made.

Helena tried to hustle me inside. I said I would be there in two minutes. Helena asked what I needed the two minutes for. I said that this carpenter here is from a village near ours, and I still have to work out the details of the remodel with him.

Helena said she would wait in front of the Mikael Agricola platform.

The whole train ride home I thought about selling my life. Did I do right or wrong? At the yarn shop I never needed to think about questions like that, because I knew that the customer would get a sweater out of the yarn, and that we were getting the difference between the wholesale price and the retail price. Everyone stayed warm.

Now all sorts of dark thoughts were running through my mind. They have a name: "moral questions". God left them to us, since he doesn't have time to be everywhere. I wasn't used to thinking about such things, because Paavo and I had lived a rather straightforward, simple life. Sitting there in the window seat, I thought, now, Salme, you've taken what they talk about so much in the business papers, a "risk".

But turning back wasn't an option – it would have been against my nature. I remembered how once Paavo and I bought a big lot of violet and orange yarn at wholesale on the risk that people might not be ready for a whimsical colour palette. We were selling that batch for a long time, but I never once thought about returning the yarn or selling at a loss. That would have been a mortifying concession to drab colours.

I bought a coffee and the most expensive pastry in the restaurant car. I wanted to celebrate that for the first time in my life I had sold something that could not be touched. I knew from my children and having watched this new world from the sidelines that there were many invisible goods for sale, but I could never have imagined that I would be charging for such a thing myself.

You always want to tell the people closest to you about big things that happen to you, but this time I couldn't. After returning home, I told Paavo that given the circumstances Helena was doing well and that I had come up with a way to improve her situation. Paavo nodded and disappeared into the shed.

I felt like crying. I didn't have the nerve to weep indoors, so I went into the back yard. Water came from my eyes, but I didn't make any sound. In five minutes I was back in dry, working order.

I called the author from our shared mobile and we arranged a meeting for the following week at a certain out-of-the-way service station between our village and the capital. I explained to Paavo that I was going on a trip with my *raanu* group. He bought it. I had taken little trips to neighbouring counties before with the other members of the weaving circle at the community centre.

The author counselled me to be as open and talkative as possible at our upcoming meeting. Apparently a book is a sort of cross between a cow and a pig that swallows huge amounts of life, which it then ruminates, softens up and digests. As a result of this process, out the other end pops a solid, compact mass packed in natural intestine, a high-quality organic sausage ready for the reader. I didn't like his metaphorical language, which brought to mind awkward, even embarrassing thoughts, but I promised to tell him his money's worth.

I was afraid, sitting there at that table in that ugly service station with a small coffee and a dictaphone in front of me, but the fear was moderated by the two-and-a-half thousand euros sitting in a neat pile next to the dictaphone. The author said that it was best to take the money off the table so the service station staff wouldn't get the wrong idea. I felt like saying that given how far things had gone already, I wasn't interested in anyone's wrong ideas, or even their right ideas.

The author looked me in the eyes and said, "The dictaphone is on now. Give me your life."

And I did.

I told the dictaphone everything, exactly how things have gone. I described precisely what my life, Paavo's life and our children's lives have been like. There weren't two words together in there that weren't as true as true can be, so I would think it would be painless to write it down. No-one could miss the mark writing such a clear account. No-one could write it wrong.

My name is Salme Malmikunnas, and I have four children. One of them died when he was four years old, but he is still my child. I have one husband, Paavo. He always has been my husband, and he always will be, even though he doesn't talk right now. We had two girls and two boys. We had that kind of luck. Unfortunately, one went and rode his tricycle into the septic tank. The service men had gone for a smoke and left the cover open. And he had to ride just there. I can't speak about it, because the words lift him up and sit him right down here at this table, and I start to think about how old he would be now and what life would have had in store for him. I'm sorry, but I'm going to keep you there in that hole for now, Heikki.

Here at the beginning I was going to say what the difference is between a lie and the truth. A lie sticks in your head. It's like a migraine. The truth, on the other hand, is like a boomerang. It hits you in the forehead, wakes you up nicely, and then continues from there off to the horizon. Truth doesn't belong to anyone. I say this because I've had bad experiences with lying. I hope the author will take this seriously. If I start to lie, I disappear almost completely. It's a sort of vanishing, lying is. The outlines disappear and before you know it you're in a big whiteness, i.e. nowhere. The boomerang knocks you on the forehead and takes you back to the world of colour.

But it isn't possible to understand a person completely. Paavo and Alfred Supinen and I talked about this a long time ago. According to Alfred, a human being is a long, symphonic piece of music. You have to listen to the overture, the principal theme, the crescendos and the finale, and then when the piece is over, there is still the silence. You have to listen to that too. Alfred thought that a person continues on even after he dies. Alfred didn't mean this in the Christian sense of a second life, but rather in the sense that the person remains in our memories.

It's difficult to speak about your own children with outsiders, because you love them so impossibly much. But I feel like I can tell a dictaphone.

The oldest of my children is Helena. No, no. This isn't going anywhere. I'm going to have to skip over Helena for right now, because of the big thing that happened. The dictaphone will have to do without that for now. I can talk about it separately. What's the saying? Off the record.

Of the boys, Pekka was born first, and two years later came Heikki, the one who isn't anymore. Then a few years went by, and Maija arrived.

Pekka was wild and free, and he enjoyed life because there was already one small person in the house. Our first born, Helena, was born to responsibility, and you never get over that feeling. That was why Helena moved away from home as soon as possible. Pekka embraced life as if it were a toy. He resembled a puppy, toddling from place to place, falling on his face, blowing his nose and then continuing on. That animation only went away later, when he started listening to strange music and got caught up in those thoughts of his. Did he start thinking about his dead brother or what? It's anyone's guess. It's peculiar how a person can disappear, even though he's still in the same house. He even disappears from himself, not knowing how he should be, sad or happy, angry or gentle. Pekka was everything all at once. There wasn't any way to tell him, though. Once Paavo did, and

Pekka moved into the forest for two days. He came back out with his stuttering problem. A problem like that, and just before puberty. Stuttering separates you from others at just the age when you start looking for connections. Of course, we tried to love Pekka out of his speech defect, but according to the doctor, love isn't always enough. It left such a deep mark on him that as an adult he still stutters when he gets into a flustering or stressful situation. He doesn't recognize it himself, but I can hear it. When the money spigot opened up in the late '80s, all that came out of Pekka's mouth was broken words. And the same thing a year later when we entered the recession. Again his throat chopped everything he was explaining over the telephone into little pieces. I'm ashamed to say it, but I read his state of mind from his stuttering.

More light flooded from Maija than from the others, just like there was an incandescent bulb behind her eyes. It felt like all love flowed over Maija like liquid honey. All children should be able to be born last. Helena and Pekka surrounded Maija and kissed her so much that for a long time she must have thought the world and our living room were paradise. And sometimes they were. When the children were all asleep when they were small, Paavo and I would sit in each other's arms on the sofa and whisper about our bliss as if using louder voices would break it.

I guess I could go ahead and say a little about Helena when she was small. When you're really looking forward to something, some of that expectation can be transferred into the thing you were waiting for. We wanted a child so badly that when we finally got one, we didn't quite know how to rejoice over her, having had to be so terribly afraid and anxious. That fear and anxiety are definitely visible in Helena. She was a serious, skittish child. She would sit up suddenly at night and look at us, the lamp and the nightstand clock with her big eyes. As if she were checking to make sure everything was true, that everyone was still alive. She would make mud pies, but wouldn't chant "Pat-a-cake, pat-a-cake, baker's man". When any adult came to visit, she would go and hide under the table and peek out from underneath. Alfred Supinen tried to coax her out, singing, "I found my gal in Karelia, found her small and sweet, hey, hey." But our gal stayed under the table. Helena laughed so little that for a while we thought she didn't like this life at all. I remember when her laugh came. On the television she saw a little man who was walking, rocking back and forth, with a little hat on his head, running into door jambs and long boards that construction men were carrying on their shoulders It was that Chaplin guy. When the programme ended, Helena said, "Again." If they had films on cassette back then, we would have bought all of Chaplin's inventions for Helena. Then later came Laurel and Hardy, but she didn't laugh at them at all. No-one in our family did. I hated those men. There wasn't any variety in how things went wrong. It was always the little one sobbing and the fat one hitting him on the head with a newspaper. Life isn't like that. Sometimes the roles change.

Helena grew up by accident. When you have lots of children, you don't realize that the first one is suddenly at the door, even though she was just sucking at your breast. One day she said seriously, "I'm leaving now." There was no rebellion or anger in her voice. It was just that serious undercurrent of hers. At the train station, Paavo and I had no idea how to be. A person isn't prepared in any way for her child to become an adult. Nor for her child to be taken away – not completely, but piece by piece. She looked out the grey window of the blue train, newborn and young woman in the same face.

Now I'm jumping from one topic to another. The dictaphone is good, because I don't even notice it. Paavo always says I can't stay on one topic, that I'm always moving on to something else in the middle of everything. Paavo can stay on one topic for a long time. His record is probably four years. Now he's going for a new record. The event this time is muteness.

So, Pekka had the speech impediment. He tried to be good at something else. There's research about this. I read in a medical book that if a person has some physical defect, let's say he doesn't have a left hand, then the right hand will grow really, really strong. The strength of the left transfers into the right. Just like blind people have extremely sharp hearing. So our Pekka was a stutterer and started to make up for it by copying people, the way they walked and their postures. Whenever a visitor came over, Pekka would sit quietly and look at him. When the visitor had left, Pekka would go over and sit in his place and begin to imitate his movements. He was talented and knew it. The other children watched like it was theatre. It was better than television. When the stuttering let up once he was older, I secretly thought he might become an actor. Pekka found his place in business, which we are of course proud of. There isn't a direct need for the imitator's skills in that field, but you do need to be able to put yourself in the customer's shoes.

Opposites attract. This isn't my own idea – it's the truth. Maija is full of light, so she had to seek out darkness. She was so impossibly fascinated with people's dark sides. It started with bottle spinning, and then came all the spiritualism nonsense, and then to top it all off, she took up with a negro. I'm using the word "negro" here, and if the dictaphone will last, I'll get this all out of the way right now. If the author sees fit to use the official name later, something like African-American, then let him, but let's go with "negro" for the rest of this session. And besides: from their first meeting the negro called Paavo "paleface".

Yes. Well. Our life changed a lot twenty years ago when Maija wrote saying she had found a love and would like to come and show him to us. When Maija stepped out of the train on the arm of a black man, Paavo leaned against me for support and whispered that we should turn back.

I dragged Paavo along, and we walked towards them. Maija smiled and said that here was her love. He was as black as pitch and looked like a spirit being. His eyes burned red in the darkness of his face and he held our daughter under his arm as if she were prey he had captured. He said something in English. Maija translated that her love had never visited the Finnish countryside before. Paavo said that he would do well to remember his first impressions carefully, because he wouldn't get a second chance.

Maija started to cry. I had to take over the situation. I felt faint, but I didn't let myself be overcome. If I've learned anything, it is forgetting myself. The world is what it is. And this time it was big and black. I whispered to Paavo that whomever our daughter has chosen, we will welcome him into our home. We walked to the car, loaded the bags and set off driving. Only humans are capable of silence like that.

I looked in the rearview mirror. I saw Maija's tears and black fingers stroking my daughter's hair. I would have liked to break those fingers and stop time and the car, but the road just went on. It always does. You can get off if you die.

We came into the yard, and Paavo walked into the bedroom and didn't come out all evening. The next morning he gave Maija a piece of graph paper and walked to the shed. A whacking sound started. He was chopping wood. He always split wood when his world was broken. I knew my husband, and I said to Maija and the black man that we should eat breakfast now without him. I asked Maija to tell the black man that every ingredient of a balanced human diet was represented on the table and that we could feel just as comfortable together as we wished.

The black man took everything and lots of it. I thought that was a good sign. A clear display of appetite engenders trust. Maija just sobbed, not managing to eat anything. It made me feel sorry for her and irritated me at the same time. She was my child of light, and she had chosen a black man from a distant continent. These two things were true, and it was also true that I had gone to a great deal of trouble over the scrambled eggs, porridge, cold cuts and fresh bread. The importance of food in easing distress is enormous. I've spoken about this with all of my children, both together and separately, reminding them that Paavo and I had lived in a world where there was no yogurt, no muesli, and none of those lovely croissants that leave butter and flaky chips of dough on the corners of your mouth to accompany your tears.

I said to Maija, "Now we're going to eat well, and then we'll have a long, hard talk. You'll get to translate a lot of questions into that foreign language. We'll sit in soft chairs and talk. We're white and he's black. We'll start from this truth and not be afraid of anything. Dad will chop wood, and we'll talk. Silence isn't golden, it's scrap iron."

Maija didn't say anything. She just held out the piece of graph paper her father had given her. It said, "You took a black man. Give me a call sometime."

What galled Maija the most was that he had the nerve to write about calling even though he knew well enough that Maija didn't have a telephone.

I took the piece of paper and said I would be back soon. I went to the shed, interrupted Paavo's swing in midair and ordered him to set the axe aside for a moment because I had something to say. I showed him the paper, crumpled it up and said, "First come thoughts, then the alphabet. On this paper the order is backwards."

I returned to Maija and the black man and said that Paavo would be coming for breakfast in a week. Maija smiled and said that her love had a name, Biko. Pronounced with as soft a "B" as possible.

And it did come softly from Maija's mouth. I asked her to translate that Paavo and I would have to get used to the new situation and that getting used to something can take a while. Biko opened his mouth and out came who-knows-what for a long time. I asked Maija to translate as honestly as possible. Biko wanted to say that he was fully aware of the influence of the colour of a black man on his surroundings, but that he had not been able to choose the colour; if he had, he would have rather chosen red, the colour of love. Biko also said that he intended to love Maija no matter what, in every condition, before anyone and everyone, even in the middle of Finland. Wood can be chopped and tears can be shed, but his love was and would remain.

I made up an excuse to go into the kitchen and then came back with new eyes and said that we haven't had much chance to practise diversity in this country, since the youth of one generation was taken up with wars and that of the next with coping with the aftermath, that because of this we had to proceed with slow steps, but looking each other in the eye the whole way.

The most important thing to me was and is that he loved and loves my daughter. I said to him, and Maija translated, that this country isn't finished yet, even though it has been built up a lot. It isn't ready for a person of your colour, since it's only just suitable for us greys. You'll have to get used to all sorts of things. If you're the touchy sort, you'll be offended the whole time. Grow a thick skin. But not so thick that you can't feel a person's hand through it.

Biko nodded and told how he came from a country that won't be finished for a long time, where a person's life costs as much as a chicken drumstick does here. He also said that it was best to think of one person at a time, not whole nations.

Out of a whole nation he had chosen our Maija, and I had to live with that fact. In this world I've never had a shed I could run to away from my troubles.

It was a big job to get Paavo to speak that time. I forced myself to speak to him constantly. Even though he didn't respond for a long time. I didn't give up. I was a peace negotiator just like our President Ahtisaari.

One evening Paavo came out of the shed and said, "Well, show me the picture then."

I took the picture I had taken myself out of my handbag. In it, Maija and Biko sat side-by-side, and they had that glow in their eyes. Paavo knows that glow – it comes from love. Normal eyes glisten with tears and exhaustion, but the eyes of love have a unique lustre, similar to sautéed onions. Paavo said, "Maija has her own life."

The dictaphone was spinning, but my head had stopped.

The author noticed the silence and turned the device off. He suggested taking a break. I realized I was dreadfully hungry. The life I had been telling had eaten up my energy. The author fetched me a big glass of fresh juice and a ham sandwich. I felt like bolting it down like at home, but I paced myself under unfamiliar eyes.

It felt strange to talk about my life and to think that it could fit into the belly of the small dictaphone. Around the author's neck was hanging the same kind of memory stick I'd seen on Helena. Apparently it could fit so many words that no-one would have the time to write that much in his entire life. Helena said once that there should always be at least two backup copies of work things. The technical wonders of this world are completely incomprehensible to me, but this I know: they don't change the fundamentals of a person one bit. There aren't backup copies of sorrows and joys.

The author was already tapping the dictaphone with his finger. I ignored his impatient gestures. I had to digest the sandwich and juice before I could go on. A hungry person can say anything. I wanted to talk turkey.

I thought about what I had said and what I had left unsaid. I realized that I didn't remember my life in order – everything was a gloop in my head, a little like that frozen reindeer haunch Paavo's friend carved pieces off to fry up that time. I tried to remember now what I had already carved off and what was still attached, still frozen.

I nodded to the author. He nimbly moved his finger to the button, and the dictaphone started recording.

My husband Paavo and I had a button shop. We called it that even though the sign outside said "Malmikunnas Yarn Shop". The sign was made of thick, white plywood, and the name was written on it in calligraphy by the display designer Alfred Supinen, who we had hired from the city and who was endowed with artistic gifts. Paavo and I were able to watch while Supinen wrote slowly and then moved back a few metres and squinted, checking the writing. Supinen said that writing four letter "A"s the same required exactness from the artist, because the letters also had to become living human creations. And indeed, as we watched we understood that there are two worlds: this visible one and the other one, which only a few ever get to peek into. Paavo was absolutely certain that if Alfred had been born in a warm southern European land, he would have become a world-famous painter whose works would have been discussed in hushed tones in well-lit galleries by people holding tapered glasses. But in this cold land the brushes stiffen and the paint freezes.

But it wasn't exactly like that. Perhaps Alfred didn't have a burning need to paint on canvases after all. Or maybe he did, but didn't know how. We'll never know for sure, since he cut everything short.

Alfred hanged himself in a cellar with a thick piece of cord. To the frayed end of it clung a yellow piece of tape that said "Saastamoinen Wholesale". It looked bad, the piece of tape. Alfred said two weeks before his suicide to Paavo, "It's all the same no matter what paint pot I put my brush into – it always comes out grey." He was depressed about a world that had changed without consulting him. The whole-saler had given notice that due to technical innovations the need for display designers was declining. Alfred didn't stay around to see the change.

Display designer. That name leaves out the most important part: beauty. A display designer makes the world more beautiful, or, if not the world, at least he makes shops more beautiful, so it's easier for people to come inside. I'm sure that some of our first customers came inside thanks to the beautiful sign.

Yarn, buttons, needles, pins, postcards, lace, ribbon and zippers. We might have had other things too. I don't remember. But that was mainly what we sold to people – useful things. We provided something that people needed. This may sound like belabouring the point, but in the '60s and '70s we each had to fight against the idea that every merchant was a thief and a predator. We took the money left over between the wholesaler and the customers. Is that a dirty trick? What do you say, Author? Nothing. Exactly. It shuts you up. No? Paavo and I could withstand the barrage, but it was hard for the children. When you get made fun of as a child, when the other children call you the spawn of a butcher or a robber baron, it leaves a mark. An invis-ible mark, and that's the worst kind of all. You can't see it, but you can feel it. I could sense it in my children then, and I still do now.

And Paavo and I didn't always stay calm either. It happened like this: by this time Helena was starting to think she knew a little something about how the world worked, and she brought a friend over to visit. Her friend was a little older and had already been to visit the big cities. She was one of those more aware young people. She put a record on the player called "A Plate of Guatemalan Blood". On it they sang about oppression and fighting, and especially about opposing evil exploiters from foreign lands, as well as home-grown ones too. It was tough for Paavo when he realized that the singers on the record were the same ones he had seen on television specifically disparaging all business people, praising the communist movement with all hearts. And there was his own daughter humming along with her eyes closed to the melodies of the spoiled brats of the urban upper class. I tried to intervene, but Paavo already had that look. His eyes narrow, he clears his throat and his hands shake. He was in the zone, as some theatre director said once on the T.V. Paavo went and tore the record from the player with such force that the needle scratched a streak across it. He went to the window, threw the record into the snow and said, "I threw it – I'll pay for it."

This led to crying, and a good while went by before Helena agreed to come out of her room. Paavo spoke to Helena about it later. He sort of tried to put his words in a row like delicate stones, saying, "Dear, we need to make our living from the shop, and it isn't like we start exploiting the working class first thing in the morning. Your parents work a pretty hard day and if you look at it from a certain perspective, you could say that we are in the working class, more or less, but there isn't anything to be gained by getting the communist movement mixed up in this, and there isn't any point in writing lamentations about it – the fruit of that movement is a country full of prisons and Siberias – I just mean how about we live our life selling yarn and buttons and then once we get close to the grave look at what the bottom line is, whether your mother and father are exploiters and blood-suckers and bourgeois devils or just the plain old salt of the earth that you sprinkle on your porridge and apparently on wounds too, and if that friend of yours wants to talk more about it, that's fine, since there are other colours in life besides black and white: there's socialism and its everyday version, the one the social democrats like Koivisto and Sorsa and the labour movement are pushing – that's a perfectly sensible operation that a small-business man like me can understand, and you don't need any Guatemalan blood for it – a plate of soup from blueberries you picked and boiled yourself will do just fine."

He had to be quiet for a long time after that, and of course Helena didn't know how to even begin responding. Every now and then

Paavo's cork pops out, but this time he was making perfect sense.

Money is one of those things people in this country don't know how to relate to. You shouldn't seek it, and you shouldn't have it, but at the same time everyone should get some, preferably the same amount. Ideologies and religions probably get scraped together just so people won't have to talk about money all the time. We didn't get any more of it in this life than anyone else. You have to practically wave the evidence from the taxman in front of people's faces for them to believe. They've come up with enough forms in this country for small-business people to fill out that you're lucky to make it to work between filling them out. I respect money, because I know how tight it is. You have to look for it under rocks. First you lift the rock out of the way, and then you start scraping at the rocky ground with your bare hands. With bloody fingertips. And scabbed knees. The moon glowing in the sky would find Paavo and me still bent over scrabbling for our treasure. And out it would come, wretched and dirty, but when we would polish it, it would start to shine. We would schlep the lump over to the taxman, who would whack off his piece with a golden billhook, and then we would carry it home and hit it with a forge hammer until it split it into four pieces. With the first we would pay for our house, with the second for the electricity and water, with the third for food and clothing, and the fourth part, that we would be really strict with. If we put it towards a car, then what kind? Not a Mercedes, because people would start to whisper. If we put it towards dressing ourselves up, the same thing. You have to be grey in a grey country. So it is that one quarter of all money isn't fit for anyone, not for yourself, not for others. It just gets stuffed in a sock, away from the sun and prying eyes. It irks a bit that, as a yarn seller, in a certain way I was helping to create those socks, at least indirectly. Money is supposed to circulate, just like all good things. It has to be in movement so everyone can catch a glimpse of it. But how can it get out of that sock all by itself? Everything is based on circulation. Gypsies, the sun, laughter, luck. They all move around, and rightly so. The poor money moulders in corners and sock drawers so no-one can be jealous of anyone else.

Paavo and I were very amused by the first rich person in the world who showed it. He had been selling things to people door to door for his whole life, putting everything in a sock. But one day he dumped the paper out of the sock, put the sock on his foot and went to the big city to buy an American car.

The rich man's name was Toivo. I won't say the family name so you won't be able to go spreading these tidings of joy, which would inevitably turn to tears along the way. If people were to find out where he lives, someone would go around and slash his tyres even though it has been twenty years.

Toivo drove about the countryside in a wide-brimmed hat and a white suit, smiling broadly. He parked in front of our shop and got out slowly, like plump people do, but he was deliberately calling attention to the idleness and unhurriedness he had worked and slaved to achieve. He came inside, looked over the merchandise and said he didn't need anything but had to have something beautiful, just like himself.

Toivo fingered the laces and the roll of velvet we had ordered for the gypsy-king's wife. I said we could only sell one yard of the velvet, but more of the lace. Toivo said that a yard of velvet would do. It was going in the car, on the passenger seat, for him to rest his free hand on nicely as the automatic transmission saw to the forward motion. I wrapped the velvet up as Toivo wandered around the shop in his white three-piece suit, the fobs of his pocket watch jingling. When he walked out the door, Paavo and I looked at each other and then out through the display window as the car swung onto the road and disappeared over the horizon as a white dot.

Now, I don't mean that Toivo was an especially dignified person, that he was better than anyone else, but he was like a breath of fresh air from some other world, a little like Alfred Supinen. At the time they were showing "The Amazing World" on the television, or was it "Wide"? It was the only programme where you could see anything even a little bit fascinating or colourful. Toivo evoked images of a peacock or penguin. I thought it was good they existed in their own way, and Paavo agreed. There was something self-satisfied and gaudy about them, but not in a way that takes away from anyone else. Or it does, of course, in the sense that it is a hard thing for nature's other creatures, the rhinoceroses and crocodiles and all the other animals made with the Creator's other hand, to watch such good-humoured types saunter about.

I was ashamed.

I told the author to turn the dictaphone off for a moment. I said I was going to the restroom. I looked in the mirror and asked myself why I had started talking about money. I've seen that it doesn't pay to talk about that. The ones who talk about it the most have the least, and I don't blame them. And the ones who talk the least have the most, but I wouldn't encourage them to be more open either.

Talking about money makes you feel dirty, even though there's nothing wrong with the instrument itself. In this country you can only speak freely about the weather, which is the same for everyone – bad.

I decided to wash my face of the matter, since my hands weren't an option. I had sold my life, and I was paying for it now with shame. I took some soap from the pump bottle, rubbed it over my face until it was white and then tried to massage the shame out. Washing your face always helps. It's a strange thing. It probably comes from the fact that life happens in a person's head, and the face is the windscreen of the head.

I walked back over to the author and nodded. "Roll tape."

You can never tell what a child will turn out to be. I mean their profession, not their final character. We have a clear system: make your life your own – we will love you. The children went out into the world and got on. That was the time in the world when there was work for everyone who wanted to do it. Then came the time when Paavo and I didn't understand anything anymore. I don't know if the children understood it either, but they had to live in it.

What I know of life, I write down on postcards and send it to my children. They believe in the written word, and even if they didn't, they could never claim afterwards that they hadn't heard or understood what I was saying. There are four kinds of cards: one has a lake, the second has winter, the third has fall and the fourth has our village high street. The lake picture was taken from the sky, up where Paavo and I went in a small plane in 1970. The same sky is still here, but with modern cameras it has become too sharp. The human eye works in generalities – it isn't meant to pick out every wisp of cloud. Modern pictures make my head hurt.

The children expect the cards. If one doesn't come for two months in a row, the youngest will ask why on the corded phone. I always say that I will send a card as soon as I know what to write on it. You have to think carefully. Figuring things out isn't always easy. The state of understanding I'm living in now has taken more than seventy years to develop. People ripen slowly.

I'm not running out of cards, even though the shop closed. I took the cards from there, but nothing else. The yarn, the ribbons, the buttons, the snaps, the elastic, the scissors, the needles and everything else I left, bidding it a fond farewell, but I emptied out the whole shelf of cards from beside the door into a big bag.

One night I counted the cards. I have a total of 657 lakes, winters, autumns and high streets. I'll run out of things to say before I run out of cards.

I've noticed that children's heads are so shiny and slippery that nothing seems to want to stick in them. Perfectly clear instructions and advice are forgotten in a matter of months. How many times do I have to write on the back of each of the four landscapes that it isn't a good idea to talk to yourself in the city or at work? People clearly draw conclusions immediately about those who mumble to themselves. Of course, geniuses and artists are another matter, but Paavo and I didn't raise our children to be that incoherent. If you absolutely have to talk to yourself, you can do it at home or in a public restroom stall, but I would consider the general rule to be: talk to each other or with people.

It was bad when all the children moved away from home. People should be given one more child to last them to the end. To be able to watch something grow again. No-one is going to feel like growing flowers forever – it's all the same: sprouting, leafing out and flowering. But a person is such a strange, wonderful thing that you can easily put fifty years into it. A child gives you a sense of scale and time. When our youngest was confirmed, we knew we would have to leave soon ourselves. The greatest injustice is that you only get to be face-to-face with them for twenty years, if that. Then they visit you with their boyfriends and girlfriends and have turned into people. A child and a person are completely different things.

One time a Polish film director was talking on the television. He had a difficult name, all "K"s and "R"s and "Z"s alternating over and over one after the other. He was chain smoking, and his face was pinched. He was clearly trying to speak the truth the whole time. He said that human sorrow comes from never being able to be the same age as one's children. He spoke the truth.

Paavo has gone without speaking for two months now. It means that I have started to talk to myself. Which is a bad thing. But apparently the amount of speech in a house is fixed. If one person stops completely, the other has to speak the full quota for the mute as well. In the very beginning speechlessness seems noble, but then the shine and the integrity wears off, and it just becomes off-putting. Paavo doesn't notice it himself. But I do understand Paavo in this situation, even though I would like someone to talk to. This is Paavo's way of getting over grief. I'm afraid of Paavo leaving before me. And he could leave, squatting mutely in the shed, watching the world with an evil eye. That sort of thing can open the door to cancer. I'm sure about this, and at least one doctor I know agrees.

Glaring at the world won't reduce the amount of evil in it. But how else but through gloomy and evil thoughts, by speaking evil, have the sages of this land risen to their positions? Or been raised. The people in the newspapers and on the television seem to want nothing more than to worship these horses' backsides, whose opinions on every issue are as extreme and as dismal as possible. I've been listening to this one fisherman for years with my cheek resting on my hand to see if even one optimistic thought might come out of his mouth to light the path out to the sauna, but no, we just hear the same invocations of the end of the world and the same invective against the human race, so much so that nothing seems worth doing for a little while afterwards. And that's the problem with evil, that it's just as disingenuous as perpetual goodness. Sometimes you'd just like to take these miserable, gloomy men in your lap and say, "Don't focus on evil. Don't deny goodness. Just go out into life and be dazzled."

There I go, all over the place. I meant to talk about the children.

Paavo and I haven't fretted over our children. There's no point in that. With two daughters, if you start shedding tears in advance, you'll start thinking your hankie was glued to your hand. Two boys evened things out. You don't have to worry about boys in the same way. Paavo said once that if you have ladies and gents in your hand and a queen in your lap, you can leave the game feeling good. Paavo included Heikki in that phrase, even though we didn't have him anymore.

I'll say one thing about Helena here in the middle, whether it's on the record or not: the oldest child's responsibility rests like a boulder on her shoulders her whole life. She was born bigger than the others right from the start, and that was not a good thing. As a young teenager she had a sort of serving disorder. Or if not a disorder, a temperament. She looked after the smaller ones, turning off lights, clearing dishes off the table, arranging hats and gloves. A servant's childhood is short. Yes, I noticed how even as a young woman she sat in the corner, even putting on her make-up mechanically, not out of a desire to be attractive. As if the poor dear only had responsibilities, not privileges. Her nails were short. The others' were red. It looked a little like when the other girls were staring off into horizon, our Helena was looking at the bus schedules. Every child of man should be allowed time for tomfoolery.

All of our children are in business, even though we didn't lead them in that direction in any way. Pekka and Maija are sales consultants. Before they were just salespeople, but at some point they became sales consultants. A thing doesn't change a bit by switching its name.

Pekka has worked in many companies, and has done well in all of them. He has done a lot of work on his stuttering. It isn't easy to give sales pitches when you have to worry about how your words are going to come out. It pains my heart to think of the situations that boy has found himself in because of his handicap, but he has got along marvellously. A little while ago, he told us he was the general manager at a firm that sells computers. Previously he sold snowboards for a living. I didn't know what those were, but when I saw one on the television, I understood that now children need to slide down the snow sideways. Pekka has finally started a family. Well, not quite a real one, but one of those blended families. He hasn't come around to show us yet, but Maija told us. It made me think about how someone could get attached to children who aren't his own, but I imagine it's possible. Nowadays almost everything is possible, even if it looks impossible.

Maija has had many jobs as well. Before people just had one job their whole lives. Maija said that she couldn't even imagine being at the same place for her entire life. That hurt this lifelong button merchant a little, but I do understand something of the restlessness of these new people. Right now Maija is selling magazines over the phone. The negro, or, rather, the Afro-American multicultural person, I mean Maija's husband, Biko, drives a bus. It's hard wrestling with these niceties. Biko has learned Finnish quickly and now gets to drive people around the city in a blue bus. Apparently Biko is aiming for a position as a taxi driver. I think that's dogs' work, driving rich drunks from place to place in an expensive car, but I might be totally out to lunch about that.

Helena is the highest up of the children. She's become an actual marketing director. She works at a firm that has a long English name and sells ideas. Helena had to explain this to us many times. The firm doesn't make anything and doesn't sell things made by anyone else; but rather, they think about other companies' business and then sell what they think to these other companies. It made my head hurt to listen to it, but Helena was patient and used our yarn shop as an example.

If, for example, your yarn shop were in trouble, customers declining and cash flow drying up, and you couldn't figure out why, then our firm could ponder this for you. Is the selection too narrow? Is there something wrong with the company's logo? Is the firm's visual image behind the times? Is the staff sufficiently energetic and understanding of modern people? Then when we get to the heart of the problem, we would create a new corporate image for you, which might mean a new general look or an expansion of your product ranges, or we might focus the need for change on some other specific area.

This clarified things, although at the same time it offended me. I said to Helena that our business image was just fine and would continue to be so, because time couldn't dull the beautiful sign Alfred Supinen had painted for us thirty-five years before. Paavo said that the most important thing in a button shop was that the products are in order and that the salespeople resemble the customers both in manner and appearance. Helena said she had used a familiar example so the thing we were talking about could be understood. She didn't mean to say that our business belonged in any way to the target audience of their firm.

In plain Finnish, Helena's firm sells something that can't be seen with the eye, and this separates me and Paavo from this world. Not that we oppose change, but that's just the way things are: Paavo and I have fallen by every possible wayside. And so it should be. There's no point in hanging on if your thoughts have already let go. The important thing is that the children can hang on at least until the next bend in the road.

I started to get tired and asked the author to check the dictaphone to see if there was enough life on it for this time. The author said that yes, this was quite enough to get him started and that then he would make up more himself. I didn't like that idea, but I didn't feel like making a fuss. My strength was almost spent, and I found myself thinking of Paavo and home.

We arranged our next meeting and shook hands. I made sure the bundle of bills was safe. It was my first wages I didn't pay taxes on. On the way home, I thought about Paavo, my life, the children. And the taxman.

THE MIDDLEMAN

The author transcribed Mrs Malmikunnas' words from the dicta-phone to paper and read them through carefully. For the first time, he had something real to write about. The problem was just how to convey the woman's life to the reader, who in the end would decide whether it was worth reading and whether the author had succeeded in transferring the life he had bought into printed form as something vibrant and interesting.

The author remembered from his childhood how difficult it was to carry a dead dragonfly home in one piece from his grandmother's house.

He had been sitting in the back seat of the small car between his siblings, holding the dragonfly cupped in his hands, protecting its delicate, transparent wings. He had got out of the car awkwardly and walked carefully up the stairs to his attic room. Only then had he dared to open his hands. A small piece of one wing had broken off. Life can't be moved from one place to another completely un-harmed.

It was in this frame of mind that he wrote a letter to the seller.

Dear Mrs Malmikunnas,

I thank you for the life which I did not have before our meeting. This is a big opportunity for me, and I hope I will be worthy of your sacrifice. I just wrote everything down on paper from the dictaphone, and now I will start writ-ing the book itself.

I am afraid, but not afraid. I am at the same time king

and subject. That is what writing is. A king rules lands and territories. A subject bows to the earth and notices the tender shoot rising from the ground. When writing, you have to be general and specific at the same time.

Perhaps it would be good at this juncture for me to enlighten you a little about why I wanted your life in particular. The writer's profession is very old. Before printed literature, there were oral stories, tales told around the evening fire. The best teller was the best author of that time, even though the profession itself did not exist. And what is a good teller like then? Someone like you. When I was listening to you there behind the conference centre, I realized that was exactly how I wanted to do my telling, if I could. This is difficult to explain, but I can pick out a good teller like a bird-watcher might recognize a rare breed after hearing just a short snippet of the song of the bird in question. My choice was also made easier by the fact that you were serious the whole time. You didn't try to entertain me, so I was entertained. A good teller never tries anything.

So, I have to start the book. This is of course made more difficult because you will read it one day. At our meeting, I got the impression that you would not like for me to add anything extra to your account.

Unfortunately, I cannot promise this, because the bare truth, no matter how genuine or personal it might be, is unpleasant to read. Now, do not misunderstand. I will try to illustrate with an example.

The whooper swan, the Finnish national bird. Imagine that one is sitting on the bank of South Harbour in

Helsinki. We see it from afar, from the terrace of the Palace Hotel. Behind the swan is a cruise ship bound for Sweden. We see a picture of a beautiful swan sitting on the bank. Our own thoughts move to the swan – we might even imagine ourselves being the swan for a moment. Up to this point, everything is true, clear and beautiful. This picture is one produced by a human, from there on the terrace of the Palace.

But then there are also other truths.

For example, the swan's truth. It may not necessarily feel like a national bird, especially when we remember that it was persecuted until the 1940s. It might think, here I sit, but how long will I be allowed to sit in peace? When will I have to fly some inordinate distance to somewhere there is more food? Again those people with their shouting and taking pictures of each other with their cameras. I wouldn't take pictures of them if I had a camera. I would take pictures of rocky isles and headlands, late in the evening and early in the morning. There is a seagull wheeling about. I know what can splash down on me out of its other end. My days are unpredictable.

And then there is still the bias related to our eyesight. We are looking at all this from the terrace of the Palace and can't tell that in fact the swan is sitting on the railing of the third deck of the cruise ship and headed on an overnight trip to Stockholm.

In short, the whooper swan needs to be depicted from at least three different perspectives: from far away, from close up and from the bird's own perspective. A picture created in this way is called a story, and, as we see, there are many truths within the story.

We will meet once again in one month. By that time, I will have accomplished something, but it is better for me not to show you the unfinished work. This I can promise, that everything you told me will be included in the story in one way or another.

I will probably start with Helena, even though you only told a little about her and were hiding something big.

Best wishes, A

A week later, the author received a postcard from Salme Malmikunnas with a lake scene on one side and the following text on the other:

Dear Author,

I am not a whooper swan. Weave your story with that in mind, and do justice to my life and my children. I don't care so much about honour.

Salme

Well now, Helena!

Don't rise above everyone else. You'll run out of air and start feeling dizzy. Eat butter and drink red milk. Or at least blue. Don't touch the light ones, or you'll float away. Stay on the ground. Like a mushroom. But don't put yourself down. That makes no sense either. Your dad made enough Karelian stew yesterday to last for days. This is a hint.

Your mother

THE NEGOTIATOR

Helena Malmikunnas was from a home the size of your palm. Now she was standing on the rooftop terrace of a high-rise, from which she could see so far into the distance it wasn't any place at all. She didn't have a sense of scale anymore. She had lost it somewhere along the way, probably in the late '80s. If someone asked her the price of a litre of milk right now, she wouldn't have remembered, even though a company she represented had bought a regional dairy in Satakunta yesterday.

Helena couldn't get a grip on anything. The granite railing of the terrace looked like clay; the clouds moved unpredictably. In her tall glass was something green and an umbrella. A brolly, Mom would say. Come on down from there, Dad would say.

The people from the firm walked by her laughing with tall glasses in their hands. Gulls wheeled over the bay. Someone stopped in front of her and was about to say something, but then moved on.

Helena squeezed the granite railing. It felt like the only thing that held true. Granite. A good, safe word. She felt like pressing her cheek against it, but she didn't want to draw attention. Yes. Draw attention. Although most of the business conducted in this city was based on that, on someone being the first one to press her cheek against the granite, drawing attention and coming up with a way to charge for it. Capitalism is made up of momentary enthusiasms. Any whimsy can be called an insight. Go ahead and draw attention, but only if you can charge for it.

Helena knew she would have to join the other people soon. The whole industry was based on that. They talked about networking. That was the only concrete concept in the industry. And now Helena was realizing she had already been in the net a long time.

Suddenly she remembered the time as a child Dad took her with him to check fishing nets. Dad lifted the dark, restlessly tossing net into the base of the rowboat. Fish wriggled and flopped. Their eyes stood terrified on either side of their slimy heads, looking at Helena in empty accusation. You took us out of the freedom of the water to gasp for breath in your miserable world. You're going to hit us on the head with a club and then your father will congratulate you for being such a big girl. Helena retreated to the other end of the boat. Dad said, "You don't need to be afraid. I'll knock them out with this club, and then we'll go and cook up some perch soup." In the middle of the net, Helena saw a lifeless, half-eaten fish – it looked like a roach, but ragged. It was caught by its gills, but in some way it belonged to the same group as the wriggling ones, and now as she stood and held the granite railing, Helena felt like that roach, badly tangled in the net, half eaten.

But these were feelings that no-one can avoid who works over-long days in a tall building so soundproofed that neither the din of traffic nor the angry words down on the street can penetrate it. Every-one cringes sometimes in the middle of company parties, thinking, what am I doing here, even though I wanted to be here? What are those gowns and jackets walking by, jiggling full of flesh and water? Where is that jingling and jangling coming from – from those tall glasses or from the overheated brains that have been stressed all autumn with new ideas, people, memoranda, working groups and endless meetings, in the middle of which everyone, at least once, has found herself staring at a lifeless bread roll resting on a high-design, wooden serving dish, between the halves of which rest ham hacked into slices, sucking the last juices out of a curved piece of red pepper?

Helena she had to shake these feelings within fifteen minutes. Fifteen minutes of privacy at a party on a rooftop terrace is the maxi-mum – after that you have to return to your co-workers and clients and demonstrate, once again, that you are able to be not only a person, but, more specifically, a unique individual. That's a difficult job for a person who would like to be staring off into space, to lapse into silence and whatever other lovely states of being there might be. Helena did not think she was a unique individual, even though uniqueness and individuality were trumpeted with a megaphone from the front door of nearly every company. Helena's view was that they had been successful because they currently had enough customers who had the same kinds of ideas as they did.

Helena turned towards the crowd and saw the core trio of her team on the other side of the terrace. Kähkönen, Laakso and Reinikka were slapping high fives and shaking their behinds to the beat of some ancient American R. & B. By their choice of music they wished to convey that the little boys, whom this cold business life had shoved into the background, were still alive and kicking in their adult bodies. They had left their sauna hats on. Their well-cut suits and the silly hats emphasized their nonchalance and folksy sense of humour, which conveyed their willingness to throw off their business armour now and then and condescend to the level of the child, the common man and the customer.

Fifteen minutes had passed, and Helena had to rejoin humanity. She attempted to avoid eye contact with Kähkönen, Laakso and Reinikka, who were prepared to pull anyone into their amorphous bumping and shaking dance, the actual purpose of which was not to imitate the music, but rather to express in broad gestures: we are now being entertained.

Helena searched the crowd for a person with whom she could talk for a moment about the granite railing, the ragged roach and the net in which we wriggle until the club thunks us between the eyes. Helena needed a serious person now. Not humourless, not dull, not funny, not sociable, not a recluse, not a moralist, but rather an old-fashioned serious person with whom she could exchange a few words about these strange emotions.

Helena noticed a quiet man next to the drinks table who was turning a stirring stick in his glass and looking around calmly. Helena did not know the man. He might be a customer or some other stakeholder in the company who had received an invitation to the Xero Party event.

Helena stopped in front of the man and recited the appropriate civilities. The man introduced himself as "just Kimmo". Helena was irritated by his self-styled modesty, and she felt like asking if the name "Just" indicated Dutch roots. It was introductions like this that usually ended up after six drinks with exclamations of bravado in which the "Just" is replaced with phrases like "Let me tell you something . . ."

Kimmo said his perspective on all of this was a little further removed than most, since he was usually looking on from Barcelona or Tallinn, depending on which home he was staying in at any given time. He said he kept a home in Helsinki as a sort of backup so he wouldn't have to use disgusting, low-class hotels. Kimmo also said, without Helena asking specifically, that he had sold his business at a good time and that now for the first time he had the opportunity to look at the big picture – from the sidelines as it were – a big picture he saw clearly, but which he tried not to get involved with anymore.

Helena noticed her full glass, drained it all at once and motioned to the waiter. She took a drink from the tray and asked the waiter to come by more often. Helena raised her glass, clinked it with Kimmo's and congratulated him on his excellent way of life. At the same time, Helena sensed the direction of the conversation and wished, although she sensed she was wishing in vain, that he would follow Helena's five-point list of don'ts:

Don't claim you made all your money with your own two hands.

Don't claim you saw further than other people and that's why you're standing on the top of the heap now.

Don't claim your success has nothing to do with the caprices of capitalism.

Don't claim that you're an independent, unique individual.

And don't say that you know a good restaurant near here that the rabble hasn't caught wind of yet and that has an absolutely mind-blowing wine list.

Kimmo made all five mistakes in ten minutes, but Helena didn't pour cold water over him. She just let him talk. One must show humility before a force of nature. If a dam breaks, stay far away from the shore. If a bear approaches, don't run all over the place, just stay where you are. If a fire breaks out in the house, don't open the windows.

Helena remembered these rules of thumb she had learned in Scouts, and let Kimmo continue. She listened, understanding that this was how it went if you let it loose: unbridled capitalism blazed exultantly, growing blindly; it made the very tarmac blossom and brought utterance to every mouth; it was limited in neither dimension nor amount; it pissed on moderation and curtsied to excess; it took credit for every jingling of a coin and blamed outmoded social contracts for any cash register that stood silent. Kimmo was the grand offspring of an ideology without ideals, the one with the best poop. His firm had had the honour of advertising for the world's largest mobile phone company, which had exploited one of the great wonders of the world: a people that was thought of as largely mute wanted nothing more than to talk to each other about personal devices that fit in your hand and do it so loudly, in so many places, and so often, that the rest of the world just had to believe: this miniature handset is not only new but necessary, handy today, essential tomorrow. And so the sea gave birth to a wave, a wave so large that Kimmo too was able to surf atop it and make money on a quirk, money the source, country of manufacture and method of production of which no-one knows, and no-one needs to know. It was enough for him to convince himself and others that the money came from his insight alone.

Helena was startled by her thoughts and looked at Kimmo. She didn't see the man anymore, just a mouth that ground and chewed and munched the material produced by its paunch, flawless and beautiful phrases, the purpose of which was to stake out their producer, a well-dressed bull, in a central place in the food chain. The mouth stopped for a moment, and the pink-and-white-fleshed tongue licked the lips to remove the saliva and wine that had dried on them. Helena didn't manage to say anything before the mouth attacked the next piece of material, constructing new words and phrases from it, the repeated use of which had ravaged of all meaning or sense, and which clinked to the terrace floor like bent nails into a steel bucket. Helena looked at the mouth and wondered if it was boundless, limitless, if it had a bottom or an end, and if it did have a bottom, was there some sort of perpetual-motion device or *machina dei* chugging away down there, which regardless of all else and without consulting its owner, produced always and forever the same mash, which Kimmo refined with his phenomenal gifts of speech into the ambrosia of the gods?

Then Helena made the mistake she should not have made: she looked past Kimmo towards the horizon. And nobody did that to Kimmo.

"Now you aren't listening."

The phrase came unexpectedly, loudly, the lightness and softness of the previous phrases absent. Kimmo hadn't bothered to tenderize and marinate this phrase, so its freshness brought to mind a bream that had just been lifted from the lake, slapping onto the bottom of the plastic boat.

"Sorry. I was just thinking about everything you were saying."

It wasn't true, but there was one right word in her answer – "you" – and Kimmo was appeased.

You.

i.e. me.

Lovely.

Kimmo's satisfaction was complete, full. It was reminiscent of coming. His audience was an attractive, sexy woman after all, not some tipsy bald guy with a title made up of a stream of un-pronounceable English fluff. Kimmo loved words and always hoped that the ground onto which words fell would be good ground, soft ground, because if this was the case, the words would grow into other new words, and, behold, before us would soon stand a meadow of lilies, amaryllis and roses, Kimmo's gift to marketing and advertising.

Kimmo looked at this pleasantly receptive woman and considered whether she would be ready to leave that repulsive, inelegant and raucous group and go with him to some more peaceful place, where Kimmo could talk in a little more detail about himself, his ideas, his accomplishments and his plans for the future, which just might include a niche for a woman with a good ear and a nice, tight arse, who had developed an exceptionally well-honed gift for listening during her long career in customer service.

Helena had to get away. Because of her position she couldn't say anything directly, even though Kimmo couldn't have any current projects with their company. Networking meant that the bream also had to take into consideration the tough zander that had slipped through the mesh of the net out into the deep. They could still surface to tell troublesome tales.

Escape was unavoidable, but it had to be done purposefully, delicately enough that Kimmo would not be put out. The industry was full of big babies, whose whims, mood swings and blood sugar spikes had to be taken into consideration. Helena thought of her seven-year-old daughter Sini and her temper, the knots she tied herself in. Helena had needed the skills of a psychological precision mechanic to unravel them. She had found help in Aikido, the Japanese art of self-defence. It emphasized the transfer of the opponent's strength past the target. The attacker's hand is diverted to the side, its force ultimately pulling the opponent over. If Sini shouted that she wanted to go outside right now, Helena opened the door, letting in a biting wind. Sini got what she wanted, but didn't want it anymore when she realized that she had wanted unwisely.

Helena thought. Kimmo wanted to talk and come on to her. Talk was foreplay, a preface. According to the basic principles of Aikido, I should divert Kimmo's will past me such that he realizes the impossibility of his wish. How to give Kimmo everything without giving him anything?

Finally Helena fashioned her trap like this: "You talk really well, but here on this windy terrace, some of the words get lost in the wind. Over beside the sauna area is a room for cooling off. Talk some more in there and when you've said everything, I'll take off all my clothes and you can fuck me like a bull."

Kimmo fell silent before these words. He had made his fortune with words, with their subtle connotations. He was a surgeon of tone and delicate shades of meaning who forced his way into the client's pleasure centre unnoticed, bypassing any defence mechanisms, opening the wallet and exiting via the same route without leaving a trace. But Kimmo didn't like coarse words – he thought people who used such words had just come down out of the tree looking for something to eat. "I'll take off all my clothes, and you can fuck me like a bull." After the charming beginning came those uncouth, base words; the content was definitely good, but incorrect word choice ruined the whole. Just like squirting ketchup from a bottle all over a meringue made of whipped egg whites and sugar.

Kimmo took a sip of his tall drink and decided to be silent for a moment. During his long career, he had observed that silence was a part of communication. Silence created meaning and suspense, and made the client think about his words.

Helena grew nervous. She remembered the sharp glance of her Aikido instructor when Helena had grabbed her opponent's hand and pulled it violently. Not like that. Do not ever show emotion. When you show your feelings, you give power to the other. Show your feelings somewhere else, not on the mat. With that last long sentence, Helena had shown her feeling of disgust, and now Kimmo had the power.

Helena realized she was at work, even though she was at a party. Actually, she was always at work, because her work was exactly this: spinning meanings, looking for words, observing moods, evaluating those she spoke with, open flattery and mild rejection, fawning and courting, frivolity and trivialities, but never anything clear, concrete or indisputable. The vagueness of the work gnawed the nervous system to shreds and built up a pounding pressure in the temples.

Kimmo was enjoying Helena's mistake. Now he had all the time and all the power. Time to wait for the next move, power to draw out the silence. Kimmo leaned on the granite railing and smiled faintly, as the well-off are wont to do. They don't condescend to guffaw, they don't snort into their fists and it would never cross their minds to giggle at a bawdy story. Their smiles have a trace of mockery, not inviting one to smile along.

Helena looked at Kimmo and thought about why men like him always dressed the same way, even though each one swore allegiance to individuality. Thick corduroy trousers, an English suit jacket cut from strong cloth with a herringbone pattern reminiscent of the deep waters from whence they hailed, a white T-shirt peeking out from beneath an expensive dress shirt, hinting at eternal youth, high-quality, patterned leather shoes on the feet and, to top off the ensemble, a small earring, in this case a black stud. The earring could be a traditional hoop, but not a big one – it couldn't be allowed to suggest membership of one of the wrong tribes, the bikers or rockers, even though they were precisely the ones, after gypsies and sailors, who set the parameters for the continuing use of the earring, encouraging the upper middle-class to join in the rite of mimicry. The black stud in Kimmo's left ear indicated that although he had made his fortune by speaking, he was also ready for action, ready to burn off steam, to express his rugged masculinity, which meant that one might find him strutting out of tapas bars humming classic American rock songs and kicking trash cans in the wee hours of the morning.

Helena sensed that all was lost, that there was nothing left to do. But what did losing everything mean in this case, on this rooftop terrace? What would happen if she said to the bull that his stall had been spread with fresh straw and that he should come along now and do what a good bull should? What was the significance of a few wrong words in a world made up of millions of words?

Everything?

If it meant everything, then you could just keep heaping anything on top of everything.

Nothing?

If it meant nothing, then could we just fill our tall glasses and continue on to another topic?

As a negotiator, Helena went over both options. Both felt bad. And what if they were combined? What would that make?

Everything and nothing.

Full emptiness.

Carnal spirit.

Globally local.

Sunny night.

Odourless shit.

Her head was screeching. And humming. Then she heard faint pops coming from her ears, like when their water seals finally burst after swimming as a child. The veins in her temples pulsed. They were little red threads that had set out from their spools and were swarming under her thin skin trying to find a way out.

Helena grew hot. This was supposed to be free time. This was supposed to be a break. I found Sini a sitter to come to this party. I put on something pretty. I took my place. I programmed my mood. I put on the expected expression.

Helena turned red. Then white. Then she moved from words to actions.

Later, Helena thought about what she had done as she stepped out of the tall, glass building for the last time. Was that act the reason why she had to leave the company? Was Kimmo one of the major investors who had become nervous about the company's profits? Had the words resonated, magnifying the act? Had Kimmo understood her small gesture in monumentally the wrong way? Had the hard zander risen to the surface and told his own version of what had happened to the other fish in the net?

Helena felt like nothing had been anyone's fault or to anyone's credit for a long time. There was no star glimmering somewhere that she could have followed. A smokeless alternative had sprung up alongside the traditional smokestack industries, an invisible kingdom of words, a wasteland of conference rooms.

In the courtyard of the office building was a stone bench, where Helena sat and tried to think. She had rejected the word and replaced it with action. In a factory, a forest, a cowshed or a field, hardly any attention would have been paid to her action, because in those places everything was based on tangible things, on physical performance and the compensation received for it. In places like that you could show anger and frustration. In the world of actions you act. In the world of words you talk. Good.

But in making the shift from the factory to the conference room, we didn't become different creatures, we didn't leave our feelings behind like a lizard leaves its tail. We carried all that anger, rage and frustration with us indoors. The problem is that there isn't any storage space for negative feelings in offices. They aren't specifically forbidden, but the message is clear that they belong to that earlier breed, the one that built the nation with hellish hue and cry.

Helena rose from the bench and decided to schedule an appointment with a consultant who specialized in people on the edge.

POSTCARD, AUTUMN SCENE

Pekka, my only son!

*I could see from your expression last time that my boy hasn't
been having luck in the world of women. Listen to your mother:
don't wear baggy trousers. And we already spoke about the platform shoes with the thick soles: ditch them. Don't offer women
alcohol. Give them food, dinner! If she eats greedily, uninhibit-
edly, she will be frisky and warm in bed too. This is a truth.*

Your mother

THE PARTICIPANT

Pekka Malmikunnas stood on a large rock at the top of a steep hill
looking down over a churchyard of people standing around dressed
in dark colours. The men scraped the gravel with the tips of their
shoes. The women hugged each other. The children raced around
their parents' legs. The double doors of the church opened, and out
rolled a black cart supporting a white casket. Four men walked beside
the cart. They were looking at the casket, evaluating any possible
irregularities in the ground before them. When the front wheel of
the cart hit a stone, the men looked at each other worriedly, as if the
deceased might have noticed the jolt. The people in the churchyard
joined the men with the cart, and the procession set off walking

slowly towards the cemetery.

Pekka came down from the hill and set off after the funeral party, keeping a little distance from them. The procession stopped beside a black pit. The priest spoke a few words, some of which were lost in the wind and the roar of the main ring road.

The men took hold of the straps and began lowering the casket into the grave. Judging from their expressions, the load was valuable and heavy. Pekka knew that sorrow increases the weight of a casket by at least thirty kilos. The casket scraped against the sides of the grave, as if not wanting to go down. Their arms trembling, the men finally got it to the bottom, after which people began throwing dirt over it. Pekka felt as if the deceased might wake at the pattering sound of the dirt, be startled by his death and try to beat the lid of the coffin open.

The mourners began to sing an old hymn that spoke of the coming endless journey and the inexpressible brilliance that awaits the traveller at its end. They sang off-key, as was appropriate. If the bereaved sing flawlessly, the ceremony loses all credibility.

Pekka walked closer and took cover behind a large gravestone. Now he was within earshot. The eldest of the pall-bearers began to speak. He let out one phrase at a time, without faltering. He spoke of his father, who had been a taciturn man by nature. Pekka wondered whether there was any other kind of man. He spoke about everyday events from the life of the deceased. Pekka made mental notes about the details. It was easy, since the deceased had lived a life nearly identical to Pekka's father's. Lives don't differ that much from each other, whatever we may think as we are living them.

The man stressed that although his father had been a bit of a peevish lout, he had also had his sensitive side. Dad had gone out to the shed three times to cry. Pekka believed him. The few times something like this occurs become events about which you remember every detail, down to the time of day.

The man ended his speech and announced that during the memorial everyone who wished could talk about Erkki informally. The procession straightened their clothes, waiting for the next-of-kin to give everyone else permission by leaving themselves.

Pekka followed the group from a short distance, going over the details of his plan. He decided it was workable. Everything depended now on what it always did: his ability to concentrate. Pekka went over the imminent performance in his mind: the dialect, the body language, the manner of being in the midst of sorrow, yet still detached from it.

Through the great windows of the chapel, he could see the mourners taking their seats at their tables. No-one had approached the bounteous buffet table yet. Apparently everyone was waiting for the family to start. Pekka walked into the chapel and found the lavatory in the foyer. He combed his hair, washed his face and inspected the details of his clothing. The suit was cheap, but appropriate. The expression was dry, but sad. He sighed deeply, opened the door and walked into the banquet room, becoming someone else, as he had who-knew-how-many times before in his life.

He walked up to the man who had spoken at the graveside, shaking his hand and saying, "Please accept my condolences. Erkki was . . . Erkki. A fisherman of the highest calibre."

"Thank you. I don't believe we've met."

"Juha-Matti. I knew your father through my hobby. I wanted to bring greetings and flowers on behalf of the fishing club. Erkki. Yes. A good man lost."

"Thank you. Can you stay to eat?"

"Thank you, I would be delighted. And I would like to extend our condolences through you to the entire family."

"Of course."

Pekka squeezed the man's hand firmly and said in a quiet voice, "Hang in there."

Then he walked to the buffet table, stopping and looking at the steaming dishes. They began to speak to him. The pork fillets lounged invitingly in a thick, brown gravy. A creamy, buttery aroma rose from the oven-poached salmon, as if the tank-raised rainbow trout were murmuring to Pekka, "Grab, eat, devour, burp, enjoy." The call of the salad bowls was even more soulful. Grape halves, pieces of red bell pepper and slices of cucumber cooed and whispered from the depths of the chopped iceberg-lettuce salad, "We are light. Eat us first. We will prepare a bed in your empty stomach for the meat and fish to lie upon." The frosty pitchers of home-brew and milk proclaimed in masculine tones, "Drink us last. We will soak everything you eat into a mass to glide through the folds of your organs, slipping into every crevice and nourishing you, you hungry, tortured soul!"

Pekka had to stop and take a deep breath. He glanced around to make sure as many guests as possible were on the same errand. He couldn't be greedy now or push in front of others, in any way giving the impression that the food had become more important than the memory of the deceased.

Pekka concentrated all of his strength on hiding his enormous hunger. He put a little green on a salad plate, added a piece of bread and then looked for an appropriate place in the hall. Unfortunately, there were no isolated seats, so he had to go to a table where a couple was already sitting. He sat next to the middle-aged man and nodded politely.

"Erkki wasn't a salad person, but the rest of us who have been left behind have to try," the man said and smiled. He said Erkki had made an agreement with the rabbits that if Erkki didn't eat the rabbits' food, the rabbits wouldn't ride on Erkki's moped.

Pekka smiled at the story, thinking back to when he had really begun to hate humour. He didn't remember the exact day, but it had been during the time when the local radio stations were just starting up, and had begun calling humour any activity that was meant to lighten a mood.

The woman of the couple was taking small bites of her salad and reminiscing about the August evenings she and her husband had spent with the deceased and his wife. They had never had any quarrels. If Erkki had a different opinion about something, he didn't raise his voice, he just went along gracefully.

According to the man, Erkki was one of the men who had built Finland with their own hands. Pekka said the country needed men like that. The man extended his hand and introduced himself as Kalervo Nygren. Pekka didn't remember his own name immediately due to his hunger, but after a second's pause he said he was Juha-Matti. Nygren wanted to know how Juha-Matti had come to know Erkki and what he thought of Erkki's most recent work.

Pekka squeezed his hands together under the table, pleading with the Almighty for answers. He didn't know anything about Erkki's profession or his latest work, but latched on to what he had heard at the graveside. He said he only knew Erkki superficially from a couple of fishing trips and that he was sad the friendship had not been allowed to continue. Nygren nodded, downcast, but reckoned that Erkki's legacy would live on because his talented children had recorded all of Erkki's burl art in digital form. Pekka latched on to this and told about being especially inspired by the burl chairs that had a place carved in the armrest for a remote control. Nygren didn't remember any chairs. As far as he understood, Erkki had done mainly birds, ashtrays and cruets. Pekka said that the chair was sort of a secret, one-of-a-kind specimen that Erkki had shown him a picture of on a fishing trip in Ahvenkoski. Nygren was surprised that he hadn't known about the chair, or that Erkki had ever gone fishing in Ahvenkoski. Pekka admitted that he might be remembering the place wrong. He had been under a lot of pressure with an intense series of meetings at work, and things tended to get jumbled up in his head. Pekka indicated the buffet table with his hand and said he was going to get a little warm food before he had to rush off to his youngest's violin recital.

At the buffet table, Pekka began to feel faint and accidentally leaned against the edge of a hot dish of fish for support. The pain was immense, but by strength of will he contained his yelp. He loaded a big plate with so much fish and pork fillet that some sauce ran off onto another serving dish. He attempted to wipe up the spillage, but in so doing soiled his fingers and the lapel of his jacket. He didn't notice Nygren, who had appeared behind him, and who said in a gruff voice that Pekka's helping did honour to the renowned appetite of the deceased. Pekka was startled and dropped his fork into the oven-poached salmon. Nygren gave a laugh and said that the pace of modern life was wearing the young men of Finland out before their time.

Pekka remembered that he had never struck anyone, even though he had wanted to several times. In his fantasies and daydreams, he had done bodily harm to a number of people, but in real life he had endured and gone along with each and every tasteless ignoramus because he had always kept a clear vision in his mind of his goal, which this time was the undisturbed journey of this lovely, heaped, steaming dish of food from his mouth to his stomach. He was prepared to humble himself in the service of this cause, to kowtow, to endure and to conciliate. He remembered what his father had said: "The customer is always right, even when he is wrong." And for Pekka, all people were now customers.

He carried his plate carefully towards the table, repeating in his mind these instructions: don't show your hunger; eat like a person, savouring; don't gulp it down – this will expose you; praise the food, but don't use folksy expressions (the girls in the kitchen sure have put their best foot forward; I'd rather eat this than get a kick in the teeth) to lighten the mood. You don't lighten the mood at a funeral, you respect it.

A young woman had appeared at the table, joining the Nygrens. She introduced herself as Sinikka, daughter of the deceased. She said she had wanted to come and meet this person she had never met before and whom she didn't know was Erkki's friend.

As Pekka said he was Juha-Matti, he shoved his hand into the pocket of his jacket, feeling for the buttons of his mobile phone and repeating the movements he had practised dozens of times for emergency situations. Just as Sinikka was starting the conversation, Pekka's mobile rang. Pekka rose, begged their pardon, lifted the phone to his ear and walked over into the lower lobby. He spoke into the mute phone, glancing at the table where Sinikka had remained to talk with the Nygrens. Pekka paced his speech with pauses, throwing in a "yes", "exactly" or "we'll see" every now and then, and said he would be there well before 1.30 p.m. As he gave the mute handset a chance to speak, he noticed that Sinikka had left the table. He ended his call, walked to the table and expressed his regrets to the Nygrens for the unfortunate interruption. A family man doesn't get to have boundaries between everyday life and solemn occasions. It was all one and the same life. Pekka apologized that he would unfortunately have to eat rather quickly, even though stuffing oneself was so inappropriate at moments like this. The Nygrens said they understood Pekka's predicament.

Pekka turned his chair sideways a little so he could have some semblance of privacy during this sacred moment. He piled mashed potatoes and pork fillet together on his fork and carefully guided the heap in front of his mouth. He glanced around one last time, closed his eyes, opened his mouth and dumped the forkful into his mouth. It was savoury and sweet. A hint of prune oozed from the pork fillet, and the butter that had been beaten into the mashed potatoes melted in his hungry mouth. Pekka would not by any means have wished to swallow the mouthful. He would have liked to wall it up in the hollows of his mouth. He would have liked to ruminate the food, to surrender it to fuel his body bit by bit, rationing it.

Pekka drank thirty millilitres of cold milk in one pull on top of his first two forkfuls. A burp signalled its arrival, but he held it in his trachea with a special swallowing technique he had learned from his father, Paavo.

Nygren leaned over his plate and asked when Juha-Matti had fished with the deceased in Ahvenkoski. Pekka had a full fork on the way to his mouth. He had to return it to the rim of his plate. Pekka said that he didn't remember the date exactly, because fishing was constantly taking him to different parts of Finland. Nygren said that Sinikka, the daughter, had just mentioned that Erkki had never, at least according to his family, ever gone fishing in Ahvenkoski.

Pekka realized he had made a big, possibly crucial mistake: he had succumbed to hunger instead of learning enough about the life and habits of the deceased, having the patience to proceed more slowly. He had not humbled himself in the face of death, and now he had to pay the dearest price of all: an interrupted meal.

He wiped his mouth, rising from the table and saying, "Perhaps we'll see each other again at another family gathering in the near future. I'll bring a few pictures from Ahvenkoski. Erkki was in his element when he lifted up his catch in that picturesque backlighting. I thank you."

Pekka walked to the cloakroom, feeling their gazes on his back. He flung a black overcoat over himself, only remembering once he reached the yard that he hadn't had an overcoat when he came. Stealing clothing had not been part of the plan under any circumstances, but in this situation he could not return the coat.

He climbed the ridge to the large rock and looked down over the darkening churchyard. He could not see through the large glass windows into the dining area, but he knew without seeing: a server was carrying a nearly full plate into the kitchen and dumping it into a black garbage sack which tomorrow would be carried along with all the other waste to a dump where it would become indistinguishable from all the other black garbage sacks. No-one would be able to guess that particular sack contained a plate two forkfuls shy of a bountiful funeral luncheon, a gigantic helping of meat and fish ladled by a greedy hand. In contemplating this loss, Pekka found himself bereft of strength, unable to think coherently for a moment. He felt faint because thirty-five hours had passed since his last hot meal, but even his dizziness was swept away by sorrow at the fact that as a result of his hubris someone's carefully prepared meal was going to waste and that no-one like him would be able to enjoy its irreplaceable nutrients.

Pekka climbed down from the rock and set off walking towards his apartment, knowing that he would again have to resort to boiled macaroni, frankfurters and ketchup.

Pekka played for time, pushing off the hunger by drinking two and a half litres of water on top of the macaroni mess. He tottered to the balcony, taking hold of the railing and looking down. It was about a ten-metre drop. Just three years ago he had been sitting in an office that was located twenty-four metres from the ground. Drunken with his power, he had demanded that the maintenance man determine the precise height.

The water washed the shreds of macaroni and pieces of frankfurter around in his half-empty stomach, and when they touched the gossamer membranes of his gut, there was a wheezing sound like a rat squealing in a stinking sewer. Vomit rioted in his oesophagus, trying to rise to his larynx, but he forced it back down by swallowing. He was forced to crane his neck like an ostrich, but finally he couldn't do anything about the vomit. A big mass comprised mostly of stomach vapours and colourless liquid gushed from his mouth onto the floor, spreading over an area of nearly a metre. Pekka could pick out a piece of pork fillet and a hint of oven-poached salmon in the mess.

He first began to clean the vomit by hand, because he calculated he could only use ten squares of toilet paper for the job. The slippery goo flowed through his fingers, but he did not give in, scooping the escaping mess back into the protection of his hands. He was disgusted, but he did not fear vomiting again, because his stomach was empty to the last drop. He dabbed the last glob away, and now the linoleum looked like there had never been anything on it of human origin.

Everything leading up to this could have been avoided if Pekka had been patient enough to do his work properly and familiarize himself thoroughly with the deceased and his background. Now, clinging to a few flimsy facts and driven mad by hunger, he had screwed up a perfectly good memorial service.

Pekka pulled himself together and began browsing through the obituaries he had cut from the newspapers. The situation was made more difficult by the fact that almost everyone who died was significantly older than him. It would have been easier to find topics of conversation, familiar milieus and common habits to use during his infiltration in the life of a contemporary. Politics, taste in music, nature, sports, women. Everything that connects people to each other, what differentiates people. If the deceased was thirty years older, it was harder to find common milieus. Ahvenkoski would teach him.

In the end, Pekka chose a fifty-nine-year-old man whose obituary came in two parts: he was missed both by his family and his company. The deceased had spent his life working as a conductor on the state railways. Pekka wrote out a bulleted list of the details he had to find out. The funeral would be held two weeks later. In that time, Pekka would be able to do his work so conscientiously, so precisely and so humbly that the events of the past day would never be repeated.

Evening darkened to night. That morning Pekka had unscrewed the light bulb in the dustbin shed. He opened the door to the shed and clicked on his flashlight. He aimed the light at the rearmost bin, where the widow Hakulinen usually put her rubbish. He lifted the lid against the wall, folded his arms and muttered a prayer. "Give me this day my daily markdowns."

Hakulinen had a habit of buying all of the prepared foods marked with a red sticker, even if she wouldn't end up eating them. Pekka had been blessed to enjoy the fruits of the widow's careless consumerism so often that he had earmarked Hakulinen's products for himself.

Pekka looked for a K-Market plastic bag – Hakulinen did not patronize any other grocery. There it glimmered, almost on the bottom. Pekka leaned over the container and stretched towards the bag. His fingers brushed the bag's knot, but he couldn't get a grip on it, and as he edged himself into a better position, he tumbled in.

He had never been in a dustbin before, but had heard of their ability to store heat. Apparently it had to do with the scraps of food still being warm at the moment they were thrown out. Pekka knew he was sitting on Hakulinen's bag, but did not rush to adjust his position. He wanted to experience with all of his senses what those who had fallen before him had reported. A dustbin was its own world, sufficiently small, relatively peaceful and in a good location. You are separated from the human world, but are still right in the middle of it. By opening the lid you can see the stars, and by closing it you can see inside yourself.

Pekka sniffed the container and found people's eating habits to be largely similar. The smells of chicken, liver casserole, trout temptation and pasta sauces forced their way through the plastic bags. He hoped there was something special in Hakulinen's plastic bag that would raise his spirits and his energy level.

He opened the lid, rose to standing position and grabbed Hakulinen's bag. The widow had tied the bag with an overhand knot, as if to bait him. If I don't eat it, neither will the rest of you. Pekka poked his finger forcefully into the knot and strained to open the bag. This time the smell was a scent. He carefully placed his hand in the bag and felt two food cartons. He guessed. He hoped. He dreamed. He climbed out of the trash bin with the cartons, picked up his flashlight and focused it on his quarry. Yes. It was true. Reindeer sauté with mashed potatoes. Two boxes of reindeer sauté with mashed potatoes.

God did exist, and God had created the widow Hakulinen.

The beautiful red stickers indicated the progress of the products' journey towards moulding, but there was still half a day left.

Pekka's hands shook, and he feared he would drop the treasures on the way to his apartment. He squeezed the cartons under his arm and stopped in front of the elevator. Calling it would cause noise. Perhaps someone would open a door onto the hallway, notice Pekka and attempt to rob him of his treasures by force. He did not want to take that risk. He walked up the stairs.

After arriving at his apartment, Pekka warmed both cartons, poured them into a bowl, took a large spoon and scraped warm mashed potatoes and shredded reindeer meat into his mouth. He thought of the potato, which had grown up in the same land as he had, and the reindeer, which had once roamed free over hill and dale as he did. He felt he was at one with the potato and the reindeer, part of all the eating and killing, living and dying, and taking and giving in the world. It was with these thoughts that Pekka fell asleep on his cot, satisfied, having received his part.

THE AGENT

Maija Malmikunnas turned the microphone attached to her head down in front of her mouth and concentrated. The basic details about four different magazines and their current special offers lay on the table before her. Maija repeated them to herself quietly, attempting to also remember the unit manager's instructions.

If the customer isn't interested, throw out some bait. If the customer is in a hurry, ask for an opportunity to call again. If the customer is grumpy, turn her attention to the bonuses. If the customer gets aggressive, do not under any circumstances become provoked and don't take it personally. If the customer has had bad experiences with the product in the past, tell her it has been revamped. But above all, remember: bait, bonuses, subscriber gifts. Maija punched in a number and waited.

Turpeinen residence.

Hello, this is Maija Malmikunnas on behalf of Periodicalls. Did I call at a bad time?

Yes.

Lovely . . . I mean, not in that sense, but in that may I say that you have been chosen in our sweepstake for a great opportunity . . .

I'm not buying anything.

Of course not, but let me just say that you have been chosen out of thousands of people for the opportunity to try at a nominal cost . . .

The phone clicked in Maija's ear.

She looked out, down onto the parking area where the cars stood covered in a wet mat of leaves. The cars were all beaten up and ugly, like all become eventually. Maija thought about what former sales-people become, the ones who can't stand to call anyone anymore. Could you pick a former salesperson out of a crowd? Do they look like the one-time pop singers who you would never believe had ever been the cause of so much youthful infatuation? Does a sales-person have an identity at all, or is she the part of the food chain that no-one ever thinks about, a bit like soy sauce, the basic seasoning in all Chinese cuisine, which you just splash into the wok as a matter of course? Does anyone remember salespeople?

Maija realized that her minute had passed. The unit manager had stressed that after a humiliating phone call it was a good idea to take a minute's break to collect yourself for a new attack.

Maija punched in a new number.

Kallio.

Hi, Maija Malmikunnas from Periodicalls here. Would you have a moment to discuss an extraordinarily attractive magazine offer?

Go on.

Good. Do I understand correctly that you currently have an auto-renewal subscription to *Hearth and Home*?

Yes, we do.

Excellent. Now you have the opportunity to try out another charming family publication, *Anna*, at a significant discount. Are you familiar with this publication?

Somewhat. It has those celebrity interviews.

Lovely. We are now offering faithful *Hearth and Home* subscribers the next four issues of *Anna* for eight euros, and, in addition . . .

It has all those celebrity interviews. I'm not really interested in that.

Of course not. I was guessing that might be the case. As a matter of fact, we have another publication that might interest you on an entirely different level, *Home Physician*.

We don't really get sick.

Of course not. People nowadays don't have time for things like that. An active, healthy person has so many other concerns. Nowadays many people consider their home decor to be a sort of safe haven. Are you familiar with the design magazine *Deko*?

It looks like my brood is about to get home from school. I should start getting food ready now.

Food, of course, but after that basic necessity comes your home, your-self, your environment. If you try out the design magazine *Deko* for six months, you will have the opportunity to participate in a draw for the grand prize of an Alvar Aalto stool.

No-one can sit on those.

A matter of taste, indeed, which I would have responded to in exactly the same way myself. In addition to the grand prize, we will be raffling off an espresso maker worth one hundred euros.

I don't drink that tar coffee.

Yes. I prefer a good old Finnish Mocha Gold myself. Which reminds me that it's best to stick to the old favourites. For a faithful, long-term subscriber like yourself, we have a special bonus offer on an old, safe favourite, *Good Company*.

It had Lauri Tähkä on the cover once.

Indeed. It may have.

It did. I can't stand his voice and all that prancing around.

Exactly, but he was just on the cover of that one issue.

That was enough. It shows what the magazine is about. It sounds like the kids are coming in from school now, so I'll have to hang up.

I could call back at a better ti . . .

A beep, beep, beep, beep came from the headphones.

You never got used to hang-ups. There was something violent and personal about them, even though she knew that the customers weren't thinking about her as they slammed the receiver in her ear. Or they were, but not by name.

Maija sighed, and, just before sinking into self-pity, remembered her previous job at the customer-service counter in a big chain department store where people came to return defective products and vent their displeasure at this one petite woman. In that job Maija was forced to confront people's disappointments and anger face to face, without the distance afforded by the telephone. As if the broken bread machines, the leaky Thermoses and the hairdryers that were making weird noises had crystallized a whole life's worth of disappointment and despair, and as if it were all Maija's fault, as if she were responsible for the hot water kettle bought on clearance that sprayed water on your legs and isn't eligible for a full-price refund, but for which our department store can offer you a twenty-euro gift card in compensation.

Maija remembered the end of that job all too well. A certain female customer had returned a vibrating device meant to firm up the midsection, claiming it was worthless. According to the woman, the device had not removed the fat stuck to her midsection at all, that it had just created false hope and consumed a ridiculous amount of electricity.

Maija had taken out the operating instructions. It promised that the device would support the owner's resolve, but that losing weight was primarily a matter of changes in diet and lifestyle. The device would speed up the process that the customer started herself in other ways.

The woman claimed that at the time of sale, she had been specifically promised that after two months of jiggling, the fat would have almost disappeared, and that the salesperson hadn't said a single word about diet or lifestyle, which for her part the woman saw no need to change. Maija repeated again what it said in the instructions.

The woman moved in closer to Maija and said, "Do you know what kin' of life I've lived, girl? There ain't been time to count no calories lookin' after four brats to make sure they survive this world, where apparently people ain't just pissin' in our eyes but also on our bellies. I ain't goin' nowhere nohow until that money is here in front of me. Don' you go preachin' to me here in front of people about lifestyles, girl. You ain't seen nothin' but teenybopper posters on your wall. Don' you go talkin' to a grown woman. You just start pushing buttons on that machine and give me my money back for this piece of junk."

Maija, who thought she was a bright, customer-oriented person, couldn't handle the situation. Tears welled up in her eyes. The pressure brought words to her mouth. The irate, sweating woman stood panting before her. Other customers peeked nervously from behind the woman. Time stopped.

Maija heard herself say, "You listen here, you cow. The best way to get rid of those rolls of blubber is to go out walking and give up chocolate. This contraption is bogus, but it isn't broken. You're broken, just like me."

After saying this, Maija left the counter, went into the manager's office and said, "Some lardarse is about to come in here and badmouth me. She's telling the truth. Here's my keycard."

Maija remembered how she had walked out of the department store. The sun had cast strips of light on the walls of the buildings, and her incipient unemployment had felt like freedom. The memories of broken appliances and useless gadgets had crunched to bits in the frozen snow, and everything had been clear and beautiful for a moment.

Maija punched in a new number.

Hello. Sisko Marjamaa speaking.

Maija Malmikunnas from Periodicalls here. Hello. Am I calling at a bad time?

Not really. I was just burying the cat.

Oh, how sad.

It isn't sad at all. Shitty kitty. It ate the baby's food.

I'm sorry to hear that.

Oh, I don't know. It was begging for it.

The baby food?

No, to be killed. I hit it with a hammer.

How about I call another time ...

Just state your business. There might not be another time. That's just what life is like. And the first time is always the best time.

Yes. I have a special magazine offer for you ...

What's the bonus? What do I get if I order?

Actually at the moment we have a very sort of down-to-earth campaign going on. I won't offer you *Pets* right now for obvious reasons, but what do you think? Are you familiar with *Wild Colt*?

Does it come with tips?

Excuse me?

Trotting tips.

No. As I understand it, this magazine approaches horses, ponies and colts from a non-competitive perspective.

The magazine can take any approach it wants, but you can be sure those critters are going to make it a competition. Speed is built into them. Just put your hand on the side of a horse sometime. You can feel it in there, throbbing, trying to get out. The speed that is.

Yes. *Wild Colt* is actually more of a little girls' thing anyway. But we are also having a special on *Hunting and Fishing*.

We already got that once. It had good stories in it. Except the ones about the old guys who let the fish go again. There isn't any sense in that. You catch it, you fry it. Does it still have stories like that?

I haven't thumbed through it all that recently, but I believe it focuses on the killing and exploitation of quarry.

What's the bonus?

At the moment, you receive a leather wallet and a map of Finland in conjunction with a six-month subscription.

How many pockets does the wallet have, and can you see Valkeajärvi on the map?

Huh. I haven't seen the wallet in question, but it is high quality, and I supposed that its value is about . . .

Can you see Valkeajärvi on the map?

Yes, I suppose so.

You suppose so? It has to be there. Will you give me your word that it has Valkeajärvi on it? My husband drowned in that lake. It has to be on the map. Will you give me your first name?

Yes, I . . .

Your whole name. I'll write it down. Oh, I left the pen in the house. That was the cat's fault too. Well, tell me your name, and I'll remember it.

Maija Malmikunnas. From Periodicalls. The number should be recorded on your caller I.D. and you can . . .

Everything gets recorded somewhere. But this is simple enough. So, this is Sisko Marjamaa here on the other end. Six months of *Hunting and Fishing*. Wallet and map thrown in. If the lake Eino drowned in is on it, all is well. Send the bill and the bonus gifts. The address is . . . do you have a pen?

Yes.

The address is Korennontie one ninety-five. Seven-o-two-o-o, Korento. Do you know what?

What?

The uglier the place, the prettier the name. What is it with that? This place ain't never seen no dragonflies. Goodbye.

Goodbye.

It was 2:45 p.m.

Maija took the microphone contraption off her head and checked her tally so far. She had sold ten magazine subscriptions. She had had the phone slammed in her ear seventeen times – eight times a customer had used foul language and one had used polite language. A normal day in a unique life. Why not a unique day in a normal life? Once polite, eight times foul. Why not eight times polite and once foul? Why not the other way around sometimes?

Maija went over to the coffee machine and picked up the new package of coffee sitting next to it. Maija scraped at the tape with a fingernail, but it didn't want to come off. Finally she caught the tape and pulled. The package slipped from her hand onto the floor, spilling the dark brown grounds all over the place. "Your daily bread will be crumbs, girl," Her father had always used to say. Maija tried to shift the pile onto a piece of paper, but was too greedy. She took too much and the paper gave way, spilling the coffee back onto the floor. Her mother always said, "We're all in God's palm here." It was starting to look like that wasn't quite true, Maija thought. We were probably on his knee once, but as he bounced us in the air we fell off, slipping between the thick floorboards and through the subfloor down to the earth. And here we are, surrounded by coffee grounds and all the other rubbish, and this is probably also where the breadcrumbs are that Dad was talking about. We just have to maintain a calm, optimistic attitude to stick it out long enough to haul ourselves back up to the floor.

The coffee percolated in the machine. Maija poured a cup and looked at the clock. She still had to stick it out for another hour and a half. She noticed four packages of coffee on the shelf. She took one of them and shoved it in her bag. Stealing gave her a strange energy. Maija had discovered this for the first time at the hair salon when she pinched a bottle of expensive shampoo from the rack. Theft is a balancing of accounts. If a hair salon grossly overcharges, then you have to take something without paying. Maija thought the same thing applied to the Periodicalls Corporation. If the commission they pay for a subscription doesn't correspond to the emotional bruises received in working with the customers, then the employee has to balance the accounts.

At first, stealing had been attended by certain moral problems, but those had been solved by a television programme. The programme had told about the compensation system for high-powered corporate executives. Their pay was tied to the profits of the company by a simple calculation. If the company made this and this much profit, the executive got this and this much bonus pay. Maija paid particular attention when one executive emphasized that through this incentive system, the executive bound himself to the company. The executive in question led a firm that had succeeded in turning record profits by reducing staff, and one and a half million euros of this profit had been lopped off for the executive. Maija drew her own conclusions from this and now considered her pilfering more of an exciting hobby than anything else. Especially when the biggest stock options were paid to the leaders of state-owned companies, i.e. in a roundabout way from the common purse. Maija remembered saying to her husband Biko that she had never been given such clear direction from any documentary.

THE HELPER

Isto Ruusutie sat across from Helena Malmikunnas and rustled his papers. Ruusutie had laid the groundwork for their session as well as possible the week before, but he felt that Malmikunnas was still reserved. It showed in her body language. She sat with her upper body bent backwards, the back of her head solidly against the wall. She had set her hands in her lap mechanically, not naturally, not relaxed. Her eyes looked towards him, but at the same time past him. Ruusutie knew the type: dutiful. He recorded it in his report: dtfl.

Ruusutie said that his professional title was "consultant", but asked Helena to forget everything connected to that word. He hoped that Helena would approach him more as a helper, a fellow traveller and a listening ear.

Helena looked at Ruusutie and the wallpaper. Ruusutie had justified the choice of wallpaper by appealing to how cut off we are from nature. Having free, lush nature on the wall of the meeting room reminds us in a charming way of our roots and our desire to return to them in due course. The wallpaper depicted marsh, anthills and quagmire. Helena didn't like the wallpaper, but found a dead standing pine on it from behind which a vernal sun glimmered. She focused her gaze on the pine tree, next to which stood Ruusutie's blond, short-cropped hair, reflecting the ambient light.

Ruusutie emphasized in particular that Helena should answer his questions as openly as possible. Openness is one of our most important tools, a little like the hoe in bygone days. Only an open mind can get us down really deep, where the human eye can't quite reach. The purpose of this session was to map out the heart of the problem, to flush it out of hiding and tame it in the service of the whole.

Our goal is not to fear the problem, but for the problem to fear us.

Ruusutie asked if Helena was ready. Helena nodded.

If you had to describe your work day in one phrase, what would it be?

Old people's home.

Can you be more specific?

The people are young and dynamic, but they say the same things every day, just in a different order. They are in motion, but standing still. This is the common illusion we all share.

Do you ever think in the morning that you would like to change your life?

Every morning.

Have you intended to do anything about it?

I have, but I never accomplish anything.

How much of your time at work is taken up by meetings?

70 per cent of all of my time.

Do you feel like you can influence the course of each day?

Everything slips out of my hands. I can't remember anymore what I was saying or what I just said. I see white. I don't mean right now, but in general.

Where do you see white?

Basically everywhere.

Do you mean a meeting room or some other space?

There isn't any space. I mean, there isn't any other space than meeting space. Everything is meeting, negotiating. When I answer the phone, I say I'm in a meeting. I've noticed that I never answer that I'm at work.

Have I understood correctly that you find you can't really concentrate in meetings?

I can't get hold of anyone anymore. Everyone loses their shape and disappears into that whiteness. They are black spots in the whiteness.

Can you be more specific? In what whiteness?

You can't make whiteness more specific.

Are you stressed?

No. Or yes. No. Because if I answer yes, then someone will be called in here to write me up a sick leave order, even though I'm well-paid and privileged. So, no. I'm not stressed. I have never been stressed. I don't count being pissed off as being stressed.

Do you feel like you would like to use coarse language more often?

I do, but then I don't, because you can't express anything with coarseness. Most expressions like that have lost all their meaning.

Do you feel like you don't have anything to give the company anymore?

I don't want to give anything to anyone. I want things to be given to me.

Like what?

Room to breathe. Oxygen. Air.

If we think of the word "meeting", what is there in that process that you would like to change?

Meet. Meat. Blood.

Now I don't understand.

Blood. Meet. Meat. Bloody meat. Or the verb "to meet". Meet your doom. Or your maker. Maker. Baker. Faker.

I mean the negotiations you find yourself in each week, if not daily.

So do I. I wanted to break it up into pieces, the word that is, so I would know what it has inside it.

O.K. We're in no rush. Our company is just studying the work environment. Take all of this with a grain of salt.

There was a field at my grandma's house. A grain field. You could see it out the window. A view. I don't have that.

Exactly. You filled out a form that talked about your subordinates. I've gone through it. You didn't comment on your subordinates in any way. In every space you ticked the option: "Don't know". I think you do know.

Yes, I do, but I don't want to say anything about them. The state I'm in isn't their fault. Nothing has been anyone's fault for a long time. No-one is sitting on the defence side of the courtroom. Everyone is signing up to be judges, prosecutors and victims. Especially victims.

But, for example, in similar interviews with Kähkönen, Laakso and Reinikka, I've got the impression that there are significant tensions and conflicts hiding there. It would be good to relieve those tensions.

The only thing that can diffuse that bomb is the power of the market itself, but it doesn't have time. It never has. It has to run from meeting to meeting. And then there are all of the children's hobbies.

You keep playing with words. Did you know that is a sign of anxiety? Trying to be clever all the time.

I did.

O.K. Let's go back to the beginning. You said you wanted to change your life every morning. What have you thought to do about it?

I would like to walk along a shoreline road on the edge of the city as it is just waking up, to sit down on the pavement and look for a moment at the ships and the birds and the other people, people to whom I wouldn't need to sell myself or anything else, especially not ideas. After that I would like to walk to the market square, to sit down there next to the pigeons with a cup of coffee and chat with someone I don't know, openly and amiably, without using any of the following words: "customer-oriented", "pace-setter" and "challenging". This stranger with whom I would speak could be a street sweeper, a midwife, an electrician, a taxi driver or maybe even a criminal, just so long as he doesn't have anything to do with my profession. We would sit there a moment, say our goodbyes, and I would continue on my way to the Maternity Hospital. Not that I would have any business there, but because to me the building represents a place where there are no opinions, just emotion. Perfectly red, white and blue emotion. Besides an amusement park, it's the only place where a person is just a person, and small to boot. The baby, the woman who gave birth to it and the dumbfounded man standing next to her. They are all small for that moment. Small before that small great thing. I would walk there and sit in the café where bulging-bellied wonderful women sit with worried, proud men. I would sit there with them all, even though I wouldn't have any part or stake in anything happening there, but in a way I would feel like I was a part of it all. Perhaps I would feel like a mother, a baby or a husband, or like the guard who says in a kind but firm voice to the men in their leather jackets that they can go ahead and smoke, but they have to move a little further away from the main entrance. That's the kind of life I would like for myself.

O.K. This is how I see things: you aren't going to be living that life, at least not in the near future. You're going to be living this life. We have to play the cards we have.

I can't see any cards anywhere, even though everyone keeps talking about them. And even if I did have cards, I wouldn't be able to play anymore. I'm not interested in winners or losers anymore, and especially not in the game. Mum sends postcards. Lately I haven't felt like reading them.

You should step back and look at your situation as part of a larger whole. In a way, I see you as having painted yourself into a corner. Do you feel that way yourself?

If I did feel that way, I would be happy. But now I don't feel anything. And I don't see any whole. If our company were to go bankrupt right now, it wouldn't hurt anything. This is the only feeling I have left.

So you don't see business as having any purpose or significance?

No. I mean this company. I'm not talking about companies in general, but rather this company in particular.

Have you expressed these feelings within the company?

No.

Do you have any forum, besides this session, where you could unload your feelings?

The toilet.

There must be some other forum?

Christmas parties.

O.K. We are clearly in a situation where you don't see any peer group with which you can discuss this difficult situation. You're holding so many things inside that soon your system won't be able to take it. You clearly aren't committed to the goals of the firm. You aren't in step with the firm. Do you remember the moment you joined the firm? Did you feel like the goals of the firm were your own?

What were those goals?

You're the one who should know them.

To make money. Ethically, but aggressively. Leading market share. But in an ethically sustainable way. Something like that. Then it got lost somehow . . . the . . .

What?

Something.

Meaning?

No. That was money. And there's nothing wrong with that. But then you have to connect some sort of . . .

Now I don't follow you.

After the money they always tack on some sort of fluff.

Meaning?

Yes, but it wasn't Finnish. Or it was ... but not really ...

Should we perhaps call this good for today?

Now I remember. It went something like this: "The purpose of the company is to take leadership in the market in an ethically sustainable, but sufficiently aggressive way, but nevertheless not in such a way as to give people the impression that all we are doing is making money, but rather that in addition to the bottom line there should also be the feeling that we care about the customer ..." Something like that ...

Yes. It sounds ... Yes ... That sounds ...

Like the N.A.T.O. option.

No, but in a certain way it captures ...

Don't start trying to translate it into real Finnish. I'm the patient here.

I wouldn't use that term. We're trying to map out the pain spots together and work out if we have a way out ...

Do you see that dead tree?

Where?

There, in the wallpaper.

Yes. What about it?

It's dead, but it's still standing. Everyone knows that it's dead, but it is treated as if it were alive, sometimes even better than alive. I remember well how whenever we were on a lingonberry expedition with Dad he would always stop in front of trees like that and say, "It isn't dead – it's resting." A person who has died standing up can't rest.

Why not?

They immediately give her a new name.

Would you like to be that dead tree? To rest namelessly?

I would like to rest as Helena.

Do you feel resistant to change?

Excuse me?

Resistant to change. Do you like to resist change?

I like to resist stupidity.

Exactly. But the management at your company has given me a paper written up by a consultancy that mentions, not by name of course, powers that are resistant to change. Do you feel like you belong to that group?

If I say I do, will you tick the box on the paper that says, "To be removed from the building right after Elvis"?

Not at all. I don't make decisions and I don't even have a box like that. I'm just mapping things out.

You're mapping things out. This is touching. I don't resist change. I don't resist conformity and freezing in place, if it's used to make a profit. I don't resist anything or support anything before I know what the plan entails. The content is what matters. Have you been to the jam shelves in the shops? They have all sorts of jars. There are expensive jams and then the cheap jams for everyone else. Do you know what? The jam in those cheaper jars is the same jam as in the more expensive ones. The jar is just different. The cheap one says Rainbow, the expensive one something claiming the jam was made by Granny Tyräkäinen. I'm one of the Rainbow people – the content is what matters.

Is there something in the way the company does business that you would like to change?

Last week I had twenty-five meetings. Five a day. That makes six litres of coffee and eighteen bread rolls and one thousand minutes of speech. This is calculated assuming that each meeting lasts approximately forty minutes. One thousand minutes of speech, of which ten minutes were important, and not even that if Kähkönen was around. I'm wasting precious time out of the only life I have going over trivial things with trivial adults, and I've already turned into a trivial talking box who clearly pisses you off, but luckily your billing is one hundred and fifty euros per hour plus tax.

I'm sensing that we should continue another day.

You have a bald spot, Ruusutie. The clock is ticking. We're down to the final hairs on our heads.

Yes.

Yes, indeed. Have you ever counted how many Easters you have left? How many Christmases, how many summers? I have thought about it. Guess where. In those meetings. While people are speaking there's time. That's my quality time. When I hear Kähkönen or Kallio starting up, I know I will have a minimum of six minutes to consider my own personal end times. Don't look at me that way. You're looking at me and thinking, here we go again, another shiny humanities graduate who lost her way in the big, bad corporate jungle and is whining about the conditions now. Another walking dead sociology dropout bitching about the credit on her social security card running out.

Not me.

Yes, you. You think I'm tired of capitalism and its laws, its cold logic. You are mistaken. I'm not at all fed up with making deals or adding value or billing or profits and losses or the jungle or all the biting dung beetles it offers into the bargain. I am tired of every new boss hauling his command staff and army in here and jamming everyone's calendar full of meetings and committees and memoranda and seminar retreats and strategy working groups and every new mid-level circus clown pulling a new PowerPoint rabbit out of his hat, droning on in American English, singing the same old refrains to new words. Every little crisis or hiccup wakes up the rats in the sewer and they climb up the drains into the executive team's offices.

I think this is all for now.

It is. Can you change the wallpaper for next time? I'm cut off from nature.

POSTCARD, LAKE SCENE

My little Maija!

Once we were walking with you in the field. There was some cow parsley growing. You wanted to pick it. The hollow tube made a snapping sound. When a person breaks, there isn't any sound. You need to keep your ears open out there in the business world. You also have to hear what people don't say. We picked a lot of apples. Your father made jam. Biko is welcome too.

Your mother

THE THIEF

Maija Malmikunnas sat in the interrogation room of the police station watching the thundering grief at the death of the princess on the television bolted to the wall.

Maija wondered why the television was on and whether the programme in question was commemorating the tenth anniversary of the departure of Princess Diana or whether it was just a normal rerun. Hysterical people cried and talked at length, incoherently and in fits and starts, about what the princess had meant to them.

The policeman asked Maija what her attitude would be about stealing after being caught this first time. Maija stared at Elton John, who had appeared on the screen dressed in a pink jacket and yellow trousers. Elton talked about how to him Diana had meant light, solace, brightness and love. Maija snapped out of it and answered that getting caught wouldn't change her attitude to stealing itself, but rather introduce a new perspective on it. Elton John said that humanity had lost its conscience with Diana, a candle the flame of which had now been forever extinguished. The policeman observed that if a young woman like her intended to continue her life with that attitude, it would ultimately be the responsibility of society to intervene in her activities with a prison sentence. Elton John was no longer able to speak – his voice faltered and he broke down sobbing. An assistant brought him a large handkerchief embroidered with his initials. The policeman said that this time Maija would get off with a fine, but that the next time the authorities would have to consider other solutions.

After Elton John, the microphone was shoved in front of the regional director of the Red Cross. She wasn't able to say anything because Elton John was blubbering behind her. The regional director attempted with her uncomfortable expression to show that she would like someone to please move the fat troubadour a little further away to continue his whimpering. According to the policeman, Maija shouldn't be playing with her life, because a criminal record follows a person throughout her years. Three men dressed in mink coats and satin trousers escorted Elton John to a white car approximately seven metres long that had a boomerang-shaped antenna decorated with mother-of-pearl attached to the roof. According to the regional director, Diana had always had enough time for the poor and unfortunate of the world, and that she had often visited refugee camps to see their harsh conditions.

The policeman extended the ticket to Maija and expressed his hope that she would look upon it as more of a caring than a punitive gesture. Maija thanked him for the piece of paper and remained staring at the television where Diana was shaking hands with a starving child. The child's arm looked like a bony magical talisman that was attached to the shoulder with a screw. When Diana let go, the arm fell, swinging listlessly for a moment and then hanging next to the frail body.

The policeman noticed Maija's intense gaze and asked whether the princess's story was familiar to her. Maija shook her head. The policeman told her that he had taped the recording himself and liked to play it at work sometimes. According to him the princess's legacy for those of us left behind was hope and light. Every one of us can do a good turn for our neighbours – it's a question of choice and willpower. In a room where so many fallen people had confessed their deeds, it was good to have the humane spirit of the princess floating in the air after the vile and filthy words were done.

Maija realized she had breached a large dam, because the policeman dug out of his desk a book that had Diana's picture on the cover. He looked as if he was preparing for a long presentation. In these cases it was good to know a person's name, so Maija looked at the fabric patch sewn above the policeman's breast pocket. Sami Niittymäki, Komisario.

Maija told Niittymäki that she had read the book and that unfortunately right now she was in a bit of a hurry because she needed to pick her child up from the nursery. According to Niittymäki, it would be good for Maija to think carefully about her behaviour, particularly with her child in mind, and the spiritual legacy that Diana left to all of us. Maija asked what that spiritual legacy was.

Niittymäki rummaged around in his drawer, taking out a C.D., pushing it into a player and asking Maija to sit. There were scratchy, reedy sounds and then after a few seconds the interrogation room was filled with a grandiloquent piano introduction, after which Elton John began to sing about a candle that flickers in a strong wind without going out. Maija remembered hearing the piece on the recording of Diana's memorial concert, but she hadn't been able to empathize with it then either. The skilful singer's nostalgic chorus stung her, but in the opposite way than the singer intended. Maija realized that she was not able to mourn Princess Diana along with the rest of the western world now – nor had she been able to at the time of her death. To her, Diana was just a well-to-do Englishwoman who died when her luxury car crashed into a cement pillar.

Maija wanted out of the room at once. Niittymäki sat in his chair, eyes closed, rocking himself into the chorus with the experienced motions of one who had listened to it hundreds of times. At exactly the same second as Elton, Niittymäki ascended from this reality to the other, lilac-coloured, good, caring world, away from the coarseness of everyday life that assaults us from every side.

Maija availed herself of the opportunity and slipped out of the room. The woman at the duty desk looked at Maija questioningly. Maija waved the ticket at her and said goodbye.

After getting outside, Maija went to a park and looked for a bench that would be as far as possible away from the gravel path that traversed the park.

She was overcome by a sick, guilty feeling, not so much for the poor children of the world, but for the fact that she had never felt anything about the princess. Maija remembered as a child being confused by the attitudes of adults towards the famous people in magazines and on the television. How could they say they loved people they didn't know, who spoke, sang, danced, played sports and wrote well?

The lady next door claimed that it was utterly impossible for her to imagine life without Eino Grön. Maija didn't know anything about Grön except for the newspaper picture with him standing on a rocky outcropping with his mouth open and the Viking Mariella cruise ship in the background. Grön looked like a pockmarked seal who was shouting for help, even though the caption claimed he was interpreting Argentinian tango.

Maija also remembered how her high school P.E. teacher had quoted javelin thrower Seppo Räty's four-word meditations during a morning assembly and said that he lived according to Seppo's cycle.

The auditorium went silent. The P.E. teacher told how between the most important competitions there were always two long years during which Räty lifted weights and didn't say a single word. The teacher said that during those two years he felt an inexpressible powerlessness and wistfulness, but as the games approached, he awoke from his elegiac melancholy like a bear, feeling a strong solidarity with the Bear of Tohmajärvi.

Maija had never experienced any connection with the people on television and in the magazines. To her they were just jabbering frogs, and the kisses of journalists weren't going to turn them into princes. On the contrary – by flattering them and building them up, their frogginess only grew. They jumped, slimy, from magazine to magazine croaking the same thing, their eyes wet with their own excellence.

Maija was pissed off, retrospectively. She would have wished that a moment ago Niittymäki had been paying attention to her, not a far-off princess. Maija thought stealing a meat pie and a hoodie demonstrated unique boldness because there were security guards on duty in both the grocery and clothing departments. Niittymäki also could have asked in a bit more detail about Maija's profession and its unique challenges. Niittymäki didn't understand what it was like to work under difficult conditions without Elton John's heartening piano, what it was like to search for an appropriate thing to steal in a country dominated by two central retail franchises whose selections were almost identical, what it was like to live when you can't share the progress of the day with your co-workers and what it was like to slog away day after day without a single word of encouragement.

Niittymäki's picture of the world had been exposed as altogether too well-defined and rigid, as if it were built out of black and white and their synthesis, grey.

Maija felt like returning to the police station and telling Niittymäki the following: shoplifting is taking something that isn't anyone's. A store's merchandise is just on its way to being someone's. If you take something from your neighbour that he has bought with his own money, that is wrong, but the goods in stores are everyone's, that is, no-one's, property. For this reason I don't consider the fine I received for stealing to be a punishment, but rather an unpleasant reminder of my carelessness. Doesn't the other word say it all: "petty theft"? Lawmakers went to great trouble to invent a word that sounds like an insignificant offence. I nicked a splinter of rock from a mountain. I took a grain of sand from a desert. I scooped a bucket of water from the ocean. I'm sorry, how can I make this up to you. To sum up: your words, Niittymäki, have a moralizing, didactic tone, and that is why they are tired, predictable and bland.

Maija realized she had regressed to ranting and remembered the card her mother had sent warning against talking to herself. It was fine for her to give advice from the sidelines, living with a man who frequently stopped talking altogether. There wasn't any point talking to her mother much about the things of this world. She understood things in her own way and wasn't shy about dispensing advice.

Maija rose from the bench and walked to the nursery. There were thirty metre-tall people dressed in almost identical snowsuits romping in the yard. The black and white one was Maija's. She waved to Saara, who jumped in the air and ran into Maija's arms. For a moment, Maija felt as if she was in the child's arms, not the child in hers.

POSTCARD, AUTUMN SCENE

Pekka, my only son!

I hear love has brought you one of those new, blended families. I'm happy for you and hope you'll be able to form a good relationship with the kids. It won't be easy since they already have a father. But I'm sure you'll get along if you really concentrate, if you really try. You can become a father that way too. But don't try to force yourself on them too much – they might be frightened and start to shy away. You father made sea-buckthorn juice. It's bitter, but it has all the most potent vitamins in it. There's a bottle waiting here for you.

Your mother

THE IMITATOR

Pekka Malmikunnas stood in front of the mirror. He smoothed the bronzing cream on his face. He pressed the moustache on tight, and thanked the late Peruvian composer Daniel Alomía Robles for a new opportunity.

Pekka turned sideways and checked his outfit one more time. Outwardly everything was in order. The rest depended on him.

Pekka had bought the black felt hat from a flea market, where in a junk box he had also found the moustache. He had borrowed the poncho from a friend from school, Pasi, who had a hippie past. Pasi had asked what he was going to use it for, to which Pekka had answered that his company was organizing a fancy dress party. Pasi had been curious to know about Pekka's current life and job, but Pekka's battery had suddenly run out in the middle of the call.

Pekka put the finishing touch on his outfit, a fringed shoulder bag he had filched from a corner in his big sister Helena's hallway. He had been forced to remove the Ruisrock stickers and the peace symbol, a relic of the domestic Finnish hippie period he remembered irritating his father Paavo so much. In Paavo's opinion, peace had been purchased in blood on a battlefield conspicuously lacking in hippies.

Pekka put a flute in the bag, looked one last time in the mirror and opened the door. The wind went under the poncho and fanned it up like a skirt. With his right hand he held the poncho down, and with his left he held the felt hat on his head. It was hard being a Peruvian.

There weren't many people around the Three Smiths Statue, even though the department store next door was having its Crazy Days sale. Pekka remembered the long passageway that went from the warrens of the Makkaratalo straight to the high street. Tens of thousands of people walked along the passageway over the course of a day. Pekka went close to the exit of the passageway and set down his mother Salme's small wooden basket, on the side of which he had written in small letters, *I am musiccian from Peru and nw homelss.*

Pekka raised the pan flute to his lips and blew. The thin, clear sound echoed in the mouth of the passageway, telling of the refugee's longing for the slopes of the Andes, away from this cold land. Pekka attempted to communicate through his playing that this was serious, that if you didn't drop some money in that wooden basket right now, the condor in the song would fall out of the sky and land on its face, terminally, that the bird had already fallen from its perch of earnings-linked unemployment payments, floundering somewhere up there in the heavens, beyond the reach of the social safety net, not over the Andes, but over goddamn Merihaka, and soon, if your conscience isn't pricked, that bird is going to come over and bang on your head with his sharp beak and ask, "Anybody home? Any humans in there? You know, the kind who are always supposed to understand a neighbour in need, even if that neighbour is from somewhere far away and doesn't wear the same kind of hat as you. This time he's exotic, an Indian with a feather in his cap, flat broke, without even a reservation to go back to."

A man dressed in a long winter coat and tracksuit bottoms, wearing a beanie with the logo of a bank stitched into it, stopped in front of Pekka, gawking with red eyes. He looked Pekka up and down and then came right up in front of Pekka.

"The fuck you're an Indian."

Pekka had prepared himself for all sorts of reactions and insults the prejudiced Finns might throw at him. That was the life of an immigrant. However, the claim made by the man in the stocking cap was sufficiently radical that it could not go unanswered. Pekka lowered the flute from his lips and sang, "I'd rather be a sparrow than a snail. Mmmm mmmm. Mmmm mmmm."

Pekka could only remember one line from the American version, but he loaded that one phrase with so much feeling that the phrase nearly came to pieces at the end. He remembered from his childhood what the display designer Alfred Supinen had said as he watched Pekka and his friend's circus show. "When you imitate a lion or a rabbit, it isn't enough to look like them. You have to become them. The audience has to believe that Pekka is a lion and Jussi is a rabbit." Pekka had understood Alfred's words immediately and become a lion so well that Jussi had fled all the way out into the yard. And since then Pekka had treasured up Alfred's words in his heart, remembering them now in his moment of need as the beanie man glared at him malevolently, questioning his identity.

Pekka sang the phrase three times, lifted the flute, played the nostalgic melody as expressively as he could, lowered the flute from his lips and said to the man, "Nachos buenos povertias."

The man was silent for a moment and then said, "Sorry. I mean, never mind. I don't have anything on me right now. Otherwise I would give you something."

Pekka smiled sympathetically and took a map of Peru out of his pocket. On the upper part of it he had made a dot with a red felt-tip pen. He pointed at the dot with his finger, thumped his chest over the heart with his right hand and said, "Houm."

The man nodded, patted Pekka on the shoulder and took a bottle of eau de cologne out of his pocket, offering it to Pekka, who shook his head. The man took a swig from the bottle, grimaced and said, "Los Kondor Paassa. Simon and Telefunken. Classic."

Then the man tottered on his way.

Pekka sighed and started from the beginning.

The previous unfortunate encounter gave Pekka's playing additional depth and made him feel even more Peruvian. He longed for the Andes, for gentle autumn rains, for his work as a herdsman, for his goat and for his beloved, who at this very moment might be selling her colourful handwork in the alleyways of Lima in order to travel to this northern land to be in the arms of her flautist.

A middle-aged, well-dressed man stopped in front of Pekka. He listened intently and then took a wallet out of his breast pocket and placed a twenty-euro note in the wooden basket. Pekka had fantasized about perhaps collecting such a sum by evening. As he stared at the note, Pekka played a couple of wrong notes, after which the man dug another ten euros out of his pocket.

"Sometimes playing off key is irritating, but sometimes it increases the believability of the distress. This was a case of the latter. The piece is good, but I've heard it approximately six hundred times now. My route to work goes right by here. The additional payment obliges you and your countrymen to diversify the repertoire. I have already become sufficiently familiar with the flight path of that particular bird," the man said, smiling and walking on.

Pekka attempted to keep his spirits up, despite his first two listeners having commented on his identity and repertoire. Pekka knew he was a pacesetter, a pioneer who would be forced to blaze his own path through the unbroken snow. He considered himself to be the first native Finnish immigrant, and in this sense his lot was even harder than that of regular newcomers, most of whom received a sympathetic reception from the authorities because of the civil wars raging in their native lands.

Pekka had discussed this issue with Maija and Biko, who had not understood Pekka's perspective at first, but after listening for a moment, Biko had been forced to acknowledge the logic of Pekka's position. In Pekka's opinion, Finland had become so different and strange in the last ten years that even a Finn could feel like an immigrant. We had been producing our own refugees for decades. Most Northern and Eastern Finns had been forced to move from their birthplaces towards the El Dorado of the South, not to mention the wartime evacuees.

Whenever he spoke of these things, Pekka had to emphasize that he was in no way anti-immigrant – he just felt that his fate was similar to theirs. Minus the exoticness bonus. Pekka was as Finnish-looking as anyone could be, and for that reason he could not appeal to the maternal or paternal instincts of empathetic people in his work. Next to Biko's pitch-blackness, Pekka's whiter-than-whiteness seemed insignificant.

An immigrant had to adjust to constant changes and the wishes of unfamiliar people. Because of this, Pekka made a concession to the previous passer-by and conjured "Guardian Angel" out of his flute, hoping it would bring the amount he had earmarked for a new moustache. The one he had now itched, and he had to constantly press it more firmly onto his skin, sometimes even in the middle of a song.

"Through the wilds of the world the lamb doth roam, a lovely angel guiding her home. The journey is long, no home is in sight, but the lovely angel walks at her right." Pekka wanted to show the Finns Peruvian hospitality by playing them a hymn that had been used to put hundreds of thousands of Finnish children to sleep, regardless of whether they or their parents belonged to the church. Pekka had last heard the piece at his big sister's house, when Helena had hummed it to Sini as she was falling asleep. Pekka had been shocked by how gloomy the piece was, because the only thing that protected the child in it was an invisible, imaginary being. Pekka had felt a seething rage towards the author of the song. If several generations had been lulled to sleep by whispering such a dark nursery rhyme, then was it any wonder there was no comfort or reconciliation to be found in the jungles of divorce and labour contract negotiations when the subconscious was pealing, "Wild is the wood and rocky the road, slippery the footing and heavy the load"?

Pekka tried to interpret the piece in such a way that the listener would have to fear for the child in the pitch-black forest. He made his voice break on purpose and gave the impression that the flute was weeping for the child.

An older woman stopped in front of the wooden basket and

lowered her bag to the ground. She concentrated, listening with her eyes closed. When Pekka blew the last breath of the angel, the woman took a one-hundred-euro note from her bag. She flashed it at Pekka and asked quietly in English if the young musician could come to her apartment and shepherd her into her final sleep with his flute. Pekka answered that he did not have the necessary professional proficiency. He was just a poor street musician from far-off Peru. The woman said that death does not concern itself with birthplace or professional proficiency. It simply comes and collects its due. But it would be nice to leave here with a pleasant flute accompaniment and the features of a beautiful man as the last thing reflected in her eyes.

Pekka hesitated. But not for long. One hundred euros was an appalling amount of money. He couldn't turn it down, even though the new task was daunting, especially given his repertoire. In addition to the condor and angel songs, all he knew was Jaakko Teppo's "Hilma and Onni", to which he didn't think he could do justice on the pan flute.

Pekka agreed.

The apartment was in a fashionable part of the city. The living room opened onto a view of the sea. Somewhere out there on the horizon was Estonia and all of Old Europe. The woman stamped out of the kitchen carrying a serving dish with savoury *hors d'oeuvres* and confections. She sat down on a velvet divan and invited Pekka to go ahead and remove his outerwear. Pekka could not take the poncho off, because he remembered that under it was a Päijät-Häme Banking Cooperative T-shirt. Pekka said he was fine the way he was.

He was trying to control himself, even though he would have liked to stuff all of the delicacies into his mouth, recognizing them as the creations of expensive bakeries. He contained himself, taking only a cream puff and a meringue confection. The woman watched

Pekka eat and poured a red drink into two delicate glasses. She said that before death it was good to take a glass of vodka and lingonberry juice. Pekka declined, saying that he hadn't had any alcohol since he left his homeland, because he feared it would return his thoughts to the Andes and make him lose his grip on the challenges of his new homeland.

The woman moved both glasses in front of herself, drank each dry at a single gulp and sighed. Then she lay down on the divan and told how she had been sober for the first seventy years or her life, but now, when all of her contemporaries had died, she had decided to give alcohol a chance.

She put four one-hundred-euro notes on the round smoking table and said, "The first is for playing, the second is for being here, the third is for falsehood and the fate of the fourth will be made clear later."

The woman introduced herself as Mirjam and extended her hand. Pekka, startled, said his name was Pablo.

"Well, now, Pablo," Mirjam said suddenly in Finnish. "You aren't Pablo, and I'm not Mirjam. I'm Mirja. The M at the end I got from the county, but the rest I got from Kontiola, my late husband. He was so rich that he didn't really know how rich he was. I am the daughter of a small farmer from Suomusalmi, who lives in her ex-husband's flat waiting to die. You are what you are. I'm not going to judge you or torment you. You're beautiful and you play well. That's enough for me. Could you play me something popular?"

"I don't know. My repertoire is rather slim. I think all I know is one piece by Jaakko Teppo."

"Is it popular?"

"Not really. Although it is a catchy tune."

"I'll pour more booze. Well now. Lay it on me."

"By the way, my name is Pekka."

"Is that so? Go ahead."

Pekka felt strange playing under his own name, but after getting past the opening theme of "Hilma and Onni" and on to the chorus, he felt himself relaxing. The flute interpreted their story with a Peruvian flavour, but maintained the pining feeling of the piece.

Mirja was swilling down big shots of the red drink and would occasionally close her eyes. When the flute belted out the melody, underscoring Onni's ultimate fate, Mirja opened her eyes and pushed three of the notes in front of Pekka.

"That wasn't exactly a pop song. It was some sort of Latin American or Spanish-flavoured love song, but that's fine. Would you like to earn the fourth hundred?"

Pekka nodded. Mirja filled her glass. The neck of the bottle clinked against the edge of the delicate glass.

"I want proof that I shouldn't die yet. I want a reason to live. Do you understand? I am a poor girl who got rich by accident. I didn't know what all Gunnar owned. This apartment and the cash in his second account and all sorts of stocks. We lived in the suburbs in a little two-bedroom apartment when Gunnar tripped on that young people's board with the wheels under it. It spun the old man upside down and landed him on his head. I'm so poor I have a hard time being rich. Well now. Listen to Mirjam going on again. Well, will you give me a reason to live? I want to see a young man naked and draw my conclusion from that. If it moves me in some way, it's worth living. If it doesn't, I'll get another bottle like this from the cupboard and Gunnar's sleeping pills. Would you do me this service for one hundred euros?"

Pekka didn't know what to say. Saliva dripped from the mouth-piece of the flute into his palm. He stood up from the chair and walked to the window. Seagulls were making wide, sweeping arcs, ending at a large rock where they stood screeching. Then one shot back into the sky, tossed about this way and that like a directionless, sharp-angled piece of rubbish and then tucked in its wings and fell like a big white bullet back to the same rock it had left from. Pekka didn't know what he should do. For money a person will make rubber boots, dig ditches, build mobile phones, sell snowboards, care for children, drive a taxi, play a flute. We do things for money, and then we leave our money behind. That's how things go, if they go right. Some people even take their clothes off for money. That's nothing special, but when he woke up that morning, Pekka hadn't prepared himself for a task of this kind.

Pekka closed his eyes and decided. If the seagulls are still on the rock when I open my eyes, I'll take off my clothes for Mirja and give her a reason to live. If the seagulls are gone, I'll walk out with my clothes on, and Mirja can sleep.

Pekka opened his eyes. The seagulls stood on the rock, screeching.

Pekka walked in front of Mirja and took his poncho off. The bank T-shirt looked stupid now – in the morning it had just felt practical. He took it off with effort, not making the gyrating motions common to these situations. Now he was bare above the waist, the tan line from the bronzing cream was clearly visible. He took off his trousers and kicked them into a pile on the floor.

A person isn't even close to naked with his socks on. But when Pekka took off his socks, he was as naked as he had ever been. You don't even notice being naked with a person close to you, but when Mirja looked Pekka up and down and down and up, Pekka felt like every part of him had been suddenly touched without permission.

"Will you turn around a couple of times and then walk like a cockerel around the room?" Mirja said.

Pekka turned around. He thought for a moment about cockerels and the way they walk. He had imitated any number of people and animals in his life, but he had never played a cockerel. He extended his neck as far up as he could, pushed his backside out, bent over slightly and began to walk a little jerkily, at the same time rocking his head from side to side as crisply as he could.

When the rooster had completed its circuit, Mirja raised her hand. The rooster stopped and straightened up into Pekka. Mirja gave Pekka the hundred euros.

"Pablo, Pekka and cockerel. I thank you for life."

THE SECOND PART

THE DONOR

I made breakfast for my mute husband, but he wasn't hungry. It made me feel anger and pity at the same time. Feelings had been mixing together often lately. Of course the best way is to have only one emotion turned on at a time, but my mind is seldom quite that orderly. My mood was also probably being influenced by the fact that I was leaving to meet the author.

I reminded Paavo that I was going to be leaving the village to look at *raanu* wall hangings again. He nodded like a whipped dog. He hasn't even been having opinions anymore. It felt all the same whether I told him where I was going or not.

I put clingfilm over the plate and patted Paavo on the shoulder. He shuffled off into the bedroom. He spent his days sitting there in front of the chest of drawers squinting at photographs, even though I had said that staring at pictures wasn't going to change it.

I began weeping on the bus. It was difficult with people all around. I concealed the crying with fake sneezes and complained to the person sitting next to me about my cold.

I arrived at the service station ten minutes early. The author was already sitting at the same table as the first time. He stood up, delighted, and asked if anything was new.

I said something inconsequential, because I couldn't tell the truth. He set the dictaphone on the table, took a stack of notes out of his breast pocket, gave a meaningful look and put the stack under the afternoon paper.

I felt dirty, even though I was doing this for a good cause. I had sent the first instalment to Helena, but I hadn't told her where it had come from. I had sent a card with the money explaining what it was for. Helena called me later and thanked me, but cried about me having sent cash. Apparently I should have sent it to her account, since cash makes you feel so dirty. I almost started shouting.

The author's finger was already on the button. You don't even have time to get your coat off before the machine turns on. I said that the first thing I was going to do after such a long trip was to have a coffee and a juice.

As I slurped these down, the author indicated a pile of paper and expressed a desire for me to familiarize myself on my trip home with the text he had written based on our first meeting and to comment on it later. I shook my head. I knew what kind of life I had lived. I was more interested in what was left ahead of me.

The author said that he had written a lot about my children's lives based on what I had told him, but that he had added things out of his own head related to the present day and the current social situation. This galled me, because I had already stressed repeatedly that the truth was enough. There wasn't any need to make anything up.

The author asked my forgiveness and said that he didn't want to annoy me unnecessarily. He said he had sold his records and his mountain bike and that this had allowed him to scrounge up an additional two thousand euros. He began to dig in his side pocket, but I told him to leave it well enough alone.

I suddenly felt faint. I grabbed the corner of a chair for support. I went completely limp. The author leaned closer and asked how I was feeling. I said something incoherent. The author put his hand on my shoulder. His hand felt like an oar I was grabbing from deep beneath the surface of the water.

I still don't know exactly what happened then, but suddenly I started telling about everything that had been happening recently, even though that was precisely what I had intended to stay silent about. Thankfully the dictaphone wasn't turned on. It might be that I had been carrying my burden for so long that I had to set it down now and then, at the feet of a stranger.

I gushed like a bottle of sparkling mineral water that's been rolling around in the footwell of a warm car for hours and then gets opened in a single pop.

I held the author by the hand and started to tell him everything that had made our good life so impossible that I had to go and sell it.

I made the author swear that everything I was telling him would stay between us and that he would under no circumstances put it in the book. He promised.

I started from the morning when I received word of what had happened.

The phone rang a little after 10.00, and there was Helena's number. Helena never called at that hour. And she shouldn't have been calling then either. I shouldn't have answered. I listened to the first words and dropped the phone on the floor. Paavo came and picked it up and listened some more and then hung up and threw the phone against the wall and walked into the kitchen and threw dishes and I heard a crash and went into the kitchen and there he was lying on the floor curled up like a big worm whimpering and then he went quiet for so long that I had to go and check if he was breathing and then I realized what my part would be – I would have to carry this thing for both of us and I became sure when Paavo got up off the floor and looked at me like a wrinkled little 72-year-old child who has had his beloved teddy bear or shovel or something else very important to him taken away and he fell against me and I was only barely able to stay upright and then we went to the couch and I tucked him in under a blanket and looked out the window at the apple trees and the grass and the potato patch and they didn't look like anything. I looked at the sky and it looked insignificant and pointless too and all of the birds I usually looked at happily looked more revolting than anything else a human eye might see and I went from the couch to the kitchen and set the coffee percolating even though it wasn't any time to be drinking coffee and I accidentally put in enough for at least eight people even though no-one was coming over and even if they were I would have thrown them out because there wasn't any point in anything and then the phone rang again even though it didn't have a cover anymore after Paavo threw it but I could still pick out Maija's number on the broken screen but why would I have answered it? I already had one crying child on the couch – I didn't want to deal with another one through the receiver and I thought about the camel they always talk about with its back breaking and I was sure I was that camel now and that our house and yard and lawn and everything I could see was the camel's dry desert sand and I was thirsty but no-one was giving me water and my back was breaking but no-one was help-ing me carry my burden and I sat on the kitchen floor and I called on that God they talk about so much but he didn't come to me, because he probably had other things to do in the Middle East or in Russia or in Afghanistan or somewhere the newspapers write about so much – he doesn't have time to come to Salme's kitchen in the middle of everything else he has to do and I had to stand up because I remem-bered I was supposed to make enough Karelian stew to last for several days and I took the meat out of the refrigerator and they looked like pieces of an animal that had been killed and I couldn't touch them and so we didn't have any food all day even though we should have because in the evening Paavo fainted when he got up off the couch to go to the toilet; I caught him so he didn't hurt his head and then the doorbell rang; I couldn't go opening it with these eyes, but the door wasn't locked and our neighbour, an electrician named Kallio, a sensible man in every way, came in and before he had time to take his shoes off I told him the thing and he let out a big damn it to hell and said he was going to make porridge and sandwiches since he was a widower and he wasn't in any rush and so he did and when he was puttering around in the kitchen just like any other day I was sort of able to give myself permission to collapse and I lay down on the couch and curled up next to Paavo and Kallio carried a stool over in front of us and on it were porridge and bread arranged so nicely that I slipped even further down because he was being so kind but I was still able to eat a little porridge and Paavo took a little piece of bread and then Kallio said he was going to take care of our household chores until this thing worked itself out and of course I sat up startled and said that we weren't about to start bothering our neighbours with our business any more than we already had, but he said it wasn't any bother and reminded us that his wife Katri had always bought yarn and needles and who-knew-what from us on credit and that apparently after Katri's death we hadn't come asking after the money and that this was just settling the account and that this thing was big enough that Kallio said from now on he was going to do what he knew how and what he didn't too, which reminded him that in situations like this you were supposed to do something that would take your mind off things for a while, and he told about how when his wife Katri collapsed on the floor in the hall with a brain haemorrhage and took her one-way trip out of here, Kallio had bought a karaoke machine and started to sing without being able to carry a tune and that was how he had got a little distance from the Katri thing but he didn't recommend singing equipment for us, instead coaxing us to go to the big city for the weekend with him for the trotting races, but we could see from Paavo's expression that there wasn't any point in saying anything more about horse racing – it would have served me just as well as anything except the thing that was in the front of my mind, right behind my forehead.

Well.

Then Kallio sat down next to us and started to sing some song – it wasn't clear what song it was – he sang so off key that he even noticed it himself and asked if we wanted him to leave, but we weren't able to want anything – the wheels in our heads were spinning – I just stroked Paavo's head wanting our old life back, the one I had before that call and when Kallio couldn't come up with anything else he went into the kitchen and I could hear chopping and he called out that he was going to make Karelian stew since it looked like the lady of the house had been interrupted and I couldn't say no and he went on cutting up rutabagas and carrots and onions and turned on the kitchen's portable radio and there was that nature programme on where those calm men answer all sorts of phone questions and there came this part where there was a question about species of birds that know how to come back to exactly the same nesting box even though they may have flown six thousand kilometres away for the winter and I stroked Paavo's head and thought about the birds and the terrible height and breadth of the sky they flew through and that there isn't anything marking the way, but they just know where to go and have the energy to flap their wings all that way and in that sense they're faithful like the bird they were talking about on the radio that comes back to that one certain tree on Lake Ylöjärvi even though there are bird boxes and nesting spots in other places too, and I thought about whether for the rest of my life I would always be returning to this day and this feeling even though there would be other days and other feelings, and whether Paavo and I would be stuck here, birds of this dark day always and forever, with this as our bird box.

Yes.

And time passed without me noticing and then soon familiar smells started to come from the kitchen when Kallio opened the oven door, apparently not trusting that Karelian stew if anything is one of those foods that you don't really prepare, it just gets ready on its own if you don't bother it, but the smell was so lovely now that it must have been ten seconds I didn't think of that horrible thing, but we weren't really hungry that night or afterwards for many weeks and Paavo and I shrank up into little raisin-shaped old people and over our eyes – I saw first when I looked at Paavo and then in the mirror – was a sort of film with a lot of water behind and it was all the same whether we cried or not; the water just stayed there waiting for the dried raisin to turn the tap on again, and it didn't care about time or place – our eyes could just tear up anywhere, and oh, how it hurt my soul when on a normal trip to the store, there at the till, it started to come and of course people couldn't know what had come over me and just figured I was crazy and thought that well she sure earned her comeuppance by taking people's money with yarn and needles and lace, and I started thinking evil of people and imagining all sorts of things, but I forgave myself for everything, and Paavo too the day he had an attack in the post office when we were sending Helena a parcel and for the address Paavo had just written Helena Malmikunnas, Helsinki, and then of course the worker asked Paavo to write a more precise address on it and Paavo said that they must know where his daughter lives down there – of course his head didn't have room for anything but our daughter and this thing, and he started shouting at the innocent worker that for fifty years he had been paying his small-business taxes and state taxes and local taxes and sales taxes and national insurance taxes and all the other stinking taxes and in the home stretch they start demanding that we write down redundant addresses, and I had to say to Paavo shut your mouth now so we can get the parcel to our girl, and after that he didn't say anything – he just froze over like a path in winter.

Mmm.

What else.

All sorts of things.

My throat was dry.

The author fetched me a mug of water.

The service station waitress glanced at us.

I drank the mug down in three gulps and looked at the author, who was solemn and pale. I suggested a sandwich and some fresh air.

He obeyed like a child and went outside.

I got some time to think in peace about what I had told him. I found that I didn't remember much of it and hoped the author didn't either. I looked through the glass as he wandered around the car park smoking a cigarette the way people who don't usually smoke do. He didn't seem to know what to do with himself. I imagine my verbal diarrhoea had found its way into his head and was sloshing around in there now.

I looked at the mute dictaphone, which without its red light looked insignificant, an abandoned box. It reminded me of Pekka's first tape recorder, which he called a boom box and on which he played that long-haired people's music. He got so into that music that it almost made me jealous. As if he had been cosseted in the music. Eyes closed lying on his cot without a care in the world about tomorrow. Or else he had so many cares that he had to escape into all that noise I guess. I pestered him about it for no reason. And then I latched on to the musicians' appearance and judged the whole thing based on that. As a mother you always hope and fear that your own daughters won't end up under the arm of one of those messy-haired men and die in a drug den, and, given that full-time fear, I didn't have the energy left over to find out if there was any rhyme or reason to the music.

The author came in looking pained. He said it was a little irritating that I had said so much without the dictaphone. That was the idea, I reminded him, saying that the truth doesn't change whether or not the machines are on. And not everything has to be written down for people to read – they have enough to carry with their own worries. That was something I had always wondered about in all this art stuff, that they have to go to so much effort to specifically dig up the worst things in life and make a big to-do about them when that energy could be directed towards describing good things.

The author said that his purpose was not to wallow in the darker side of my life, but that there also wouldn't be any sense in keeping them covered up either. He thought the whole thing was a game of light and dark, that then in the afterglow of reading the book's reader can mull things over and decide which one comes out on top.

I noticed that I couldn't keep up with his notions, especially when I had already spoken much more than I should have. I made a sort of concession that from now on the author could write the more sensitive things I said into the story, but only from memory.

Let the dictaphone stay off when Salme is on.

We came to an understanding about this, but it wasn't easy continuing about Helena, especially when the matter had taken new twists after the trial. I tried to think where I would start. It felt like everything started with Helena and ended with Helena.

It made me angry. I knew that I still had to tell all sorts of things for my money and trust that it would go into the book right. I was sure it wouldn't. It had become clear that an author's job is to invent, to exaggerate, to lie. The truth wasn't enough for him.

But there weren't any alternatives.

I hated the person whose fault this all was. If that one horrible thing hadn't happened, I could be sitting at home with Paavo weaving rugs and *raanuja*. All sorts of things can happen to a person in life, but nothing as big as happened to Helena. Paavo and I had been near bankruptcy many times when they slapped those presumptive taxes on the yarn shop, but we got through our troubles since we had something else behind it all. And what was that something else? The children. It was for them that a person worked and toiled and pinched pennies. It was only just that their lives not be taken away.

The author waited for me to speak, but I didn't know where to start. He suggested that he could present questions for me to answer informally, touching on changes in the economy and the progress of my children's careers. I expressed my surprise that he would inquire about that in particular. He said that by answering some general questions we could get back out into more open water after the logjam Helena had caused. He presumed to say "we", as if he and I were engaged in some sort of common cause.

Well, so be it.

The children don't tell us much about their affairs. They all work in business and are always busy. When we call them, there is always roaring and hissing where they answer. I haven't heard from Pekka in a long time, but I suppose he has moved from the computer store to somewhere bigger. At least he said he had his sights on getting a position in some big company's . . . what's the word? Operations management.

Of course it worries me sometimes, how they are getting along in their lives down there. Like my parents were worried about how I would get along. My mother was born in a smoke sauna and didn't live long enough to see a computer. When I told her that Paavo and I were starting a yarn shop, she was shocked. She said, "Salme, you can rest easy if you work for someone else – don't go building sandcastles with the bank's money. People could stop knitting altogether soon and then what will you do, all that debt and shame hanging around your neck?" This is the pattern. The next generation is always doing things the wrong way. I haven't understood everything my children have done either, like, for example, the way Helena went to sell ideas at a company with a foreign name.

The author interrupted to say that he didn't intend to turn the dictaphone on for the whole time we were meeting. As he said this, he took a notepad and a pencil out of his pocket. I said that he needed to put those away while I was speaking as well. The author shook his head and reminded me that he had paid for goods that he would be taking with him in some form. I gave him permission to write, but decided to speak as fast as possible so he wouldn't be able to get it all down.

The economy. My children's careers.

I had never thought of these things, at least consciously. Now I had to say something about them for money. Paavo and I hardly thought about work anymore – the yarn shop took and gave everything that we needed. The bottom line didn't leave us with any debt, and there was enough profit that we could hold our heads high. It was just everyday small-business life, hand to mouth and out the other end. Living a life like that you don't get a chance to raise your kids. They were always there in the middle of everything. They saw and heard everything, learning what they learned. Now that the end is in sight, I can say that I don't believe in any kind of child rearing. At least in this country. Of course it is a different matter in countries where peace has prevailed uninterrupted, where people get to stand around next to the fields watching the oats grow, without any wars.

Or in countries where the riches of nature force their way up out of the ground: oil, ore, gold, natural gas and whatever else. Just build roads and railways to them and then sell them to those of us with rocky fields and boys coming home with shock from the wars. In rich countries like that they can raise children, try different kinds of plants and cook more complicated meals. By saying this I don't mean to relieve myself and Paavo of the responsibility for raising our children, but just to say that a country's history has some significance.

Look at Sweden.

Once Paavo and I travelled by bus across the middle of it and good heavens was it tidy! Flowerbeds stretching on forever, the shoulders of the roads manicured just so, the yellow and red houses with fresh coats of paint, flaxen-haired children under the feet of carefree adults. And of course they had taken care not to be tied down by too many children, with only two in each yard. Out in the country in Finland in the old days, every family had at least three, and we had four before Heikki fell in the well. You can raise children – I'm not saying that – but there has to be some limit to how much you're going to chase them around. And to human understanding. Humans aren't that special.

I mean in terms of sense. When it comes to feelings we're at the top of the heap compared to the rest of the animal kingdom. They claim that horses, cats, dogs and cows feel some things, and they are supposed to have the ability to be hurt or to be happy, but I don't see anything in that which would make them comparable to us. When you talk about feelings, humans are a ten out of ten. Nothing else compares to the concoctions we brew up. A human is perfectly capable of feeling shame, joy, sorrow, boredom, envy and jealousy all in one sitting.

But in terms of sense, humans are what they are.

And for this reason raising them is a bit hit and miss.

Children learn by example – it's like running into a chair leg for them. And in a family like we had, they ran into small business. Even though no-one ever used that word. The children just learned that we were in the workshop, as Paavo had a way of saying. And we were almost always there. And the children came there.

I mean they were brought up with the idea that a person really had to move for his bread. But we didn't say it out loud. They could see it. Just like everything else in the economy in those days. The products we were selling were on the shelves, the money was cash and the credit ledger was a blue notebook. You could say that we only believed in what we could see. And we proclaimed that faith to the children as well. Unknowingly, I mean. Whether it's sound doctrine, I don't know. At the time it was the teaching and the custom of the land. All of our male relatives had made it through the war by the skin of their teeth, and there wasn't any point in talking to them metaphorically about bread and fishes.

This all started with child rearing. Or the economy. It's all one and the same life.

I looked at the author, who sat hunched over, writing as if his life depended on it.

The big graph paper notebook was filled with messy scribbling – my life.

"Everything starts in the middle and gets cut short," Alfred Supinen said once. Paavo and I looked at each other, confused. Supinen explained that there is no clear plot in life. That we get dropped into the middle of life, we get startled awake and start to live it and then when we start to understand things, it gets cut short.

At first I was put off by what he said, but when I realized that Supinen didn't mean anything bad by it, it started to make sense.

Even though it did leave out God, whom my mother considered competent and able to arrive anywhere in the nick of time. Mother thought God's influence extended everywhere, even though it didn't show.

Paavo's older brother Juhani came home from the war proclaiming at every opportunity that there wasn't any God – there was just the Devil, who took Kauko Hänninen's guts out of his stomach and spread them all across the Karelian Isthmus. I said to Paavo that it might be best not to invite Juhani to each and every family party. This offended Paavo, and he yelled about how we were glad enough to be living in our own country, but couldn't stand listening to the opinions of the men who defended it.

In a way Paavo was right, but my heart broke for my mother each time Juhani would spend the first hour of the party or funeral sitting in the corner of the room before jumping up to condemn everything.

He even interrupted hymns. When we were burying Mum's sister, and we were at the part where we sang "Abide with me; fast falls the eventide; the darkness deepens; Lord, with me abide", Juhani yelled out that the lords weren't going to be spending the night because they were too busy butchering the working man.

Juhani's anger was pitch black and frightening. Once when the children were playing in the garden, Juhani climbed on top of the playhouse and yelled, "Everyone knows how to hit. It takes a different kind of person to take punches!"

The children went quiet. What could they say to that?

Everything Juhani said came from a completely different world, but no-one talked about psychological problems in those days. It would have been too much to start calling the boys who had been in the war crazy. Enduring horrible things like we did meant that when other problems came later, we didn't know how to react to them or empathize with them, since the war and the price we paid for it was so fresh in our minds. You could see and hear the price tag in Juhani.

And while I'm here, with an author sitting in front of me, I should also say we could have done without all those war books. They became such a burden. As if the truth wasn't enough of a cross to bear that you had to go making things up to add to it. It was a hard thing for Juhani when *The Unknown Soldier* came out and then they had to go and make a movie about such a fairy tale. Juhani got really upset about the book and said he had never guessed amidst all the blood and tattered flesh that there were such humorous, quick-witted men living in the next dugout. "That boy Linna has quite an imagination," Juhani said. "They must not be too busy at the mill if he has time to be reinventing the war during working hours."

The author stopped his pen and began defending Väinö Linna. According to him, Linna gave a face to the war and the men who fought in it. I said I could give him Juhani's phone number if he wanted to talk in more detail about who provided a face and who provided a mask. I also said that although Juhani was in bad shape, basically a prisoner of his bed, he would get up for this discussion.

The author said that he wasn't about to start arguing with a war veteran who had given all he had for us, but that he would gladly tell me what Linna's depiction of the war was all about.

I said I knew without him telling me. It was about making the war something other than it was. War is killing. Period. An onion is an onion even if you pour honey over it and wrap it in tissue paper.

The author stood up, raising his voice. No-one could say that Linna poured honey over things or wrapped the world in tissue paper.

I raised a hand. The author sat back down on his chair.

The waitress glanced at us.

I suggested that we proceed with my life and leave our discussion of what kind of life Linna invented for our broken boys for later. The author said that was fine by him. And added that it wouldn't hurt for me to stick to the truth in my own story and leave out the honey and tissue paper.

I stood up.

I stood there, unable to speak.

I sat down.

I stood up again.

No-one had ever spoken to me that way.

I said that this session was over and that I didn't need any more money.

The author appeared calm. That made me even angrier.

The author said that I had lectured him several times about truth, but that I hadn't stuck to it myself. I answered that he had one minute to justify that accusation and that after that I was walking out of that place and never coming back.

The author said that he had run into a Malmikunnas about a year before and claimed that I had modified the truth a bit, but said that he understood completely, because every parent sees his or her children through the eyes of love, not truth. He didn't think there was anything wrong with this. Everyone tries to build his career to the best of his ability, sometimes succeeding, sometimes not. And every child protects his parents from worry and care.

It made me feel like vomiting to hear talk like that.

I knew the author didn't have a family and so had no concept of what it was like to watch a child's life from the outside. I fidgeted with the good luck charm hanging from my handbag that Sini had crocheted and tried to think what to do.

Nothing.

Alfred Supinen always said that the worst thing was not to be able to do anything. There was nothing to be gained painting yourself into a corner – there should always be an open door. Well said, Alfred, but then you didn't have a family.

My grief started coming back. Just a few months ago everything had been good, the children in good jobs and well fed like ducks in a row. Now I was sitting at the corner table of an ugly service station accused of twisting the truth.

I started to collect my things.

The author stopped me by putting his hand on my shoulder. I flung the hand away.

The author begged my pardon for his choice of words and swore he held my truth in high regard even though Pekka had caused him to doubt it.

I felt dizzy. It felt bad for a stranger to say the name of my only living son out loud.

The author said he had taken his computer to be repaired at a certain shop, and that the machine had been worked on by a man named Pekka Malmikunnas, who, according to what I had said, should have been the general manager, not a repairman.

Is that so?

I didn't know what else to say straightaway, but after drinking my glass of juice, I did.

If my son is a repairman, then why don't you write him as a general manager like Väinö Linna would have done, eh? If they had to embellish the war, then let's embellish peacetime as well! Give him a new life. Don't leave my son languishing in the repair shop. Make up a proper position for him!

The waitress started walking towards my shout.

The author told her nothing was wrong and that we were just

trading opinions. I corrected him, saying that we weren't trading opinions, we were trading lives. And this gentleman right here is going to make my son's life completely different in exchange for money. The waitress shook her head and disappeared into the kitchen.

Silence fell.

I tried to hate Pekka, but in vain. Then I tried to hate the author and myself, but nothing came of that either.

I gave up. I didn't have the energy anymore.

I told the author he could go ahead and turn on every dictaphone in the world and write whatever he wanted, that it would suit me just fine so long as I got to hear my eldest daughter laugh one more time before I died.

I don't know if it's even possible anymore. Right now it feels like it isn't. Paavo will speak again – I know that – but I'm not sure about Helena laughing. A person is built to withstand everything and then nothing at all. There is a limit somewhere. You have to know that limit. And now I do. Now, Author, you've had your lot, and I've had my fill. I will talk to you for one more hour and then afterwards I will leave here with that money and go home, and we will never meet again. You can live in your world making up new lives, and I will live out the rest of this life of mine. I wish you all the best. I do not think ill of you, because I have learned in life that evil is catching and good floats in the air. Go ahead and turn on the dictaphone. I'm going to tell you what kind of sendoff our Pekka got for his teenage years, and maybe you'll understand his current situation better.

It went this way. When Pekka went to confirmation camp and they had to read the Bible out loud, everyone in turn, and when it came to Pekka's turn, the Holy Word came from his mouth one syllable at a time, and as a man of words you can understand how that would sound. The priest there beside him of course thought that

Pekka was intentionally trying to amuse his friends by mocking the Word of God. The priest put Pekka in detention in a shack by the lake without food for the day and then let him go to bed hungry. In the night Pekka borrowed a friend's moped and drove home, taking some bread from the cupboard and then hurrying back to the camp. In the morning he gave the soft, fresh bread to the boy who had lent him the moped and to everyone else, and the priest found out. It meant no good for Pekka for the rest of the camp.

Then came Confirmation Sunday and all the young people knelt before the altar in their white frocks. The priest came to Pekka with the bread and wine and mumbled about the Blood of God sacrificed on your behalf. Just as the chalice was placed in front of Pekka's mouth, he said he couldn't drink because he would be driving his moped.

Afterward the priest came to Paavo and me in the churchyard, and before he could open his mouth, Paavo said that the whole family had come on that same moped.

That was our Pekka's foundation for adulthood.

A human is a fledgling bird alright. It has to leave the nest even if its wings are transparent. I often thanked Paavo for those words there in the churchyard. Those words were wings. And a stutterer has the advantage compared to the rest of us that he remembers the things people say better than normal. Without knowing it, Paavo had been raising his son in that churchyard. He took his side.

You can't understand this exactly since you don't have children.

Or you may if you go home and think after you leave here.

Alfred Supinen said once that he had no-one and everyone in this world. I didn't understand immediately, but he explained that as a person without a family, he treated all small people, whether they were children or those otherwise diminutive in stature, as if they were on loan to him, just like life is in general. With our children Supinen acted as if he had always been there, even though he was just visiting. He took the children seriously and answered their questions matter-of-factly and with precision.

Of course Helena, Pekka, and Maija fell in love with him and were constantly asking when the display designer was coming. Pekka in particular followed him around, and even as an adult has marvelled at why a person like that would want to hang himself. We didn't expect it either, because you can't see inside a person, even though it claims in the Bible that God can see all of our thoughts. That book exaggerates. Claims like that set God up as an utterly impossible being. No-one sees everything. It would ruin your eyes.

At least we couldn't see into Supinen, even though he was so luminous. Sometimes the children were dazzled by how much time he had – or maybe he didn't have any more than everyone else, but he took it. For each child he made time stand still. Children remember things like that forever.

And of course I hope that now that I've told my life, you will go home and break your clock for Salme and think that for a little while there will just be this one old woman in the world and I will concentrate on her.

A person only needs two traits: the ability to concentrate and imagination. Concentrate on what you are doing and imagine yourself in the other person's position. That's all – everything else will follow.

I'm saying this too late and as an aside. In this world there isn't time to raise your children, and once you start working things out, it's already too late. I'm not even sure about my postcards. It could be that the kids throw them in the bin without reading them. I send them because I believe in the word, like you in a way.

Apparently they actually print in the instructions for my children's mobile phones that they have to answer no matter what. Maija even answered in the shower once. Find the sense in that. That was why I started sending the cards. So they can concentrate on reading them.

Now I'm going to take this money and turn it into good energy.

Before people used squirrel pelts as money. It makes you sad for the creatures now, after the fact, but it was for a good cause. I'm going to turn this money into squirrel pelts and cover my eldest daughter with them when she gets cold.

THE STORYTELLER

The author came home, transcribed what the dictaphone had captured, scanned his notebook and began to put the story together. He knew the task would be difficult, but possible. He incorporated into the story everything he knew of the world and everything he had only begun to suspect.

He took out a large sheet of paper and drew Salme and Paavo and their children, Helena, Pekka and Maija on it. Around them all he drew a large box, which he labelled "Society". Inside the box he drew ten more "X"s, which signified the unknown factors that always influence people's lives.

Then the author concentrated. He closed his eyes and thought about his own life. It was small and insignificant. Not much happened in it. But he decided to incorporate part of it into the story, and it was in this frame of mind that he wrote a letter to the person who had donated her life.

Dear Mrs Malmikunnas,

Our last meeting has been weighing on my mind. My purpose was not to offend, but I am sure that I did.

I ask your forgiveness. This profession of mine is difficult. I have to serve both truth and falsehood at the same time. Perhaps you will not understand, but for me truth and falsehood are twins. They avoid one another, they shun one another, but they cannot live without one another.

When you sold me your life, I am sure I did not explain

sufficiently clearly that I would be making my own version of it. Your truth is your own. My truth is the reader's truth – assuming the book is published. If the book is not published, your truth will remain the only valid one.

But one thing unites us. You need money for a good cause, and I need this book. Without a book I disappear. Without a book there is no me. You may think that might not be such a terrible loss, but in my profession the fact is that an author only exists through his books.

During our meetings you lost your temper with me several times. This was caused by the fact that we have such different views on literature. Or more correctly, and excuse me for saying so, by you having no view at all. You suppose that writing a book means putting down on paper everything someone has seen and experienced. That system would give us some pretty thick, unreadable books. But I want to believe that if and when you read the book made from your life, you will understand what I mean. In my previous letter I used an example of a whooper swan, attempting to explain from how many different perspectives it would have to be described for both the reader and the swan to be satisfied.

Now let me use a pig as an example.

We see it in the pigpen along with others of its kind. It grunts and roots around, scraping at the ground. It evokes strong feelings.

If I were to write a story about it, I would begin with the assumption that it is there in the pen for us. Before long we will be killing and eating it. I would describe it from this perspective and feel empathy towards it.

This is the human perspective. The pig has another.

We do not know what the pig is thinking, but I suppose it does not think of the future, living only in the moment. It pushes others out of the way, trying to get to the food trough and out to walk around. If it sees a bird in the yard, it might be jealous. Perhaps. We do not know. Perhaps it would think the bird is an optical illusion, because it supposes there is nothing in the world besides the pig itself and its master. The pig does not remember yesterday, does not consider the future, and yet senses something when the rubber-suited men approach it. The pig fears the men, and with good reason, because the men will soon be applying an electric shock to end the pig's life.

Then there is the perspective of a child. In the pig, a child sees Christmas, but not its path to the Christmas table. A child thinks the pig is cute, calling every pig "piggy". Piggies have even been the main characters in films, because adults remember their own childhoods. Children's books are also full of their socket noses.

Now we have three perspectives of the pig's life. If we were to write a story from only the pig's perspective, the story would be short and unconvincing. If I succeed with my book, we will see the sow and the boar in the pen. Their children, that is their piglets, have left the hog house and gone out into the world and are trying to get along and avoid the slaughterhouse. The life of a pig has changed from previous times such that the sow and boar are no longer able to keep up with everything that happens to the piglets. Then something bad happens to one of them (let me remind you, Mrs Malmikunnas, that

I am speaking metaphorically now, and that of course I do not consider you a pig but rather am simply attempting to describe my intentions as though in a fable), but luckily the other pigs and a monkey come to the rescue.

And so on.

If I succeed, your life will become rich and full, something that others besides the permanent residents of the hog house will be able to relate to.

Best wishes, A

Four days later, the author received two postcards, an autumn scene and a lake scene. The text was split between them.

Dear Author,

I am sitting here in a beautiful place with Helena not feeling any desire to quarrel over ugly things. By the way, do you eat berries? Nature is constantly giving us tips for a better life. Lingonberries, blueberries, sea-buckthorn berries and the rest. Paavo and I eat them daily. This is a hint. And I have one request as well. When the

(Continues on lake scene. Didn't fit on one card. Sorry.)

book appears, could you say at the book fair or wherever it is presented that it is completely made up? I could even pay you a little for this favour, since we sold our old car. This is extremely important to me. Did you know, by the way, that the sea-buckthorn berry has almost all the vitamins a person needs? Salme

THE SPEAKER

Kimmo got into the car, taking hold of the sturdy door handle and pulling. The heavy door thumped closed so tightly that none of the commotion of life could penetrate it. He had paid 55,000 euros for the car, but now it felt like every single one was paying itself back. In fact, he knew he had paid a small sum for the soundproofing and the ergonomic seat that conformed to every contour of the human body. For the same money he could have bought a small studio apartment in a bad part of town, but the accessories could easily have included noisy neighbours and junkies in the stairwell.

Kimmo worked himself deeper into the cupping seat and thought: For the first time, I have a car that accelerates from zero to one hundred faster than its owner and whose torque in the lower gears is stronger than its owner's pull against a customer's biases. Kimmo was so deeply happy about his new vehicle that he closed his eyes and imagined its path from the production line to his driveway.

Two months before a Turkish finisher named Turkai Göz woke up early in the morning on the outskirts of the city of Ingolstadt, trimmed his sideburns, said goodbye to his wife, drove his little Volkswagen Polo the twenty-kilometre journey to the Audi factory complex, clocked himself in, walked to his line and crouched next to an Audi S3 automobile.

Turkai knew that he was the last person between the factory and the auto dealership. After him the car would move to the delivery hall and then on to the dealer, who would sell the car to the customer. Turkai felt important and responsible, even though it didn't show in his salary. Professional pride made up for the missing euros.

Kimmo thought of Turkai with warmth, although he did slightly dislike the thought that his car had been inspected by a Turk who smelled of kebabs rather than a German with millimetre precision, but in a world of freely moving capital and labour, one couldn't whine about minor blemishes.

Turkai inspected the locks, the seals, the seat rails, the chrome surfaces, the details of the control system, the brakes and the remote control. He placed a protective covering over the driver's seat, sat down, turned on the car and went over the computer. Everything was in order. At this point Turkai often found himself thinking somewhat childishly: I deliver you to the road and wish that your journey be not so full of thorns as mine and that of my family, but that you move lightly, without so much as a backward glance

Turkai collected the protective coverings from the front and back seats and pressed a button. The Audi S3 jerked forward, and immediately another, identical, appeared in its place. They only became individuals in the driveways of people like Kimmo.

Kimmo blessed Turkai and his family and the whole of the German-Turkish minority who toiled in a foreign land so that all European nations could have the opportunity to partake of the fruits of German engineering. Kimmo thought sympathetically for a moment of the Islamic faith, although he shunned the basic idea in all religions that there is some greater purpose behind everything. There was no hidden purpose, but at that moment, sitting on the leather seat of his new car, Kimmo vouchsafed Turkai Göz and his family the shreds of comfort they received from their false religion and the calls to prayer of their muezzins echoing from the minarets.

Kimmo started the car and pressed on the accelerator. The car growled. He floored the pedal. The car howled. He lifted his foot. The car hummed. Yes. That was right. It was an animal that he had tamed. It obeyed him, but without discipline it would run wild, bolting off wherever it wished. You have to make it clear to an animal right from the beginning who's boss. If you don't set limits for an animal, it feels insecure. The Audi now knew that Kimmo had the power. And Kimmo knew that an Audi can be a rowdy scallywag if you give it any slack.

Kimmo set off driving along the coastal road. The Audi obeyed his every command. Sometimes it would sniff a Japanese or Korean rump, but then it would brush past at Kimmo's command. The road extended towards the sunset, with Turku beyond. Kimmo didn't have any business there, but the Audi had caught the scent. He gave the car its head, but took care that it didn't run too fast. One hundred and eighty kilometres per hour was just the right speed. It let the animal's temperament show through, although its true personality naturally lurked at an entirely different speed range.

The Audi sensed it was approaching its native pastures – a motor knows the motorway. Its four paws, which in this case were sheathed in low profile tires, probed the road, conforming to its every dip and depression. The Audi wanted to run as fast as it could, but it also wanted to obey its master, who was clearly lapsing into a deep, contemplative state. This always happens to the Master when he takes time for himself and goes out roaming in nature. Of course I'm still a pup and can wait for my real time to run, but my paws are already itching for it. Mountains and rocks have been blasted out of my way and a smooth path has been laid beneath my feet. It rankles to lope along at half power, especially since some upper-crust French mongrel just cruised by and Master didn't let me follow him. On the other hand, the mongrel was screaming his head off, obviously giving everything he had to show me his backside.

Kimmo decided to creep along at 140 kilometres per hour all the way to Salo so he could think about life.

Life. After having lived two-thirds of it, he understood it as a story. Life isn't interesting – the story is. Especially when he had recognized that not all successful people's lives are stories by any means. They were usually a creamy mixture of privileged background and obvious choices, lives that only leave behind cold numbers and carefully cropped close-ups. If you're born with a golden spoon in your mouth, there's every chance of losing your sense of taste early on.

Kimmo had started out the only way possible for a good story: from nothing. When you start from nothing, you're sure to know fulfilment when you find it. "I came to this city as no-one, with nothing, from nowhere." He used that phrase at the beginning of his presentations, most recently during Idea Days.

From nowhere.

Yeah.

In retrospect it was possible to see purpose and meaning in it, but then, ten years ago, everything had just felt hard and unfair. He had delivered newspapers, toiled away on building sites and at the docks, collected empty bottles, cleaned stairwells and sat in a draughty car park tollbooth.

Personally, he considered the turning point to have been the moment when he had finally had his fill of toil and poverty. Millions of people have that same moment, but only one in a thousand seizes it. In that moment Kimmo had decided that he would never again in his life dirty his hands. He decided to make money with his head.

Something grey flashed in his field of vision three hundred metres ahead. Kimmo braked. The Audi acquiesced to a speed of 100 kilometres per hour. The greyness took on the form of a moose climbing up the embankment towards the road. Kimmo put the brake pedal to the floor. The shocks compressed, the car coming to a stop at the last second. Kimmo saw a brown, tapered mass in front of him, swaying back and forth in slow motion. It was a head, and the eyes set on each side of it were moist and drowsy.

The moose stared at the windscreen and the creature behind it. The creature had its mouth open. Its forehead was against the glass. The moose had seen these creatures before – they came into the forest to collect berries. Sometimes they flew through the glass onto the road, his late father's brother had said. More of us die than them, the moose thought. Even though they sometimes have shells and glass around them, they still die. They're flimsy and wobble around on two legs. They build these strips through the middle of our forest. They come with shells, but their shells break easily. My father ran into a creature like that.

Kimmo was shaking. He removed his hands from the wheel and placed them on his knees. The moose rocked into motion. It traipsed across the road and forced its way through the bushes off into the darkness. Kimmo hated it. Not because it was a moose, but because it represented chance and irrationality. A moose could just appear out of nowhere and end your life. Because of this Kimmo never ate any food made with moose, even though he generally enjoyed all meat dishes. Once he had been served a moose stew but had refused it, saying, "I will only eat this enemy if I have killed him myself."

Kimmo patted the Audi's dashboard and whispered, "It's alright. Calm down. We're still alive." He started the car and accelerated to 120 kilometres per hour, even though he knew the Audi hated going so slowly. One moose often meant others, and Kimmo did not want to take the risk.

He rewound his thoughts to the turning point in his life, to the moment when he had decided to make money with his head. He had thought that going to a college or university could open up superb possibilities, but that was a slow, rocky path. And there wasn't necessarily a money tree growing at the end of it.

He had realized the importance of capital. He had to get capital. *Capitalis. Caput.* Head. Capital. That one word captured everything. He had built up capital by working three jobs simultaneously for a year. After that he had slept for four days with the aid of sedatives and then marched into a bank with his capital. He had used it to take out a loan and purchase a dilapidated studio apartment. He had guessed right. Money didn't grow on trees – it grew in buildings made of stone. Assuming the building was in a good location. And a good location is where there are jobs and people. Money accrues interest in buildings, and even if it doesn't, it doesn't disappear anywhere. In a few years the price of the small studio apartment had tripled. He had sold it and, with a small additional loan, purchased two more even smaller studios. He moved into one and rented out the other.

Once his tenant had called to inform Kimmo he wouldn't be able to pay his rent. Kimmo had said he would call back soon. He had seen an opportunity where someone else would have just seen an inconvenience. He informed the tenant that everything would be O.K. if he would agree to make two payments the next month at ten per cent interest. The tenant had agreed. Over the next three years, Kimmo had taken rent at interest several times.

Capital. Interest.

Two important words.

Interest on capital. Just putting one bit of interest in front of another, as Kimmo sometimes had a habit of expressing it in selected company as Friday turned to Saturday in an upscale restaurant.

During the two-studio period, Kimmo had supported himself as a taxi driver and a doorman at a restaurant. In those jobs he had found himself possessed of a special gift: he knew how to talk in such a way that people were entertained, laughed, calmed down and started talking themselves. He spent his days standing at the door of the restaurant and his nights sitting in a taxi. And his mouth worked. He was a machine grinding out phrases about the weather, T.V. programmes, the price of gas, refugees, what the opposition was doing, retail oligopoly, equality, football and Formula One. If a customer started in on a subject that was unfamiliar to him, he jumped on board, agreeing and easing himself into the new topic. He would say a few words, but was careful not to disagree with the customer. Soon he developed a large regular clientele, who never entered the restaurant or sat down in his taxi without uttering some light turn of phrase. And thus Kimmo gradually learned to understand the importance of speech in all human communication. Without speech there was only action, and action was from the old world, where everything was done by hand. Action is a good thing, but it has to be flavoured with speech.

Property and speech had value. Kimmo knew he had been born into a good world. He also very quickly realized that speech is valued even more if the speaker has status. Of course people listened to Kimmo's stories at the door to the cloakroom and in the back seat of the taxi, but they listened even more intently to people who were somebody.

Somebody.

That guy.

You know.

From that show.

Kimmo learned quickly. He decided to get status. He cut his taxi driving time back by half and began to study at the university. He graduated with a master's degree in economics in three and a half years because he read with the intensity of a starving man and with the instincts of an animal. He didn't internalize anything, but knew everything by heart. If he had been able to choose, the piece of paper would have said "speaker" instead of "master".

And from then on, licensed by that piece of paper, Kimmo had spoken for everything he wanted. First a job in an advertising office, and then a partnership, and then the whole office, the sale of which now allowed him to live without doing anything.

He had done things right and wrong, he had succeeded and failed, but the most important thing was that he had spoken. He had talked himself into situations and out of them. He had used speech to change frogs into princes and crises into opportunities. He had continued to speak even after everyone else had stopped. He had understood what this was all about: it didn't matter what the product was like – it mattered how you spoke about it.

Kimmo had a habit of speaking using examples and metaphors. Rich countries have ore, oil and other natural riches. Poor countries only have folklore. But thankfully those traditions are full of metaphors and illustrative stories, which Kimmo used as the basis for his marketing speeches. For example, primitive man didn't buy an axe, he bought fire. The axe was the tool that ancient man used to get fire, light, warmth, the ability to cook food, perhaps even a woman, who might come to him drawn by the glow of the fire. That is, don't sell the axe, sell everything that comes with it.

Downtown Turku shimmered on the horizon. Kimmo slowed the Audi and glided towards the heart of the city at 80 kilometres per hour. He stopped on the edge of the market square, but did not immediately turn off the engine. He wanted to listen to the car, which had just covered a 165-kilometre trip at an average speed of 139 kilometres per hour. The sound of the engine was dispirited, but not broken. Kimmo sensed irritation and sorrow in the sound at having had its natural abilities sold short, that it had been forced to take into account speed limits set by the rabble.

Kimmo turned off the engine and pondered contradiction. Contradiction is salt. Without contradiction, life has no flavour. And the last thing that had added flavour to the pot was that woman at the party.

Blonde hair attractively attached to an intelligent head, trim frame, tooth jewel, large black watch, generally relaxed bearing. But the woman's speech and especially her actions did not fit the whole – they were more appropriate for toothless, bad-smelling people who had already given up and fallen out of sight.

She had pulled his ear.

Children were pulled by the ear. Or animals.

Was there some symbolism in it? A hidden message?

Kimmo was over being offended. Now he was considering the matter from a distance, clinically. At the same time, he also enjoyed the position of victim. By her poor behaviour the woman had driven herself into a trap: she owed Kimmo – not money, but an explanation or an apology. Kimmo liked people to owe him things. Debt tied people to each other more strongly that anything else. The glue of debt held.

Interest and debt, debt and interest. The Siamese twins of the market economy.

Kimmo knew the woman was attainable. Everything was. Sooner or later.

The winner was whoever could afford to wait. For prices to rise, for the next slump, for forgiveness. Before long whoever bites your leg will come trotting back to sit at your feet. And this time she wouldn't bite, she would stroke and massage and spread balsam oil over those feet.

The square was quiet. The cobblestones glistened wet. Steam rose from a manhole.

Kimmo imagined a tribe living under the square, ignorant of our civilized society. One day it would rise from below and make everything anew. Our habits, the structures of society, our precious law and order.

But not yet.

Kimmo started the Audi. It rumbled angrily at the tribe living beneath the square.

POSTCARD, HIGH STREET

Pekka, my only son!

Don't play with fire. No fooling around on the sea. Take responsibility even if it isn't offered. Look people in the eye. We don't buy Korean compass saws (Dad's advice). In addition to these instructions, I also have to say: don't mock your mother. Maija said you don't have a blended family. Why would you tell me something like that, you brat? You're good enough for me just the way you are. I'm making rosehip soup for the weekend.

Your mother

THE CONNOISSEUR

Pekka Malmikunnas wandered the streets of the city, blowing here and there like a discarded plastic bag, driven by the weather and his moods. He found himself in parks, in alleys and at the harbour, in places where he had never been before.

On really cold days he gravitated towards the large department stores, whose buzzing entrances sucked all sorts of passers-by into their warmth. Pekka had no way to buy anything, but even with empty pockets he was able to enjoy the material abundance. All sorts of jars, Christmas decorations, gadgets, gizmos, implements and contraptions had been produced for the enjoyment of man. It was fun to fiddle with them and think that had the stars aligned differently, he too could stroll about in a smoking jacket like that and open a bottle of red wine with a hundred-euro corkscrew. With good luck he too could wrap himself in the cashmere a goat plucked from his wanderings on sunny mountain slopes had surrendered for this very purpose.

Pekka's senses became more finely attuned when he experienced want. He saw everything he could not buy and smelled everything he could not eat. He preferred to roam near the meat and fish counters in the food departments of the stores, but he avoided eye contact with the salespeople. He looked at the red meat and thought for a moment of the cow that had sacrificed its body on our behalf. A memory of his grandmother's house flooded into his mind: the sun, the field and that cow next to which he had fallen asleep long ago. He had supposed that his grandmother's house had its very own sun, different from the one in other places, but his father had said that it was the same sun everywhere. Learning that made the world smaller.

Pork chops lay next to the pieces of cow. He looked askance at these, because the life of a small pig had made him feel bad even as a child. The narrow pen, the squelching muck under hoof, the dirty snout, bellowing and squealing until someone whacks you in the head with a shock pistol and cuts your stomach open. The effects of a life like that carry over to the other side, i.e. to the food processing plant, Pekka thought. The pork chops retained the aura of that short, sad life.

One day, which was supposed to be just like every other day, a new world opened up for Pekka. He noticed a man dressed in a chef's hat and white clothing standing behind a separate refrigerated counter. The man seemed to be speaking to himself, but upon closer inspection, he was speaking into a small microphone which curved from behind his ear in front of his mouth. He was announcing that at the counter before him he was offering genuine, authentic Jelpunen Brothers' Processed Meat products: sliced ham, sausage, frankfurters and jellied aspic, and that all these things were free for the sampling. He said that meat was always the star in Jelpunen products and that only insignificant supporting roles were reserved for fillers.

Pekka carefully approached the counter, ending up behind two older ladies. The ladies grabbed toothpicks on the ends of which jiggled jellied veal. When one of the ladies shoved the toothpick into her mouth and flicked the nugget down her gullet, Pekka began to feel hunger in every fibre of his being. He had last eaten a hot meal the day before yesterday – ever since he had been living on white bread, oats mixed with milk, and water. He suddenly felt like shoving the women out of his way and chomping down every last piece of aspic on the counter. However, he contained himself. He knew that if he proceeded with patience, the tasting table would offer him lasting happiness.

He looked at each product carefully. He did not know how to decide which of them would be the best and the most flavourful. Each seemed to radiate savour and nutritional value. His mouth began to water and then went dry. His gaze moved from the ham sausage to the sausage links and from there past the aspic to the frankfurters.

Then Pekka began to inspect the man who stood behind the counter smiling, moving his tongs from one product to the next, as if attempting to guess what the customer's next choice would be. There was a name tag on his white coat that read "Kauko Pyrhönen, consultant". He looked like his products: full of flavour, easily approached, jelly-like and clearly a family man. He exuded a fundamental happiness, as if he had been born in a sea of frankfurters with a little sausage crown on his head.

Pekka drove out these feelings of jealousy, for in his innermost self he felt that he and Pyrhönen belonged to the same tribe, even though they approached the matter from different sides of the counter. Kauko represented bounty, and Pekka represented hunger. The world could reverse their roles in a second. This is what had happened two months ago when Pekka had said goodbye to his sports coat and hello to the windbreaker.

Pyrhönen brought his tongs to a halt over a piece of aspic and tapped it in a fatherly way. After this they had a conversation that stuck in Pekka's mind, if only for the reason that it functioned as foreplay for an extended act of pleasure.

"What shall it be today? As I just said, the Jelpunens don't skimp on the meat. This is a matter of family pride. Old man Jelpunen would rather cut back on other expenses in the business. You don't see any Mercedes in their car park. So, what sort of treat would your tummy fancy today?"

"I don't really know. There's so much to choose from."

"People have been liking the aspic. And of course the ham sausage. And the meaty frankfurters are always a hit with the children."

"The twins have been trying to get over an ear infection."

"I'm sorry to hear that. We need to have tubes put in ourselves. What about pâté? It has everything a body needs in a compact form. Even for the most gentile table."

"We just had it last week when our eldest had his confirmation."

"We wouldn't want to repeat ourselves then. What about sausage links? An old favourite. No additives, not too much filler, Jelpunen's speciality. Shall I cut you a little three-centimetre head start?"

"Well, I guess I could have a little."

And so Pekka tasted a piece of sausage. He tried to chew the bite with as much care as he could. His empty stomach was a brittle-walled canyon into which he did not dare dump large servings all at once; but rather, filling it had to be started by dropping little pieces in along the sides.

Pyrhönen watched Pekka's fervent chewing with an expectant expression. Pekka nodded in approval and moved his gaze to the aspic. Pyrhönen sensed his customer's desire and cut a two-centimetre slice from the jelly. Onto the cutting board fell a memento of the cow and pig that just a short time before had been sauntering about their farm in southwest Finland, ignorant of the fact that they would soon end up encased in jiggling jelly on the end of a toothpick.

Pekka felt the salty, moist flavour of the aspic in his mouth. He felt like closing his eyes as he did as a child when a fresh sweet roll and cold milk mashed together in his mouth. He did not close his eyes. He waited. He knew that the moment would yet come when he would be able to enjoy the jelly privately.

Pekka nodded to Pyrhönen, who snapped up three slices of ham sausage with his tongs. Pekka was not able to focus on the nuances in flavour of the product because he was already thinking feverishly of what would follow. He superficially praised the marriage of ham and starchy fillers and then said he was going to meet the rest of the family in the textiles department and would contemplate his final purchasing decision for a moment. Pyrhönen smiled and said he would be at the counter until closing, ready to expound upon the eternal marriage of man and meat, which began during the stone age when our forefathers saw both a threat and an opportunity in every approaching bear.

Pekka promised to return to the hunting grounds before closing time because the Jelpunen's products had made an unforgettable impression on him. Pyrhönen smiled and traded his tongs for a long sheath knife, which he used to spear a frankfurter out of the bowl, offering it to Pekka. Pyrhönen was of the opinion that it was an uncomfortably long way to the textiles department, so provisions for the journey were in order, provisions which could at the same time also function as a sort of amulet, a good luck charm.

Pekka thanked him for the frankfurter, walked slowly behind the fruit and vegetable displays and leaned against a large pile of oranges. He calmed the pounding of his heart and slowed the racing of his thoughts. He had to come up with a plan. He had to see past hunger and pleasure. He had to separate the important from the trivial. A piece of advice from his father came to mind: if you have to choose between a rose and an onion, choose the onion.

In ten minutes his plan was complete, and he was relatively satisfied with it. The main ideas were straightforward and logical, and there were no holes in the overall framework. He believed the details would work themselves out in the course of a practical trial.

He walked to the clothing department and chose a pair of khaki trousers, a brown sports jacket and a baseball cap. When he came out of the dressing room, he looked like a carefree consumer who had already made up his mind about what he was going to purchase, but who did not yet care to exit the world of possibilities for the frigid winds outside.

He stopped in front of a large mirror and was pleased with what he saw. Making a decision changes a person immediately. His face loses the reddish flush of cheap soap, his hair seems as if it has found its place on the lumpy surface of the crown of his head and his ears no longer stick out from the sides so unfortunately, looking like they were pasted on as an afterthought. The overall impression is of a person who has found his place in the world and intends to keep it.

Spurred by these uplifting thoughts, Pekka moved his plan into its second phase, to the electric razors. The machines were connected with long, black wires to the wall. His brow furrowed, he rubbed his scruffy stubble thoughtfully. As did those who were seriously considering what to buy. Philips or Braun? Which is the more sensible purchase for you in particular? What are your requirements? Do you shave every day or is once a week enough? In order to make the decision easier, Pekka decided to try his different options. He noticed a fan on an adjacent shelf, which he turned on in hopes that its noise would cover the sound of the razor.

The smooth, cold steel mesh felt good on his skin. The small, buzzing blades under the mesh removed the uneven layer of hair from his jaw and cheeks, making Pekka's face brighter, as if for a moment he belonged there. He flipped up the trimmer using the switch on the side and used it to remove the fuzz from his ears. The last traces of the ape were thus removed.

Pekka did not notice the home appliance salesperson who had appeared behind him, and who very kindly informed him that although the razor was plugged in, it was not meant to be used for shaving, particularly not for removing such significant tracts of stubble. Pekka apologized for his behaviour, appealing to the appalling number of meetings he had been having at work, which often left him nearly out of his mind. A person cannot keep so much complex, interconnected information inside for so long without some ill effects.

The salesperson listened empathetically and then asked what Pekka thought of the Braun in question. Pekka thought it was the market leader, unsurpassed in terms of its price to quality ratio. He said he had already made his purchase decision and asked the salesperson for a warranty certificate. As the salesperson left to fetch it, Pekka exited the area and walked towards the smell.

Pyrhönen was at his station, introducing two tracksuited women to the myriad manifestations of meat. Pyrhönen noticed his new client and called for the gentleman to come closer. "These animals don't bite anymore."

Pekka was so relieved by his successful metamorphosis that he ate greedily from each container without paying any attention to Pyrhönen's speeches. He noticed a couple of empty paper trays in the rubbish bin. He picked them up with his left hand, raised his right hand and searched for the proper tone of voice.

"Would there be any possibility of getting a few samples in these trays? You see, my family is waiting in the minivan because our youngest has an ear infection."

"Of course. That's very good of you."

"Thank you very much. My wife and I always come to this counter in particular. It feels almost like the Jelpunens are friends of the family."

"That's nice to hear."

Pekka waited until Pyrhönen turned to serve the ladies again and then filled his trays with product and walked to the fitting room. He retrieved his clothing from under the bench, redressed as himself and looked in the mirror. Everything had gone according to plan, even better than he had expected. His stomach had received the nourishment it needed, his mind had been enlightened and a new idea had sprung up among the sparse, slightly wilted thoughts he usually entertained. Pekka remembered what his father had said about new ideas: test them out in practice immediately. Pekka sent his regards to his father mentally as he popped a rolled-up piece of ham sausage into his mouth.

Over the following days, Pekka ate well in six stores. Meat products were available, but he was also able to sample yogurts, soups, confections and breads. In one store there was no clothing department, but he was also prepared for this eventuality: he carried three different woollen hats in his backpack, which allowed him to adopt different guises. He chatted with the employees, determining their routes and schedules.

Pekka devised a careful path, traversing approximately ten kilometres and five supermarkets, after the completion of which one could say he had eaten products from every food group excepting salads. He wrote a memorandum on the subject using a mechanical typewriter and then went to the library and made ten copies. He regretted having sold his computer and printer during a previous period of famine, because the copies cost twenty cents apiece. But he believed that before long he would be able to bill a healthy sum for his insight.

The next day Pekka hurried to the Park of the Fallen to present his case. To his consternation, most of those present were so drunk or incoherent that there was no way to present them with any new information. They were spread all over the park, not forming a cohesive group, as if the Creator had sprinkled them here and there like pine nuts.

The strong wind blowing in from the sea clinked empty bottles against each other, and tattered plastic bags flew here and there, hissing. The Fallen were sprawled on the grass, the walking paths and at the foot of trees. Now and then one of them turned over with a groan or tipped from his side onto his back.

Stretch, who Pekka remembered had spent the last year living in a Nissan Cherry, had dragged his lanky body half onto a bench. His right leg lay on the ground, his left partially on the bench. His head lolled sideways, and in some way he had managed to pass out such that his backside was partially in contact with the grass and partially with the bench. Pekka knew that although Stretch looked unconscious, he could still register voices and smells. Stretch was famous for the ability to bounce upright from a deep coma if anything or anyone threatened his privacy. Stretch had been drinking for so long he wasn't drunk anymore, but rather in a long, seemingly endless state, a sort of waking dream, which he maintained mechanically and chemically.

Pekka stopped in front of Stretch, nudged him carefully with the toe of his shoe, introduced himself as Pekka and said he was here on business, that he had a new idea.

Stretch opened one eye, judged the newcomer to be familiar and harmless and rose, not quite up, but into a better position, which meant that he folded himself onto the bench like a sheet. Then he opened his other eye as well, raised his right hand in the air and nodded in assent.

Pekka began to present his memorandum, which he said he would sell for two euros a copy. With the help of the memorandum, the customer could eat a varied, flavourful diet in different parts of the city; admittedly, several of the free food spots were located on the outskirts.

Stretch was a master of business administration by training and known for his computational abilities. He had worked in import companies, as a purchasing agent for the Stockmann men's department and for a short time as a marketing manager for the Silja Line cruise company.

He nodded. Pekka could continue. If Stretch had closed his eyes, it would have meant that the proposal was uninteresting and that it should be cut off immediately.

Pekka focused his sales pitch on the advantages for the consumer.

With an investment of two euros, the purchaser would be introduced to the flora and fauna of the culinary world, and for this small amount of money the purchaser would not only receive a full belly but also an indispensable storehouse of information about the offerings of the city centre and outlying areas. The purchaser would benefit from this storehouse when times became more favourable again and the purchaser climbed back onto the wagon he had fallen off, naturally through no fault of his own. When good times arrived and roles reversed, the owner of the sampling memorandum might, depending on his moral disposition, either sell or donate the memorandum to another.

At the end of his presentation, Pekka extended one copy of the memorandum to Stretch, who thanked him and began turning his head back and forth, evaluating the content of the sales pitch. He closed his eyes, which at this stage was a good thing, because as he did so, Stretch dived into the inner recesses of his head, there considering each aspect of the overall proposal, shielded from prying eyes.

Pekka waited. He knew that Stretch never, even in the most profound state of confusion or malnourishment, uttered anything precipitously. One could expect only carefully weighed opinions, relevant far beyond the matter at hand or the current situation.

Stretch opened his eyes. He looked Pekka in the eyes and cleared his throat. This was a mistake which Stretch made from time to time. The act awakened his throat and the clumps of mucus slumbering there. A hacking, rattling cough began, one which buffeted the lanky man like a marionette, forcing him to lean over on his knees, and there he coughed and hawked and spat nearly twenty-centimetre-long globules which clung to the corners of his mouth, and which, as they fell to the grass, formed strange shapes like molten tin dropped hissing into cold water on New Year's Eve. There was no need for augury in interpreting the globules this time. It was clear from them what rolled cigarettes, sweet wine, and beer did to an organism. Finally Stretch managed to clear his throat and begged Pekka's pardon for the scene, which according to him resulted from the poor air quality in the city.

According to Stretch, the basic idea of the memorandum on offer was tenable, but he saw certain problems with its resale value.

"First of all, the clientele is physically limited in places, as most of them do not have the wherewithal to travel long distances without tiring or losing their way, which suggests the possibility that the distances between the free samples may be too long. Second, some of those belonging to the target audience may have trouble disguising themselves – they may have insufficient brain cells remaining for such an activity. It requires, you must admit, a certain stoutness of heart and spryness to find one's way to a dubiously small dressing room in a clothing department, the likes of which the client may have last visited in the 1990s, if ever. That is, the market for this memorandum is, and I say this without any desire to offend my brothers and sisters in tribulation, made up of the most lucid and fit among us. Thirdly, the memorandum does not contain, at least not based on my quick perusal, sufficient carbohydrates, which we humans need for activities of extended duration."

Pekka understood the issues Stretch had raised, except the last mentioned, which he considered irrelevant, because of course Pekka had no influence over the selection of products being offered. Pekka also felt like commenting on the issue of carbohydrates in general, the overconsumption of which made one fat and lazy. A good balance between protein and fluids was the foundation of well being, a support upon which you could lean to find fulfilment in life.

Stretch noticed Pekka's slight melancholy and quickly added,

"All in all the idea is splendid and worthy of further refinement. I consider its greatest merit to be that you have seen beyond the ordinary and found an opportunity in a thing in which many see only a prosaic event. That's no mean feat, especially since I know you have been operating in a state of severe hunger and without any of the start-up capital or moral support offered by the state to other small enterprises."

Pekka thanked Stretch for his support, but was curious to hear what sorts of further opportunities he saw in this still-nascent idea. From his experience of work, Pekka knew that anyone could spout ideas, but that their further development and implementation required tenacity.

Stretch asked for time to think and closed his eyes. He opened them quickly and asked whether Pekka happened to have any samples of the nourishment in question left over. Pekka offered Stretch a paper tray of aspic and ham sausage. Stretch upended the tray into his mouth, ruminating loudly and greedily. Between slurps and smacks he managed to report that a day and a half had passed since his last meal. Stretch washed the mass down by knocking back a large bottle of water. In conclusion he cursed about how water didn't agree with his stomach, which had become used to other sorts of beverages.

"There is something altogether coarse and unseemly in water these days. Too much piss in the Päijänne. But where else is the city supposed to get water? But back to your innovation. If I were you, I would look elsewhere for your target audience, which is not to belittle those fallen and slumbering about us, but only to suggest there is want and distress and people on the edge in other social classes as well. On the edge. That's a good phrase. About to fall off. On the borderline. They are not yet what they are becoming. And the best thing is they don't know it. We didn't know it either. Ignorance is not only bliss, it is freedom from prejudice. I might suggest retirees, for example. They might be an excellent audience, some of them in even better condition than we ever were. And besides, they will know immediately what this is all about. They have been to the events in question. Pekka Malmikunnas, I say to you: go to them – make your accounting. With these words I bid you on your way, for more than this I cannot say at this time without a deterioration in quality."

Stretch extended his right hand horizontally and made a shooing motion with his fingers. Pekka thanked him and promised to get Stretch more food samples at the first opportunity.

Pekka walked towards his apartment in the darkening evening. On a side street he noticed an abandoned American van with its side windows smashed out. Pekka peeked in through one window and established that the van was serviceable, although cigarettes had been put out on the red seats and there was a little water in the footwell. Pekka thought that if he ended up having to give up his rented apartment for financial reasons, he could perhaps turn this van into a decent place to live. He opened the front door, which was already cracked. The door squeaked and a bird burst out from under the front seat. That was a good sign. Pekka remembered reading that birds choose their nesting sites carefully. The bird had tested the van and found that it was good for itself and therefore also for a human.

At home Pekka turned on a small nightlight and drank four decilitres of room temperature water to stave off his hunger until morning. Then he curled up under a blanket and pondered in his heart Stretch's wise words.

THE RIOTER

On that morning Kimmo Hienlahti turned forty-nine years old and knew that he did not necessarily ever have to work again in his life. His was the opportunity to simply stay in his leather easy chair from the designer with the name that was difficult to pronounce. If he wanted to he could sauna and potter about in his bathrobe for the rest of the day. He could get out of his chair, but even that was not imperative because he could order food, drink and people to his home with the telephone that lay on the armrest. But he did not feel like any of those things. He felt hollow, and as a person of verbal precision, he was irritated that only one sound separated hollow from wallow.

Kimmo pushed off with the big toe of his left foot and rocked.

He began to think about wealth and money. What did it mean in practice? If you discounted everything visible: the house, the stocks, the cars, the second house and all the other junk? What was wealth? What do you need to be prepared for if you plan to be wealthy? What do you have to give up? What do you get? What do you lose? And is there anything left to hope for or to look forward to? Was this everything? Had the line been drawn? And who had drawn it? And what did you get if you wanted?

When a person becomes wealthy, he unwittingly also becomes lonely, independent, an island. He is at sea – everyone else is on land. A wealthy person can't guess how much else will come along with the wealth. And that everything else comes first with responsibility. First responsibility, then freedom. And the more wealthy you are, the less freedom there is. The price you pay for wealth can be surprisingly high.

Rich is different from wealthy. A rich person is rich for a little while, a wealthy person for the rest of his life. The history of riches is short, colourful and embarrassing. During the first economic boom in the 1980s, a tradition of imitating riches was born. People pretended to be rich using borrowed money. I'll be this – you be that. A familiar pattern from the playground, with adults playing the parts.

A rich person is tasteless because he wants to taste everything. No sense of taste develops. There isn't time. A rich person flaunts it – a wealthy person conceals it. Every truly wealthy person expends a great deal of time and energy concealing his wealth. The history of wealth is a history of camouflage. The most wealthy person is the one who can buy distance. Distance is unquestionably the best thing that money can buy. Income disparity is distance.

Kimmo realized he was thinking himself into a frenzy. He could have said all of this to a seminar audience, but he didn't feel like speaking anymore.

Kimmo was wealthy, but because his wealth was neither old nor inherited, he wasn't on a first name basis with it yet. When he was moving among people, he watched and censored himself, finding himself keeping such a low profile that it hurt his back. He envied the nouveau-riche who rushed about, cavorting, squandering their resources, blustering, smelling of sweet perfumes, and just generally running amok through life as if it were a town square paved just for them. The nouveau-riche spent without any regard for business cycles or the laws of economics, which at any second could splash sleet on their silk shirts and horse shit on their patent leather shoes. They didn't care if they were mocked as social climbers. They didn't pay any attention to the hoots and jeers. They looked neither to the left nor to the right. They just went straight to the sales counter and bought everything useless and shiny. The nouveau-riche and those living on borrowed money took their cues from the Russians, who have always known how to display their riches. Especially now, after finally getting rid of their seventy-year social experiment, the Russkis were flooding into Finland and showing the amateurs how money was really burned. The Russkis were teaching the Finns a new proverb the hard way: holding your cap in your hand makes you feel like buying a hat for your head.

Kimmo was watching all this from the sidelines. He controlled himself and behaved properly and cast about enviously in every direction. The nouveau-riche were running amok, the rabble shouted. When he glided in his car through a bad part of town, he saw the bread line that snaked around the block, and only a couple of kilometres away the nouveau-rich were peeling out in their German luxury cars. He felt isolated between these two tribes. The old world had disappeared, and he couldn't figure out the new one. Kimmo felt like he had been born at the wrong time.

His business associate Nyström had been born at the right time. At barely thirty years of age he had been blessed with a new life: in 1988 the financial markets opened up, spread their legs, and out popped cheeky little Nyström, who from his very first cry seized hold of the new world, sped on his way by the virgin forests he had inherited, which soughed in the breezes for only a moment and then fell headlong at the feet of Nyström's fancy. Nyström put his fortune into residential properties and the rest he used to disport himself, but he used another term entirely: he invested in "quality of life". There was no technical gadget or gizmo invented anywhere in the world that couldn't be found in Nyström's pocket, car or home, and he generously and unstintingly gave Kimmo advice on how to splurge and squander, terms which he did not prefer to use because they had an unpleasant, plebeian ring to them. When Nyström's money supply dwindled, he got more from the bank as fast as they could print it. At his worst or his best – the tone depended on the person doing the telling – Nyström owned three education centres, an empty nursing home and one manufacturing plant. Nyström didn't know what industry the manufacturing plant was in, but it was located in Loimaa. Kimmo hated Nyström. Not because he had money, but because he shuffled the deck. In the olden days, the rabble knew their place, as did the gentry. Then came a time when they got all jumbled together. The rabble could borrow as much as they wanted from the bank. And oh how they wanted. The rabble began to resemble the gentry outwardly, so much so that the gentry were discomfited and began to stagnate. They had become too used to walking birch-lined lanes whistling "Rich man, poor man, beggar man, thief". Luckily for the gentry, interest rates rose and the homes the rabble had managed to buy lost their value, and the rabble returned to their starting point, i.e. zero. But then the ground thawed again, and the nouveau-riche tribe crawled out of some gutter and reshuffled the deck again, and no-one could tell a knave from a king anymore.

Kimmo rose from his chair and walked over to his enormous window. The sea roiled, dark and uncaring. On the other side of the bay he could just see the enormous high-rise apartment buildings where thousands of people lived one atop another. None of them was visible from this far away. Income disparity is distance.

He dressed himself in clothing that bore the name of no designer. He didn't like the clothes, but he didn't want to have anything on that would attract attention on this journey. He said farewell to his house and glanced at his car in the driveway, cold and quiet, looking strangely melancholy. He looked at the plantings that the landscape architect had chosen and which the Estonian men had planted. Kimmo had paid them eight euros an hour under the table, and after the work was done he had given the men two bottles of vodka, which they hadn't wanted. Instead they asked Kimmo for a euro an hour more. Vodka was no good; they begged for more money. He knew the world had changed.

Kimmo didn't know how to act on a bus. Were you supposed to buy a ticket in advance? How much did it cost? Where is the button you push to get out immediately?

The blue bus curtsied, and the doors hissed open. Kimmo stood before the driver. He was black, and the identification card that hung at his breast said Biko Malmikunnas. Kimmo looked questioningly at the driver, who said the price in bad Finnish, "Two twenty." Kimmo only had hundred-euro notes, the crispest of which he extended to the driver. The driver sighed and shook his head. Kimmo thought that he could just as easily shake his head with a sigh and tell the driver in his good Finnish what he thought about globalization, which he used to support but didn't anymore. If I had known that in practice it would mean freedom for everything and everyone, I would have opposed it.

The driver set a stack of change in Kimmo's hand. He shoved the whole wad into his trouser pocket and swayed his way along the aisle, looking for an appropriate seat. There was one person sitting on each double bench. Kimmo was forced to sit next to a drowsy, middle-aged man.

He was dressed. There was nothing else Kimmo could say about his clothing. He stank of sweat, liver casserole and mustard. Kimmo tried to at least turn a little to the side, but it was impossible because the pudgy, formless man flowed against Kimmo's side. The man reminded him of a ringed seal who had strayed onto dry land and whose birthplace was revealed by the blue algae that had dried on his skin.

The negro took a curve so fast that the seal rocked towards

Kimmo and they both fell into the aisle. Kimmo felt like kicking him, but he noticed that there was already one bruise on his temple. Kimmo extracted himself from the man, leaving him lying in the aisle. The negro said something in the microphone, but Kimmo couldn't understand. Apparently his job description also included pointing out the more important sights in the city. A youngish man got out of his seat, gave Kimmo a nasty look and lifted the lifeless seal onto a seat. Kimmo held on to a pipe and swayed with the motion of the bus. The trip felt endless, even though the bus was already approaching one of the main roads into the city centre.

Suddenly Kimmo had a strange panic attack. He was sure that at any moment the negro would push a button to close the doors of the bus and that no-one would ever be able to get out again. That the world would come to a stop in the bus, and the bus would be the whole world. It would be led by the negro, its prime minister would be the mouldy seal and the other passengers would serve them. The negro would announce into the microphone that all of Kimmo's property had been confiscated on the same grounds as the Russian oligarch Mikhail Khodorkovsky's once upon a time. The mouldy seal would stand up and slap Kimmo on the cheek with its slimy tail. The negro and the seal would force Kimmo and the other passengers to scour the centre aisle clean and start to dance the tango cheek to cheek. The dance would never end, because there is always land across the open sea, as its lyrics claim.

Kimmo came to his senses when someone pushed the stop button. Kimmo slipped out when the doors opened.

Now he was in the middle of a bad part of town, and he didn't have a steel-shelled car to protect him. His distance had been crumpled in on itself. It was time to get to know the world of the rabble. The gentry could disappear from the world, but the rabble never would. In the animal kingdom the rabble could be compared to rats and the gentry to geese. Rats leave sinking ships, scurrying to dry land and reproducing. Geese honk for a moment in the oil pond and then drop to the ground with their beaks blackened.

The rabble had something that Kimmo didn't: others like themselves. Every member of the rabble knew that just around the corner there were a hundred people just like him. Kimmo didn't have anything in common with other wealthy people. He had come from the dairy to the drawing room, but a bit of manure had fallen on the floor from the soles of his shoes and he had been found out.

The rabble wandered about carrying plastic bags, footloose and fancy free, completely ignorant of the cares of the wealthy. They strung up their social safety net and rocked themselves to sleep in the afternoon sun after a few beers. Society had built them a complicated but functional system which made it possible for them to give up at any moment and fall, back first, arms spread-eagled, off the roof of their rented apartment building, sure that below a net woven of unemployment compensation and income supports awaited the next person who wanted a turn in the hammock. The state existed for them – it was for them it had been established.

My job is to pay taxes so that every strand of their safety hammock will bear all of their weight. Kimmo was working himself into a rage. That was a bad thing. Rage takes away your judgement and lowers a person to the level of the target of the rage. But inside my own head I can do whatever I want. I can't do anything anywhere else. I have to bear all of this because I am wealthy. Or fortunate, as that vilest of terms goes. What does fortune have to do with this, you cretins? I've made everything by taking risks, and I bore those risks myself. I bore the risk and now I bear the cross. Jesus bore a cross in the fairy tale, but I bore my risks literally. It could just as easily have been that my speeches wouldn't have hit the mark and that I wouldn't have been able to send anyone an invoice. Then I would have fallen straight on my head, from plenty high up. And they don't set up safety nets for wealthy people like me.

Kimmo felt like talking. He walked through a small, littered park and noticed a being sleeping on a bench. He couldn't say at once if it was a man or a woman. The being wore a large, wide-brimmed hat concealing the face beneath. Kimmo sat down on the next bench over to be on the safe side, since he wasn't sure what contagious diseases the being might possibly be carrying.

A straggly German Shepherd slept at the being's feet. The dog opened its left eye, established that Kimmo was harmless and continued sleeping.

Kimmo was bothered by the being's androgyny, so he cleared his throat loudly. The being took the wide-brimmed hat off and was revealed as an old man. Grey stubble extended down onto his neck. Black hairs sprouted from his ears. Neck hair protruded from beneath his purple collared shirt.

"Moses. We have a visitor."

The dog became alert, looking questioningly at his master. The man scratched his dog, which then returned to its slumber.

"Was that a cough or a comment?" the man asked.

"Neither really. I'm not from here and was thinking I might converse a bit with the locals."

"So that's how it is. Are you some sort of researcher?"

"No."

"I only ask because nowadays it's difficult to tell who is who. Everything is guesswork. Everyone pretends to be something else or turns into something else. Only the heavenly bodies abide. What do you say, Moses?"

The dog pricked up one of its ears for a moment, but didn't open its eyes.

"I'm from the coast, and I'm wealthy," Kimmo said quickly, but in the same moment realized the statement was flawed. It was missing a gentle introduction to the meat of the message and a cushioning follow-up.

"Showing all your cards up front. Good. But being wealthy isn't a profession, is it?"

"I'm a C.E.O. The main shareholder of a company. Or I was. I sold my company, and now I'm looking at what I could do next."

"Do you have a first name, or did that go along with the company?"

"Kimmo."

"Armas," the man said, extending his hand. Kimmo hesitated to take the hand. Armas noticed. "I don't have any diseases, and my shower works," Armas said. Kimmo blushed and took the hand. Armas squeezed so hard and so long that for a moment Kimmo was afraid he would be attached to the old man forever.

"To begin with, Kimmo, I'll say that I'm not jealous of anyone's money. I used to have it. I've sniffed as many notes as Moses here has people's shoes. But now things are slightly different."

"You mean you live at the mercy of society."

"This boy is hot. Did you hear what he said, Moses? I would phrase it a little differently myself. I'm resting on the arm of society. The same arms that have borne you up as well. By the way, do you know how to stand on your head?"

"What do you mean?"

"Just what I said. I'll show you."

Armas stood up straight, stretched for a moment, sprang into a handstand and then slowly lowered himself so his head touched the ground. He shook, but he stayed upright. He stayed up for ten seconds and then flipped back onto his feet.

"Like that! You know the saying: it wouldn't matter if I stood on my head! And now I showed you one of the great truisms of life in honour of a beautiful night and all the gymnasts of Helsinki. I admit there was an element of trying to stand out from the crowd, but the heart of the matter is that sometimes you can't do anything about the way the world works no matter what you do."

"But some people don't even try," Kimmo said.

"Sure enough. And then there are those who skim off the icing even though they've never even seen the cake. Did you hit the lottery, or are you just messed up otherwise?"

"I'm not messed up. And I've earned everything I have by the sweat of my brow."

"So they all say. Now you have time to learn to stand on your head. You can show the routine to the next generation after all of your stocks have disappeared."

"My wealth isn't in stocks."

"It has to be somewhere, since it isn't in your head. Sorry. But remember that you started this brinksmanship. Moses and I were sleeping and waiting for summer when you came."

"Fair enough. But I'll say this much that all I got from home was my mother's homemade berry juice and advice from my dad. Whatever was on the bottom line I made. This whole thing has spun around on its axis now. My father thought the bourgeoisie were exploiting the working class, but I think the working class are exploiting the bourgeoisie."

"Father and son are both right and wrong at the same time. There isn't one truth anymore. And because of that I ran off the road for a while too. Since there wasn't anyone to blame. It's best to look carefully at the flag you go waving out there. You should choose a flag big enough that in an pinch you can make a tent out of it."

Armas looked under the bench and look out a large bottle of water and a bag of meat pies.

"Are you hungry, Mr Wealthy Man? Hydration and blood sugar. Those are the same for everybody."

Kimmo's hunger faded immediately when he saw the familiar, smashed meat pie, the kind he had eaten so often to stave off his horrible hunger as he toiled for his second studio apartment. His appetite was ruined completely by the way Armas mashed the pie in the front of his mouth and smacked his lips cheerily. Kimmo was reminded of his father from the old Finland, the one built amidst a hellish stink of sweat and pine resin. His father had a habit of eating standing up, quickly, as if food were just about to run out in the world.

Armas strained with his tongue at the bits of pie that had got stuck between his teeth and then rinsed it all down with water. And at the end of the ceremony came what Kimmo predicted, overcome with disgust: a burp, which came from so deep and with such a resounding noise that Kimmo was afraid it was going to bring the food back up with it.

"Unfortunately I don't have any alcohol to offer since I gave up drinking two years ago. I started feeling terribly dizzy, and I saw all sorts of things in the mornings. Once a boa constrictor came out from under the rug. They don't exactly thrive in these latitudes, but it turned up there anyway. I don't mean under the rug – I mean in my head. I had to upend my cup so I could see other things. I came into this world sober, and I'm going to leave it sober. The same with tobacco. I smoked for thirty-seven years, and one morning I started to cough. The worst piece of phlegm was forty-seven centimetres long. I stopped cold turkey. For two weeks I tossed and turned and shivered under my sheets, but I didn't chew any nicotine gum. I don't chew anything I'm not going to swallow, on principle. Well, what do you say? How are we going to sit out the rest of the evening? Should we talk about politics or something real? I know one thing. Nothing is certain. That's why I'm sitting here in this slightly shabby clothing with this scruffy dog. Sorry, Moses. There never has been any certainty. And there never will be. No-one knows anything perfectly. Except that he's going to die. That's why I'm going to be sitting here until it comes."

"Death?"

"No, summer."

"Summer?"

"Yeah. I decided in '92 when my firm went under. I didn't have a clue what happened. And neither did anyone else. Not the bank manager, not the government ministers, no-one. The experts stood with microphones at their mouths stiff as boards and gacked something incoherent. The country sank like a sheet of ice, so deep that no-one could see that far down. You were probably in high school then. I decided then that there would be one more time in my life when I was in the right place at the right time and knew something with perfect certainty. Today is the seventh of May, and it will be here soon. Perhaps tomorrow night. And Moses and I will be on duty. We will see it. We will witness it."

"What?"

"When the trees leaf out. We will be able to say that we were there, and we saw it with our own eyes. Actually, I won't promise anything about Moses' eyes, since he's old enough that he's always falling asleep. If you happen by this corner again within the next couple of weeks, I'll be able to tell you precisely when summer came to Finland. Isn't it somehow comforting to be perfectly certain about one thing? What do you say, Kimmo?"

Kimmo didn't know what to say. He was reminded of a similar situation years ago in a conference room when he was supposed to present a sales strategy to a client. Kimmo opened his mouth, but nothing came out. His mouth hung open. His left arm went numb. The outlines of the people and the bluish screens of the laptops lurched in his field of vision. He had to sit down. His assistant managed to get a chair pushed under him at the last second. The attack lasted only a minute, but it was enough. He had lost face, and it took half a year to create a new one. Later, when meeting with the same clients, he told them he had experienced a panic attack because he had sensed so much resistance to change around him.

"I should probably be going now," Kimmo said.

"Don't go disappearing after the appetizer."

"I really have to. It was nice to chat with you."

"Yeah. Remember to learn to stand on your head. It's a matter of balance. Like everything."

Armas waved. The dog opened one eye, looking at Kimmo for a moment and then continuing its drowsing.

Kimmo walked from the park to the road and sat down on the steps of a shuttered chemist's. A decal on the display window flapped in the wind. It said "Take time for yourself". Kimmo tried to assemble his thoughts, but it felt like trying to collect the twigs that fell from the birch trees in the windy yard of the home he had left decades before. There was no end to the twigs, and they were impossible to tell apart.

Kimmo stood up and walked across the intersection to a secluded pathway.

A gang of young riff-raff swaggered towards him, covering the width of the path. They were boisterous and carefree. They seemed to find support and safety in each other. Kimmo's head was full of talk, but after Armas he couldn't get a single word out of his mouth. In his mind he spoke to them gracefully and humanely.

I understand you. You have just graduated to unemployment. I understand that your expressions and gestures are not meant as an affront to me personally, but are rather simply some of the innate advantages of your position and age, clothing you in a certain haughtiness and pride. These characteristics form a thick wall between you and organized society, especially as a pack. And although I say I understand you, I can in no way conceal my contempt, which springs from the fact that I worked hard for the money one-third of which goes to supporting people like you, although I am comforted by the fact that due to the capital gains tax rate I am in a slightly better position than a middle-class wage earner. But the thing that most especially concerns me is that to some extent my future depends on you. I refer now to my pension. If your generation does not work, society will not have the resources to pay for my retirement, and for this very reason I have been forced to purchase second homes and other property to secure my old age, because I can't count on you at all.

Kimmo had not realized that part of his internal monologue had dribbled out as a mumble and that the group of youths had stopped to listen to the strange wanderer.

The leader of the group was a pockmarked man tattooed up to his jaw. He looked Kimmo up and down, trying to find a place for him in his gallery of humanity.

"What's this guy mumbling about? Were you talking to us, or were you getting in touch with outer space?"

"Sorry, it was nothing. I was just thinking . . . or, I wasn't thinking

... or, I was thinking ... that, that what you ... or, to say it in a word, I approve of you ... "

"That's wonderful news. Now all that's missing is for us to approve of you. Are you a communist?"

"Me! Not in any way, shape or form. How could you even think ... ?"

"It shows, doesn't it, boys? You've come to convert us, right? You think that you can get our votes, but you're wrong. There aren't any votes to be had here. We keep our opinions to ourselves."

"On the contrary, I represent the opposite extreme ... "

"What do we hate even more than communism, boys? People who don't dare stand behind their opinions. C.C.C.P. Not U.S.S.R. C.C.C.P. Cold Calculating Communist Pig."

"There must be some misunderstanding. I vote National Coalition!"

"No, we vote Coalition. You vote Communist! Every last one of us is an entrepreneur. I'm an electrician, but I have my own company. These others are in the cleaning industry, and they have their own company. Everyone has a company nowadays. Do you know what a company is, comrade?"

"Listen here, I've had three companies. I've been an entrepreneur my whole short life. You can't lecture me!"

"We're off. Someone has to do the work around here!"

Following their pockmarked leader, the group left Kimmo on the path. He had never been left like that. Of course, he had often been left alone with his opinions, but he found this to be much worse, because he did not feel physically safe.

He noticed a street sign on the path that indicated the road was ending. He had always hated road signs. Their messages were always fixed, final. The roads don't end and the traffic doesn't stop, no matter what it says on the signs.

Kimmo set off walking down the path. It ended in the car park of a large, old brick building. According to an ancient, partially disintegrated placard, the building had once served as a match factory.

Kimmo sat on the massive concrete steps and thought about his life. Half of it was over, and he didn't know what he would do with the second half. If you strike a match once, it's gone, but you can scratch and tear and wear out a life. It's never completely ruined. But Kimmo understood that his life had been a working life. There was nothing outside of that. No family, no friends, no hobbies. His family was the company, his friends were his business associates and his hobby was golf, which he hated but played because all of his business associates relaxed on the greens. If he didn't, he might have missed hearing some important business matter. He remembered how he had wandered for kilometres over the endless grass fields, stopping every now and then to listen to Nyström in his plaid trousers commenting on how the torso guides the swing and how one foot should break fluidly in the direction of the stroke. Nyström also thought it was of the utmost importance to remember the irregularities in the surface of the grass and any variance in wind conditions. Even while playing Nyström found time to fiddle with his phone, which he switched for a new model at six-month intervals, always recommending the same update to Kimmo just for the sake of keeping up appearances. The same for the plaid trousers, the pink V-neck sweater and the spike-soled golf shoes.

Kimmo noticed himself losing his temper in retrospect. He had never known how to show his feelings in the heat of the moment. Now he felt like striking a match on the wall of the factory, using it to light a torch, walking to Nyström's loft and turning his two holes into eighteen. Kimmo wanted to smell burned flesh and see black holes.

Rage rioted in his head, smashing all of his wants and desires and dreams into an unrecognizable, gurgling, stinking pulp. Suddenly he wanted to start a family, to get divorced and to be granted visitation rights. He wanted to drive his kids to their activities and stand as one of the anonymous fathers waiting in the car parks of ice-skating rinks and the lobbies of music academies. He wanted a normal life he could ruin with his selfish behaviour. He wanted a rented studio apartment in a bad part of town and an unregistered car. He wanted income support payments and an ugly girlfriend. He wanted earnings-linked unemployment insurance and prepackaged liver casserole. He wanted what he hated. He hated what he wanted.

And he agreed with himself that it was all Nyström's fault.

He began to hear a creaking sound on the path.

A young boy was pushing a wheelbarrow full of broken tape recorders, bread machines and electric water kettles. Just a few years ago they had been the latest thing, what every consumer was supposed to respond to with shouts of joy. The idea came immediately. Kimmo rushed over to the boy.

"I want to buy those."

"This is trash. They're going to the recycling centre."

"No they aren't, if we can agree on a price."

"Do you have both oars in the water, mate? These are worthless."

"They have utility value for me. Is that phrase familiar? I'll use them as an extension of my desires, so I'm willing to pay for them. I'll give you one grand if you cart them to the address I give you and dump them out front. No-one will be home."

"A grand?"

"Two crisp five-hundred-euro notes. Do you know why I like the five-hundred-euro note in particular? Because its pictorial motif is the modern era. Do you like the modern era?"

"I don't really know."

"I do, and after this I'm going to like you too. I'll write down the address where I want you to take this junk. In addition to your reward, I'll give you fifty for a taxi."

Kimmo dug his wallet out of his breast pocket, handed the crisp notes to the boy and wrote down the address.

"My friend collects old electronics. I only collect experiences. Isn't it great that you're about to walk into the sunset one thousand euros richer? When I was your age, I walked back and forth along the same dirt road with twenty pennies in my pocket."

"Aha."

The boy left, the wheelbarrow creaking.

Kimmo was in a good mood again.

Evil does a body good. Evil is energy. Evil is the beginning of everything good.

His rage subsided.

His mood levelled off.

Joy welled up within him.

Kimmo called the taxi control centre and asked for the longest, whitest car they had. The controller said that what showed up might be brown and short, but it would have four wheels. Kimmo asked the controller's name and said he was going to complain about their service to the Taxi Association. The controller encouraged him to do so, but reminded him that even brown taxis didn't like coming to the address in question, because there weren't any residential buildings in the area. Kimmo said he had just bought the whole area and that he was going to build residential units there once he had a free moment.

The controller was silent.

Kimmo laughed and said he was just joking, because no-one could sell anything in this world anymore with a straight face. Jokers have the heaviest wallets, if you know what I mean, miss. The miss said she was a missus and that the car was on its way, and that its make was Škoda. Kimmo said he was happy because the blossoming capitalism of the Czech Republic will line all of our coffers in the end.

The Škoda came.

It was driven by a man whose first syllable betrayed him as an Estonian. His head was shaved and there were red insect bites on his neck. He turned towards Kimmo. His left eye was glass. Kimmo was taken aback. He was sure that the power of the damaged eye had been transferred to the other, because the gaze of the right eye was so sharp. People with two eyes look. People with one eye aim.

Kimmo said the address, which the Estonian punched into the G.P.S. A green road appeared on the screen. At the end of the road was an arrow. The car jerked and then glided along the green road through the ugliness.

Kimmo thought about Nyström, who had called the week before, inquisitive about Kimmo's luck with the ladies. Kimmo had said something inconsequential. Nyström had reminded him that men have a biological clock too, and he said he could hear the ticking of Kimmo's a mile away. According to Nyström, Kimmo should start his facelift with his mobile phone. Using a two-year-old model signalled to women that his voicemail was full.

Kimmo thought about Nyström and everything money could buy.

He asked the Estonian driver what he would do if he got a lot, really a lot, of money. The driver looked in the rearview mirror with one eye and said he might buy something useful for his wife and children. Kimmo said he had just bought a lot of something completely useless, which would probably give him more pleasure than something useful.

The driver didn't reply. He sped up.

THE ESCORT

Helena Malmikunnas looked at Kähkönen and the sea. She should have only been looking at Kähkönen, but Helena was drawing strength from the sea, which was glistening far off outside the window, able to do whatever it wanted. The sea surged and rippled and raged. A person who sat admiring the sea, awaiting its next whim, could accept anything. But when the market economy follows its whims for a moment, the person rebels, whining, "This isn't what I ordered when I asked for a force of nature."

Helena looked at her watch. She had half an hour to tell the man sitting in front of her that there was no longer a place for him in the organization. 47-year-old Kähkönen was a marketing professional, an extrovert, optimistic and energetic, but in the diagram drawn by the new C.E.O., Kähkönen's spot was blank. Helena had hoped that the guillotine would have fallen five millimetres above Kähkönen's balding head, since he had three school-aged children and a house with a mortgage.

The new C.E.O. had emphasized to Helena that he didn't like doing this, but that they had to react to the new market conditions. Kähkönen is an embolus, a drag on the company left over from the old guard. The investors will wait, but not for long. If we don't exercise, soon we won't have any abs at all. But remember, we aren't firing anyone, we're just coming to an understanding.

Helena looked at Kähkönen as he clicked his pen and thought about what turn of phrase she would use to come to an understanding with Kähkönen. Helena felt like saying things just as they were, but if she did, next week she might be sitting where Kähkönen was.

Helena stood up and said she was going to get her calendar. She walked from the conference room straight into the office of the new C.E.O. without any regard for the secretary, who waved after her. The C.E.O. said into the phone that he would call back in a moment and looked inquiringly at Helena.

"Imagine a problem like this. I have in my hand a pig made of clay, and I'm supposed to say that it's a deer. How would I convey it?"

"I don't think I understand what you're getting at, Ms Malmikunnas."

"Kähkönen. How do I convey the boot I'm going to give him? He's sitting in there waiting. Since this is an exceptional circumstance, can I just speak in plain Finnish?"

"Finnish is a very flexible language. You can water it down a little. You don't have to pour the coffee in his lap if it's possible to pour it on the floor. It's a matter of the difference between escorting and shoving. A difference in tone – you understand that. In general what I meant by conveying was how you formulate the message when you deliver it to the staff."

"Fair enough."

Helena walked back to the conference room and said to Kähkö-nen, "There isn't a place for you here anymore. You're fired. The new C.E.O. is the one firing you, but I had to come and tell you about it. This is just how the market is now. Don't ask me how that is, because no-one knows. Do you remember the days when we laughed at the humanities types because they didn't understand anything about business or the economy? No-one is laughing now, because even the economics gurus don't understand. You can leave now, but I'm going to spin the whole thing so handily that it will look like you wanted to leave."

Helena walked to the window and looked out at the sea. Ships were trying to leave their mark on its surface. In vain. The sea was invulnerable and overpowering. The ships looked like little scraps of steel on it.

Helena heard Kähkönen clearing his throat and turned around. He was white, sitting hunched over.

"I . . . I didn't do anything . . . wrong . . . At least I haven't received any especially negative feedback from clients . . ."

"Of course not. No-one has done anything wrong. That hasn't been what this is about for ages. The old world of guilt and innocence is gone. Do you have any suggestions about what sort of wording you'd like to use in the memo I'm going to write to the staff?"

"How can this be happening so fast? I'm not just going to roll over and accept this . . . this diktat! I've been here almost twenty years . . . Helena, you can't . . ."

"No, I can't, but I have to. I have a template ready for the memo. I wrote it for myself. You know my nerves haven't been exactly in the best shape lately, so I was sort of expecting this for myself. But it could work for you too. Listen."

Helena took a piece of paper from a folder and read.

"'Helena Malmikunnas has resigned from her position as marketing director and is moving on to new challenges. She has been heavily involved in reforming the company's business practices and moving the firm towards greater participation in the new globalized marketplace. Malmikunnas will be replaced by Tapani Kähkönen who has previously served . . . and so forth.' Your name is in there now, but we'll replace it with someone else's. I don't know whose. Something like that. How does it sound?"

"I haven't reformed anything and nothing is moving towards greater participation in the globalized marketplace."

"Of course you haven't and of course it isn't. They're just words, Tapani. I have to write something along these lines. Or would you rather that I write that the old nags and dead wood had to be got rid of and that Kähkönen happened to represent both groups?"

"No, I don't. But you know just as well as I do that there won't be anything for me after this. I can't go on to new challenges – I can just go home. Or into a ditch. Preferably home. And what will happen there? If this is what I take home, we're going to have to sell the place. What do you say to that?"

"Nothing."

"Nothing?"

"Nothing. Or, well . . . for years I've been clipping help-wanted ads from the newspapers. My favourite is for a job as a substitute bingo hostess at the Itäkeskus Mall. Now don't get excited, Kähkönen. I'm serious. My brother has had all sorts of jobs since he slipped and fell out of the business world, through no fault of his own. He was innocent too. The worst thing for us is how well off we are. How can you go out there on the street and bray about how the politicians need to wake up because you just got tossed out from your six-thousand-euro-a-month salary? Those are two things you can't demand at the same time, money and empathy. Would you leave your laptop on your desk when you go so we can look through the material on it? You can pick it up next week. We'll be having our own discussions about a send-off party. In these economic conditions all we'll be able to manage is some anonymous retro rock band, I'm sorry to say. And I've come to an understanding with myself that you'll get six months' severance."

Kähkönen took the Timo Sarpaneva vase from the table and threw it at the Kuutti Lavonen painting on the wall. The vase sliced open the plangent Madonna's cheek, falling onto the Indian rug, in which it left a crease. The vase split into six pieces.

Helena looked at Kähkönen, who had tears in his eyes. The total cost of the Sarpaneva, the Lavonen and the Indian rug was around ten thousand euros. She couldn't say that to Kähkönen yet. In fact, she couldn't say anything to Kähkönen. She was supposed to have soothed Kähkönen, but Helena couldn't do that. Kähkönen should have been escorted to the seashore and shown that most imponderable of all the elements. Kähkönen could swim in the sea. Kähkönen could become a seal. Kähkönen could swim to Estonia and perform as a human freak of nature, a victim of the free enterprise system who, always adaptable, had succeeded in middle age at combining the habits of a seal and the intellectual world of a human.

Kähkönen walked out the door. Helena felt like a large group had just left, leaving her alone.

She waited a moment and then turned off her computer and looked at her calendar: Sini's music lesson. She walked quickly to the elevator. She looked left at the front door. On the corner a man was walking slowly against the red light. Kähkönen. The cars honked. Kähkönen didn't even spare them a glance, just continuing forward mechanically, shuffling a little, as if he had aged ten years in fifteen minutes.

Sini was waiting in the hall with her violin case. Helena clasped her in her arms. Sini asked her mother to stay in the room to listen this time. She had taken Sini to her music lesson every single time and always had to return to work for the hour, but this time she agreed.

Their route went through the park. The old maple stood doggedly in the same place. Trees stood their ground. Helena had had a habit of sitting under the maple long ago when the line between work and free time had been clear. For the last ten years Helena had been walking through the park to get a baguette sandwich before the next meeting, for which she was already six minutes late.

Sini took her hand. The violin swung gaily in her other hand. Sometimes in her weaker moments Helena envied her daughter's complete, unsullied lack of concern.

Sini went ahead into the music room. The teacher, Sinikka Tammilehto, shook hands with Sini and Helena, and asked Sini to take her violin out of its case. Sini removed it slowly, with an air of dignity. Ms Sinikka drew her attention to the position of the violin between her neck and jaw. If this position could be made relaxed and natural, the player could concentrate on drawing out from the instrument what the maker and the composer had hidden in its inner recesses.

Helena admired Sinikka's way of speaking to her small students. She took them seriously, wanting to show them the path towards the pain and beauty of the music. When words aren't enough to express something, we take out the violin, Sinikka had a habit of saying when talking about the power of instrumental music. The violin teaches us everything about patience and concentration. When you learn the basics of playing the violin, you will become strong in the face of life.

When Sini began to play, everything else disappeared. Helena did not remember Kähkönen, nor the irritating man whom she had been stuck talking to at the party or the volatile, unstable feeling at work as the new C.E.O. laid off workhorses and hired tigers. Everything disappeared in the music. Helena closed her eyes, hearing the mistakes, the screeching sounds, the long, perfect notes, the small girl's sighs, the teacher's calm voice. Soon Helena could no longer differentiate the individual sounds. Everything melted together into one and the same humming, as if the sea had withdrawn from the shore and was roaring out there somewhere.

Helena awoke with a start to Sinikka's calm voice.

"I'll take your falling asleep as a sign of praise."

"I'm sorry."

"It's nothing."

"Work has been a bit of this, that and the other."

"The power of music is inexplicable. It can put someone to sleep or wake them up. It lifts and it lowers. It soothes and it jostles. You don't ever have to say 'I don't understand'. Isn't it lovely? My husband, who is the most rational, intellectual animal I know, never demands everything from music he does from literature: intelligence, emotion, structure, significance. He never accosts Magnus Lindberg to demand an explanation. He doesn't like all music, but he never says, 'I don't understand'. Everything else he subordinates to understanding. But now we're wasting lesson time. You go ahead and sleep. Sini and I will continue."

Helena was both ashamed and amused. She remembered what her mother Salme had drilled into her children: always sleep when you can. Gather strength like your father gathers firewood.

Sini played one two-minute piece from start to finish, concentrating hard. Sinikka stood next to her humming. When the violin had gone still, Sinikka said, "Thank you."

Sini looked at Sinikka and Helena seriously and then smiled. She put the violin in its case carefully and nodded to Helena. Helena shook hands with Sinikka.

They walked the first little way without speaking, but at the park Helena stopped and asked Sini to sit for a while under the maple.

Sini sat down, wondering why her mother wanted to sit just here. You didn't always know what Mum was about. Sometimes she had odd things in her head. But sure, we can sit here. Mum began to say something about changing jobs. She said there wasn't anything wrong with the job – there was something wrong with her. It felt strange, but then when she put her hand on my shoulder, it didn't anymore. There wasn't anything wrong with Mum. If there was, I would notice. I notice everything. Mum doesn't know. I even notice invisible things.

Helena thought, I can't say things like this to a child, but I already did. It isn't appropriate to go on. I have to regulate how much of what I have jammed inside I let out at one time. If a child is given too much to carry, she can become an adult too quickly. I think I did. A leaden-shouldered worrier. Like me.

The violin music had stuck in Helena's head. She watched how Sini swung her legs, kicking the leaves. Nine years old. Carefree. But when she puts the violin under her chin and plays, she grows into something else. Or maybe she doesn't grow. She is carried away by the music, which makes me happy and sad all at the same time. She's already playing her own life into existence.

"What do you like about playing the violin? Does it feel hard or easy?" Helena asked.

"I want to play forever," Sini answered.

THE HUMAN PART

POSTCARD, LAKE SCENE

Hey there, Helena!

Helena, about your shoulder pains. You sit hunched over at your computer. And you're letting your rear end sag with too many meetings. Once a day spread your legs apart sitting on your chair and lower your arms, outstretched, slowly towards the floor. The tail bone. That is where all the tightness comes from. All of the webs and nerves and other important wires start at the tail bone. Believe me. And if you don't, ask Ritva. She's one of the masseuses over in the next parish. She even has your father reaching for crumbs on the floor nowadays.

Your mother

THE EYEWITNESS

Kimmo Hienlahti drove around the city, unable to get the woman out of his mind.

It was 8.00. He had left home just after 6.00. He drove up a ramp into the car park of a late-night service station that had been built over the ring road, and parked between two Japanese models, even though he knew that his German one wouldn't like it.

His bloodless, flaccid legs took a moment to get used to the ground. He flexed them and heard a crack just like the one he had heard from his father's legs so long ago in the yard of the ugly house he grew up in. He remembered deciding that he would never be as old or as anything as his father.

The large, glass door of the service station opened automatically. Inside sat a bunch of people dressed in ugly clothes.

He got in line and flowed along with it to the coffee cups, taking one and setting it under the dispenser. He accidentally pressed cocoa and then tried to cancel, but the machine wouldn't stop. Kimmo shifted his cup to the side and half of the hot chocolate ran into the grate.

Kimmo pushed his demi-cocoa in front of the cashier, paid with a tenner and was just about to say "Keep the change" when at the last moment he remembered he was out among the rabble, where a gesture like that would be taken for arrogance.

He tried to act as normal as possible, as if nothing had happened. He looked around, trying to read from people's expressions and glances whether they were seeing through him. Kimmo was sure it was obvious by looking at him that he had never had any of the things they had – no woman, no children, no nothing.

A couple was sitting at a corner table. The man was looking outside, the woman at the wall. Before them they had two halves of a sandwich and large Cokes. Kimmo felt like walking over to them and saying, "I haven't got what you have, but do you know what? I'm happy and relieved, because in you I can see where love ends, how the cream is going rancid and the flies are starting to swarm above your heads."

The ring road ran along below, outside a large window. The cars zipped by in both directions. They were clearly in a hurry to get to their destinations – to Grandma's house, to the cottage, to a lover, to somewhere where everything stops for a moment and all you can hear is the soughing of the wind in the trees along the shoreline.

Kimmo felt like he wouldn't find peace at the end of any road.

The cocoa had grown cold. It tasted like chocolate water. Light-coloured splotches had formed on its surface, reminding him of the frost-bitten cheeks from his childhood up in the cold North.

Kimmo stood up and walked over to the slot machines. He fed four euros into the machine and chose the largest bet, one euro. He hated oranges. From experience years ago he knew that if one of them stopped in the window, the game was over. They were putrid, the same ones he had seen in front of the filthy shops on the sidewalk on the one and only tourist vacation he had ever taken. He remembered how he had kicked one of the rotten fruits, and part of its yellow-green muck had stuck to his shoe.

Two strawberries stopped on the payline. He covered the third space with his hand and played a game: if a third strawberry stopped there, the woman would be his. He heard a click and opened his fingers: orange. He kicked the machine and glanced at the cashier. He felt like saying to her, "I could buy this whole service station and all of its employees and you and your scabby two-bedroom apartment and still have money left over to buy every strawberry patch in this whole country!"

Kimmo was ashamed of his thoughts and walked out. The remote control opened the car door. He sat down and turned the key in the ignition. The car jerked awake like a cold deer.

He decided to drive to the woman's apartment and say immediately at the door, "You are mine, even though I hated you at first. And I still hate you, but I hate myself even more. Would you mind fucking me? You heard me right. Fuck me. I have brains and money. You can fuck them out of me right up front. And then let's see what's left. I don't use vocabulary like this. Usually. Now I do. Life is not short – it's so long that I can't see to the end of it. Life is boring. I'm short sighted, so I'm rich. I didn't have the patience to wait. I was brutal and fast. And now the time is ripe. In large part everything resulted from luck and constant talking. I have never been quiet in a place where there were people. People are always clients – not immediately, but before long. Do you think this is boring? If you do, say so, and I'll disappear. No, you won't say so, because you can't get a word in edgeways. I control the airspace, and there isn't any other space here. If you control the airspace, you control everything."

Kimmo drove for half an hour before he came to, realizing he had been mumbling to himself.

He looked at the G.P.S. He was getting closer to where the woman lived, even though he had been driving carelessly, this way and that. Something drew him there. She was the end of the road.

Now carefully.

Right here.

Then left.

Clint Eastwood's voice, which he had ordered for the G.P.S., said he was approaching his destination.

Be careful.

But were you careful when you kicked the saloon door open, biting your cigar and shooting everything that moved? Who are you to say that to me or especially to this car, which our Turkish friend built to drive faster than its fellow creatures?

Suddenly something flashed in front of him from the left.

He hit the brakes and closed his eyes. When he opened his eyes, he saw everything. Slowed down. Sped up. But not rewound.

Something green flew through the air and thudded to the ground somewhere over there.

Where?

On the grass.

Alive.

Surely.

I can see it with my own eyes.

There isn't any water coming from them.

My eyes, I mean.

The Estonian taxi driver had a glass eye.

You end up with one of those if you cry for the old system.

I had a green light.

I did.

And I do.

It was crossing on a red, the thing that flew.

I was moving.

Not too fast, but fast enough.

A car with two exhaust pipes can't be driven at a crawl.

It's a law of nature. Anyone who says differently doesn't know nature.

Joggers don't expect a soft paw from a bear.

The woman lives here somewhere.

I can smell it. I chose her by smell up there on the terrace.

Even though I tried to convince myself it was about intelligence and beauty.

We are animals inside and humans outside. I want to get inside a human.

I will never meet that woman again.

We will never become a couple. I will never become a father.

I will never become anything ever again. I have already had everything.

No-one gets to come into my car.

Someone is trying.

Someone crazy.

Or wise.

You can't tell them apart anymore. They are one and the same. Like the political parties.

If I ever meet that woman again, I won't say anything crude like I was just planning to.

I will be different.

I promise.

I don't have any other option.

Anymore.

I used to.

What got into me? Why did I speed up?

Nothing. It was already in me.

Everything is in us, in us humans.

The question is just what we put into use.

The crazy person is kicking my car.

There is blood coming from my forehead.

I hate red.

It reminds me of communism.

What if the woman is a humanist type?

She must be.

It's good that I'm not going to see her.

I'm not going to see anyone.

Anymore.

Now I have to speak well.

Not a lot, but well.

THE CLEANERS

Kerttu Rinkinen sat down, afraid. She had never sat in the back of a police car and spoken to a police officer before. It felt strange, as if she were being accused of something. Komisario Niittymäki said that Kerttu could relax.

"We're just interviewing you as an eyewitness. We'll take your statement and then you'll be interviewed again because of the seriousness of the case. Can you tell me as precisely as possible what you saw?"

Kerttu felt like saying that she was just a cleaning lady – just let me go to work and do what I know how to do.

"Yeah."

Kerttu began. She immediately wanted to stop. There are things you can talk about and things you can't. This was something Kerttu had learned as a cleaning lady. She had been working as a cleaning lady on the executive floor for fourteen years. You hear a lot there. Even if you aren't listening.

"I was standing there, and the traffic lights were green. For the cars. The girl was there next to me. I don't have my own children. I would have liked to, and so I always keep a close eye on any children around me. Like this one. Quick eyes. Hair in braids."

The president of the company had once told Kerttu that leadership meant keeping almost everything inside. Saying only what you had to say. Saying what no-one else dared. I'm paid a lot of money for saying hard things, the president of the company had said to Kerttu.

He spoke to me because talking to a cleaning lady is easy. It's the same as talking to the mop or to the floor scrubber I push along the hallways. A mop never spreads rumours. There is another reason. The president of the company is from Pihtipudas, just like me, and feels at home with me.

"Then the lights changed. Green for us that is. The little green man was there on the post. I remember it clearly. I never go when the little red man is there. We had green, no matter what the driver says. The girl and I started across in single file, and then the girl disappeared from in front of me. She flew in the air. She was up there for a long time. In the air."

The president of the company said once that his salary included a one-hundred-thousand-euro shield bonus. I asked him what on earth that could be. He said that he had to stand as a shield for all the shit from the fan to spatter on. I said that you're using dirty words with the wrong person now, since I have to clean up shit all day long. He wanted to tell me more and invited me to sit down. He said that part of the job of the president of a company was to accept everything that came his way. From outside the company, from management, from the staff, from everywhere. He had to accept it all and endure it all. That if Kerttu ever wondered about their salaries, they always include a shield bonus.

"I won't try to guess the car's speed, but he was certainly speeding, and not just a little. I kicked the car at least ten times. I admit that, and even if I go to jail, I'm not going to pay a red cent for the dents. I couldn't get the car door open. He must have locked it. I would have dragged him out and punched him. I have strong arms after carrying and dragging cleaning tools and lifting and moving furniture year after year. And people like me who have never hit anyone, we're the ones who hit the hardest. And don't know when to stop. Thankfully the door didn't open. And thankfully he's sitting over there in the other car now."

Komisario Niittymäki listened to the elderly woman, looking at the other car where a middle-aged man sat hunched over. Niittymäki tried to control his emotions. There were so many that shepherding them was work. The sound of the ambulance departing the scene still reached them from far off.

Niittymäki liked beauty and virtue. He liked them so much that he was ready to do almost anything for them. And that scared him.

Niittymäki wanted to know a few more things. The woman stared ahead. Niittymäki repeated his questions.

Kerttu Rinkinen thought of the president's shield bonus. We all have to accept what life gives us, and we don't get paid anything extra. We each have to clean up the shit that rains into the fan. Kerttu remembered saying to the president of the company, to the boy from her village, that he should be careful with his stories. Don't go talking too loud about that shield bonus of yours. He thought that Kerttu's ears were matchless, beyond compare. I never speak to anyone else the way I do to you. Kerttu had been a little taken aback, because that had sounded like a line from a movie. They speak differently in movies than people do in real life.

Then the president had lowered his voice and said that if he got fired, it wasn't a normal firing. They would shake my hand at the door and in the hand of the person who did it would be gold nuggets. That's why they call it the golden handshake. The gold nuggets are a fairy tale. The truth is in the paper I signed on the day I walked into the building for the first time. On that piece of paper it says that if they give me the boot, I get one-and-a-half year's salary in compensation. Do you know what that means in euros, Kerttu? It means three hundred and eighty thousand euros. Shield bonus and golden handshake. You I can tell about this.

Niittymäki clicked his pen, waiting. He recognized a typical eyewitness. The accident they see gets into their brain and shakes it all up. It's hard to form sensible sentences that an outsider can use to piece together the chain of events. Niittymäki remembered again the accident that led to Princess Diana's death, an overall picture of which was impossible to stitch together from the eyewitness accounts, because the people being interviewed were so upset and emotional that they couldn't tell rainwater from tears. Kerttu Rinkinen, who was the first eyewitness being interviewed, did not belong to the victim's circle of acquaintances, but for some reason she was still acting illogically, slightly irrationally. The accident had obviously opened up something inside her, and whatever had been behind those locked doors was now being disgorged onto the back seat of this police car.

"The girl flew . . . and to be totally honest, I can't say anything more about it right now . . . I mean, I can, but I don't know how . . . and that man stayed in his car like I said and locked the doors. As if he was in a different world in there than the rest of us are out here. And I guess he is. There are any number of different worlds here. I'm sure you know what I mean, Komisario. I see at least six worlds every day at work on that one floor. The president of the company's, his secretary's, the three heads of department's and my own. I clean there, you see. On the top floor they have a sauna suite, which I clean up after parties. I know how to read dirt and trash. They tell me what kind of parties they have. What was I going to say . . . oh yes. There are plenty of different worlds. The girl . . . since I don't have my own . . . it felt like my own daughter had been sent flying . . ."

Kerttu stopped when she realized that nothing was coming out of her mouth.

That her head was empty.

And in a strange way she felt like something inside her had been permanently lost along with the girl flying in the air.

Even though it wasn't true.

I stayed here in this world and will soon get out of this car without being accused of anything. I will walk to the big building and start cleaning the executive floor and will hear what the president of the company has on his mind this time. I would like, but I don't have the courage, to ask the president of the company if he could pay me extra for listening to him, for unburdening him by taking his burdens upon myself. Could I have a burden bonus? Could he pay me a lump sum of one tenth of the golden handshake he would be receiving on the day they kicked him out on his arse, for example? One-tenth of that sum is thirty-eight thousand euros. That isn't so much. The president of the company made about that much in stock trades after the merger. He didn't tell me that – he told the phone. But I happened to be there at the moment cleaning the windowsill. He spoke quietly, in a low voice. He was making an insider trade. I'm not stupid – I'm Kerttu. With that sure knowledge I could walk into his office and say, "I will gladly carry this burden, but I would be happy to accept any help you were to offer."

"O.K., Ms Rinkinen. Thank you. We will most likely be contacting you later and when things progress to a certain point, you will receive a summons to appear as a witness at the legal proceedings," Niittymäki said and nodded to his colleague. He opened the door for Kerttu.

Kerttu got out of the car and for a moment did not know what world she was in.

Niittymäki looked at Rinkinen as she wandered around the car in a daze and prepared to interview the driver.

Niittymäki had to take two minutes of personal time.

He thought of beauty and virtue, because he was surrounded by ugliness and evil. When it rained, he thought of the sun. When a little girl flew in the air, he thought of a swing. But when Niittymäki thought about the man sitting in the back seat of the police car, he thought about the man sitting in the back seat of the police car. He couldn't make it change into anything besides what it was. There was no place for this man in the world of beauty and virtue.

Niittymäki grew furious.

Suddenly he hated this man, and hate did not become Niittymäki. He shunned hate, and hate shunned him.

His colleague noticed and asked Niittymäki why he had bitten his fountain pen so hard that fragments were splintering onto the seat and blue ink was dotting the light-coloured upholstery.

Niittymäki jumped. He got out of the car and walked over to the other vehicle.

The man looked shy and startled. He wanted to look that way.

He was playing at humility.

He was mimicking a person in grief.

Niittymäki took two steps back, thinking.

Be a policeman.

You are on duty.

You are on the side of beauty and virtue.

Niittymäki opened the door, sitting down on the front seat and turning back towards the man.

"According to an eyewitness, you were speeding, but you denied this just a moment ago in the car. Is that true?"

"I don't believe I was speeding as much as was claimed."

"But you were speeding?"

"Perhaps a little. Everything is in the eye of the beholder. I would say I was speeding just a touch. When you measure speeding, you use a ten per cent margin of error. I suppose I fit within that margin."

"And you drove through a red light?"

"Yellow. Or actually, it was a late green."

"Right now only the leaves are green. You drove through a pedestrian crossing even though the pedestrians had a green light. This is a fact. We have three eyewitnesses lined up. One has already been interviewed."

"My understanding of things differs from yours. It was a sudden situation, for all of us. Truth is a relative concept – everyone has their own views. It would be best to find the average of the truths . . ."

"Do you have children?"

"No."

"I don't either."

"But how does that relate to this?"

"It does relate. Fundamentally. Do you have an imagination?"

"I don't follow you."

"Imagination is the passport into the world of humanity. And it's good that we have it. It allows us to be human. We can imagine. We can imagine how others feel. We estimate that you were driving thirty kilometres over the speed limit. In a forty zone."

"As far as I can tell, my speed was nowhere near that. As I said, everything happened so fast."

"According to the eyewitnesses, the speed of your black Audi A3 was . . ."

"It's an Audi S3."

"Excuse me?"

"The model is S3. It's a completely different car from the A3."

"The body style is the same."

"Yes, but it is different in every other way from the stock model."

"Would you perhaps like this clarification to be entered into the official interview record?"

"Gladly."

Niittymäki opened the window to get some oxygen. There was too little of it. He opened the door and got out of the car for a moment. His colleague in the front seat looked at Niittymäki, who indicated by his expression that he would be O.K.

Niittymäki got back into the car and turned towards the man.

"There are three eyewitnesses. I have heard from one of them. The role of an eyewitness is a difficult one. To see with their own eyes. You have eyes as well. It's nice to have eyes and ears. They are for paintings and for music. They were not created for seeing and hearing things like this. Do you understand?"

"I don't quiet grasp what you're getting at."

"You are mocking my ears by talking shit into them. Excuse me. My language is inappropriate. Don't write this down, Mirja."

His colleague in the front seat sighed.

"You killed a child. You didn't murder, but you did kill. The official name will be something like reckless endangerment, vehicular manslaughter or some other vague mishmash. Excuse me. The fact is that you murdered a child by driving too fast through a red light. Tell me this is how things are."

"I didn't have any intention . . . you can't use terms like that. They do not in any way even begin to give a correct picture of this ambiguous situation. And, as I said, I had no intention . . ."

"Is there any way you can stop producing that filth with your mouth? In a healthy person material like that only comes out the other end. No-one ever has any intention of behaving badly in this world! I have a mind to do some tidying up because I serve beauty. To get rid of all the trash and ugly things. I feel like cleaning you out of this world. You can continue this, Mirja. I'm going to get out of this car now and request a leave of absence."

Niittymäki threw his notes into the footwell and got out of the car. The spring wind whipped against his face. He bent his head back and looked up. The white, fluffy trail of a fighter jet floated in the sky. That was how he wanted to see filth. As something beautiful.

THE DRIVER

Biko Malmikunnas stopped his blue bus in front of the Ateneum Art Museum and opened the door with a hissing sound. Expressionless people pushed their way in through the doorway. No-one said a word, not even the ones who paid with cash. They threw their coins or notes onto the tray and waited for Biko to give them their tickets and change as quickly as possible. Six months ago, Biko would have said hello to every passenger, but he had given up the practice after realizing that hardly anyone said anything back.

Biko turned on the blinker and guided the heavy, rocking bus on to Kaisaniemenkatu. When the tarmac changed to cobblestones for a moment, the bus bumped and rattled.

There were a lot of people at the Kruununhaka stop. Biko noticed the rising hands in the nick of time and braked. The mass of humanity rocked against each other. A group of young people with buds in their ears entered through the front door. A young woman attempted to enter through the middle doors with a baby carriage. When the woman had gotten the buggy in with great effort and fastened it to the railing, she began looking for a place to sit. The group of youths had occupied the seats next to the buggy. The woman pointed this out, but the group ignored her.

Biko saw the situation in the mirror and said into the microphone, "Can give woman place?"

"What the fuck did that cocoa cock say?"

The boy in the group of youths with the biggest beanie took air supremacy and began to abuse Biko with many and varied turns of phrase, of which Biko understood fewer than half. He understood the tone, but ignored it, speaking into the microphone again in hopes of getting at least one of the passengers on his side.

"Eyes on the road, tar baby! I wanna get home sometime this fuckin' century!"

Biko had no desire to employ all that skill and knowledge which had allowed him to be alive and sitting behind the wheel of this blue bus as the evening turned blue-grey on this smooth road in this northern land. Biko would have just liked to drive people to their homes and to their offices at a steady speed, in a good mood, rejoicing with all of his heart for the one and only life he had.

None of the passengers paid any attention to the incident. Biko tried once more over the microphone, because he knew what it was like to stand up in a bus rocking back and forth after a hard day of work and a trip to the daycare.

"Could give the seat if think a little?"

"Could go jack off in own country and come back when can speak language!"

This response from the boy with the big beanie evoked great rejoicing among his followers. The other passengers drowsed uncomfortably in their seats.

Biko set off driving, thinking of the beautiful things his new homeland had brought him. Maija. The rutabaga. Warm apartments. Fried vendace. Small lakes. The zander in all its many forms. Fried perch. Pete, the owner of the bowling alley. Roads. A job as a bus driver. The Hakaniemi market hall. The February sun when there was snow.

Biko glanced in the mirror at the boy with the big beanie, who was whispering something to his companions and pointing in the direction of the driver. Biko knew what they were planning. The group was touching in its grandiosity. They thought violence was a game and that you could blow the whistle to start the match for any reason whatsoever. This time a black driver was enough of a reason.

Biko had experienced so much violence in his life that he knew it was a fire best left unkindled. It was easy to burn your own hair and clothes, even if the purpose of the joke had been to set alight the neighbour's barn.

Biko knew the plot of the game and was only worried for the boy with the big beanie and his tribe. A poorly chosen leader spoiled the whole barrel. Biko knew this from his childhood, from his own village. The most enthusiastic and quick-fisted were always put on the back row. At the front stood a calm, aged soldier, to whom the village had assigned their collective brain-usage rights. This saved unnecessary bodily harm.

Biko tried to drive the full bus calmly, avoiding any violent side-ways movements. The people had done a hard day's work and had earned a comfortable and safe trip home.

They approached the final stop. Only the gang was left on the bus. The stop was in a dark place at the corner of a housing development. Biko swept up to the stop and looked in the mirror. The tribe of the boy with the big beanie strode towards Biko following their leader.

Biko opened the driver's door, turned his chair towards the approaching group and said, "I say once. You start. I only finish." The boy with the big beanie stopped. He let out a forced laugh and took a stance he had learned from the movies. Biko recognized the stance as Eastern, but it lacked the linearity of an experienced fighter. The boy with the big beanie had only copied the hand positions from the bad action movies.

Biko struck like a snake. His fingers hit the throat. The beanie flew. The tribe shrank back. The boy jackknifed with a wheeze and fell to the walkway. Biko knelt next to him and hit him on the back with his palm in such a way that his breath began to flow again. Biko raised him up and sat him down on a bench.

"All good. Tribe take you home. Have good weekend."

The boy stammered. His kinsmen came and led him away. Biko closed the doors and sat in the driver's seat. His hands were shaking. He closed his eyes and prayed forgiveness from his great teacher who lived 6,893 kilometres away in Biko's home village but saw into the heart of each of his students.

That which you taught runs onto the sand. The sun that you showed me is covered by cloud. The life that you gave me now resembles death. Forgive me. This was my first time.

Biko opened his eyes, started the bus and continued his route.

He could not get the boy with the big beanie out of his head. After the blow he had become himself, a sixteen-year-old who lived with his parents in a small row house. The boy with the big beanie would remember the blow and would tell his own story about it, and that story would defeat Biko's story. This was how all black-and-white stories began, Biko thought, accelerating the blue bus up a gentle hill.

His shift ended on the fly in front of the Ateneum.

Biko walked to the R-Kiosk cafe. On the small television on the wall, horses were warming up and preparing for the starting gun. Black and white men talked in loud voices about bets, different races and sure things. Biko recognized Estonian, Russian, Somali and Finnish men in the group. Biko purchased a small coffee and sat on a tall stool bolted to the floor. The horses' muzzles steamed. The drivers sat in their carts and prepared to hit the horses. Biko hated trotting, but didn't say so out loud.

He had learned to keep his opinions inside. His head was full to overflowing with them. Biko knew that if he kept storing things up in his head endlessly, before long the same thing would happen to him that happened to many Finns – everything would come out at once. Biko also knew that his reserve was a result of the language.

Even in his beginning Finnish course, Biko had sensed that he would never learn the language well enough to be able to express himself perfectly. Language is a cane that keeps the cripple upright. A cripple standing in the entrance to a shopping centre unable to get in to admire the immense selection of merchandise.

Biko would have liked to share his thoughts using long subordinate clauses. He would have liked to master all of the subtleties, the nuances in tone and the detailed adjectives. He was infinitely irritated that there was only one person in the country who knew exactly what he felt. Maija. All other people were a long language away, somewhere far off on the horizon.

The men shouted. The horses ran. The drivers sitting on their delicate carts hit the horses, who ran around the track, manes streaming and muzzles steaming. Suddenly one of the horses broke into a gallop, and the men in the kiosk swore and shook their heads. Biko saw in slow motion how the horse that had bounced into a gallop raised his muzzle, shaking his head and attempting to say, "Enough is enough. I want freedom. I want nuance. I want variety in my life." Biko was that horse. He trotted around a track, carrying mute Finns to their jobs and to their homes. He languished in a prison of three-word phrases – his tongue was his bridle. And the last person to pull on his bridle had been the boy with the big beanie.

Biko was sure that with perfect language proficiency he would have been able to get out of the situation and not have had to strike the boy in the throat. He would have been able to say to the boy, "You think that I am a threat to your employment and romantic prospects, but I can assure you that I am not, because presumably you will not be entering the bus driving profession and because I have Maija. I won't be laying a finger on your women. I am just a little black nuisance for you in this world. The really colourful troubles are to be found somewhere else entirely. You are touching and cute. I was just like you at your age. I ran in a gang and looked for something to bully. Anything small and the wrong colour. And if we really combed the savannah, we could find something too. And if it is any comfort to you, I can tell you that I am a racist as well. I think of you Finns as simple people. You kowtow to people's faces and whimper behind their backs. You take revenge on your neurotic bosses with your wives, husbands and children. By the time you throw your hat in the ring, the bout is already over. You fight your civil wars in your families, not in the workplace where the grousing and self-defensiveness might actually bring some benefit. You never work up any real rebellion. I won a book about your history in a raffle, and I have been reading it on my breaks. You had one real civil war, but it seems you were just following the example of a larger country. Poor little things.

"And you take every single word so seriously. Perhaps it is because you have so few words that every one of them means so much. To you.

"Yes. I consider you an inferior race. But I must pay tribute to the fact that you have managed to stay alive alone here in this appalling cold. And you have never been able to force your way in anywhere, since the Bear has always been lurking on your borders. I don't even count Sweden as a country – it is merely a recreation area. Did you know, by the way, that I can read you like an open book? You think that you conceal so much with your silence, but oh how much you end up revealing. On the night bus I can say after a single glance how a passenger's evening has gone. You don't jump up and down, but I can sense your joy, which always has a touch of self-satisfaction. Your luck is always stolen from a neighbour. Is it that you have not had neighbours for very long, that you have always lived kilometres away from each other? Otherwise I cannot understand why your neighbours are the be-all and end-all for you. If things are going poorly for you, and you hear that things are going even worse for your neighbour, you start to feel better. This is both adorable and incomprehensible. What was it we were supposed to be talking about, boy with the big beanie? Oh yes, about whether you could please be so good as to give the young, tired mother a seat. No. Because a black driver is asking. No. Because a white driver is asking. No. Because someone is asking. No. You won't. Did you see what I did there? The parallelism. Not bad for a negro, eh? Yeah. You make life so hard. Because you don't get it. Life. That it is a sun. You can't just stand in front of it."

A horse named Jonkka's Eikka won the race. One of the men, a Russian judging by the lumpy nose, shouted and raised his ticket in the air. Biko finished his coffee and left.

At home Maija asked how his day had gone. Biko said that the day had slipped from his hand and turned into night. Maija made Biko a large sandwich and stroked his head. Biko took Maija in his lap and softly crooned a song in his own language in her ear. It told of a shepherd who had lost his tribe and was wandering in a strange land.

Maija told Biko about a letter that had come which was waiting on the nightstand. After Maija had fallen asleep, Biko read the letter. From it rose a sun which Biko could not tell Maija about.

The next morning Biko called his boss, told the story of the boy with the big beanie and suggested that he be fired. The boss said that he already knew about it and reported a witness statement according to which the gang of youths had started the row.

Biko tried to explain to his boss that finding the guilty party did not help him because he had transgressed against life and tampered with the sun. He could no longer continue in the position of trust that had been given him. He could no longer transport people from their jobs to their homes and from their homes to their jobs.

The boss said that it would pass.

"What?" Biko asked.

"It. The bad feeling. Take a few days off."

"You don't understand," Biko said. That was all he could get out, even though he would have liked to say more. He would have liked to explain to his boss about the birth of the sun, its rising and setting, and what the great teacher had taught. Only strike the throat in the greatest distress. If you strike sooner, you lose purpose and meaning. You cause the sun to set. The duty of man is to hold power within himself and keep the sun in the sky.

"You are a good driver. The kid in the hat touched the wrong guy."

His boss didn't understand. Or he did. But wrong. Biko squeezed the phone. His boss didn't get it. Purpose. Meaning. And honour. I want to keep face, even if I lose everything else. I come from a land of light. I could tell about my father-in-law. He hated me immediately, passionately, but I did not make the mistake of taking his anger away from him. I gave it time to melt. And it did. The sun melts ice. I had to wait in the shadows and let the sun do its work. I cannot take that work up myself. Now my father-in-law likes me. Or at least he tolerates me. You do not know what kind of letter he sent me. Sent from his heart. He would never have sent it if on that first night I had responded to his anger like I responded to the anger of the boy in the hat. My father-in-law gave me a task. A difficult task. Thankfully I do not have to do it alone. But it is an honour, a position of trust for which I must prepare like the eagle prepares high in the heavens. Below on the earth no-one knows yet.

"Are you still there? So you'll take some time off and then come Tuesday evening?"

Life has to have purpose and meaning. Honour comes with them, but not before them. Your land gave me purpose and meaning, but I shoved them into the throat of the boy with the big beanie. But I still have a chance to get them back. I will make it all up to the sun.

"Malmikunnas, is that clear? Can you hear me? Don't make any rash decisions. Guess how many drivers have felt like doing the same thing. Are you there? I'm hanging up now. I'll see you on Thursday."

Biko heard a click. For a moment he thought it had come from his own head. Maija came into the room and asked who Biko had been silent on the phone with for so long. Biko told her.

Maija slapped him instantly.

And cried.

And then she stroked him and wailed about what was going to happen to them now.

Biko said that everything would be fine.

How can you say that?

Because we O.K. because love.

Yeah, but if we don't have any food, idiot.

I drive taxi. Vroom vroom. Fancy cars. Mercedes.

How can you say that? Who's going to hire you just like that? And what was the letter?

Some go around thing.

A chain letter?

Yeah, that.

What did it ask you to do?

If put ten euros in now, get hundred in six month.

You aren't fool enough to go along with that, are you?

No. No worry. Come lap.

I can't. I'm too angry.

Maija. I calm angry.

What's going to happen to us, dammit?

I cut forest out of way of sun.

THE QUEUER

Maija Malmikunnas saw it in the distance. It was like a technicolour snake that wound slowly around the block. Muted conversation and coughing came from the bread queue. Maija thought, if I take a place at the end of the queue, I will be declaring myself a member of the tribe. Someone I know will walk by and connect the dots. That person will tell another, word will get around, rumours will start and the truth will fall over the family like a dirty, rented tarpaulin that will cover us completely, and we will never seen the sun again.

Maija had turned down any and all assistance offered by society. Her pride was no traditional immodesty or disdain – it was a question of honour. She did not see herself as one of the fallen. Maija tried to think whether her attitudes had been influenced by her father and mother's opinions or whether she had come up with her position on her own. She was forced to admit that the influence of her home was visible in her thoughts, but not so much as in Pekka, who would under no circumstances ever admit his defeats. Pekka said that he believed in the free market, but that the free market didn't believe in him.

Maija was now forced to compromise her sense of honour because Biko had resigned from his job. It had been difficult for Maija to accept, especially since the boss had called on two separate occasions asking Biko to return to work. As his reason for resigning, Biko had said that his sun had set. Maija had asked Biko not to phrase it that way to the employment office personnel. You're going to be disqualified from receiving benefits for a while anyway. Biko had claimed he could get work in a taxi anytime because now that G.P.S.s were common, the drivers didn't have to know addresses anymore.

Maija pulled the hood of her coat over her head and took her place at the end of the queue. She tried to be air. Like she was. The woman standing in front of her turned to Maija and stared her straight in the eyes.

"Are you afraid of something? Are you hiding or something?"

"No."

"Then stand up straight and take what they give you. I heard a load of meat came from Kesko today. With stickers. But it won't go bad for a few days. Buck up."

"But I'm not supposed to be here. In this queue, I mean."

"None of us are supposed to be here. Don't even start, because I know the rest already. Let me guess. You fell from pretty high up, higher than Batman ever did. You weren't supposed to fall, because your genes, your degrees, your background and your work experience point in an entirely different direction, right? You were God's chosen, not one of us chained to this rock of a slum. But then the fairy tale took a turn. The Big Bad Wolf came along the forest path, took you by the neck and threw you back to the end of the queue. And now you want to hide what happened to you. You want to pull your hood over your head. You listen to me – hold your chin up and uncover your head. There's a load of meat from Kesko today."

"Is that so?"

"Just so. There are bad days and there are good days. And this is a good day. A meat day!"

The woman clapped Maija on the shoulder and turned away. The back of the woman's light green jacket said "Turkey Welcomes You".

Maija considered the woman's words and the situation. What did I want when I came to the city? How has everything turned out the way it has? Is there a storyline in all of this, some unavoidable chain of events that is meant to end at the back of this queue?

I wanted to succeed moderately well and honourably. I wanted things that everyone should have, even though in wanting them I knew I was privileged. Privileged. That word is ugly and has brought me much sorrow. Privilege, *etuoikeus*. *Etu* and *oikeus*, advantage and right. An acquired advantage. I've never had any advantage because my parents never acquired anything they could have passed on to me. The only golden spoon I have I won in a five-kilometre ski race.

And then rights. Whose? The rights of the strong or of the weak? Neither, because I've never felt strong or weak. The rights of the one in the middle, the rights I've earned by my labour. By my boring labour. My dull drudgery.

"Move forward. Or do you want someone to cut in there?"

"Sorry."

Maija stepped forward, trying to understand what was happening. She glanced nervously at the roofs of the buildings. She didn't see any cameras. But they could be small, too small for the human eye to detect. The previous day Maija had called the welfare office, the church and the organization that ran the queue to make sure it was neither photographed nor recorded, and that no record of her visit would be kept in any kind of registry. Everyone had assured her that nothing was photographed or recorded in any way.

But you never could be sure. It would be a miracle if no trace of this was left in any official file, Maija thought. She was startled when the queue suddenly moved forward by at least ten metres.

"They opened the doors."

The woman smiled broadly, and Maija noticed her tooth jewel. The woman realized that Maija had noticed it.

"You saw it. Isn't it pretty? It's a reminder of my previous life. The one that ended the year before last, that is. That was my fourth life. Which one is this for you? This is how I count them: my first life was the one I lived in the country, the second was when I came to the city, the third was when I got married and the fourth was when I got rich. The jewel is from that last one. I lived in Lauttasaari, and I was with a company that designed content for mobile phones. Games, I mean. I had some sense that it couldn't go on forever. But I was getting four grand a month and drinking bubbly whenever I was thirsty. Now this here is my fifth life. But the fourth one left a mark on my teeth. I think it's nice to have at least something left over. A lot of people in this queue don't have teeth at all. Sorry I'm talking so much. It's a bad habit I picked up from my job. I had to talk to the bosses over at Nokia nonstop every day about the virtual widgets we were designing. Hey, but now we're moving."

The woman turned and walked forward briskly.

Maija followed her.

The queue sucked and drew them along.

Maija felt like someone was pulling it. Just like all of society and the whole world. Someone was pulling, but no-one knew who. Someone was pulling the strings and the queue. Maija realized what she was thinking was childish and chalked it up to exhaustion.

Her mobile phone vibrated in her pocket like a small animal. It showed Salme's number.

"It's your mom. Where's my girl?"

"I'm in Stockmann. In the women's department. How come?"

"What's all the noise there? It sounds like you're outside."

"I'm never outside . . . I mean . . . I'm sorry . . . what were you calling about?"

"More than can fit in such a small telephone. I thought to call to ask if you knew anything about Pekka. I can't get hold of him."

"I don't really know. I imagine he's at his office."

"I've been getting the idea that he doesn't have an office at all anymore."

"Well. He must be working for someone new then."

"Where?"

"Listen, I don't really know."

"It's strange how none of my kids seems to know anything. Even though they're all educated. They don't even know about their siblings' lives."

"It's kind of a bad time right now."

"It's always a bad time when I call. I so want for you to have a good time for once."

"I just don't have the energy right now, Mum. I have to go and get the meat . . ."

"In the clothing department?"

"For a meeting . . . a new blouse for a meeting, I mean."

"What's that in your voice?"

"What?"

"The tension. We should really sit down and talk. I have the money now. That we talked about, about how to help Helena."

"Well ah ya gonna take the fawkin' round roast or not? I'm not gonna fawkin' wait here all day!"

The man standing behind Maija pushed his hand past her.

"Who's swearing there? Who's saying that? Hello . . . Maija?"

"This is a little bit of a bad time. I'll call tonight."

"No, you won't. You know you won't. Where are you? You can tell your mother. They've never sold round roast with fucks in the Stockmann women's clothing department. Don't deceive your old mother. You're even making me be coarse now."

Maija cut Salme off with a press of the red button and grabbed the roast. The box also included sliced turkey, ham rolls, sausages and light salami. All of the packages had a red sticker, almost the same colour as on the Japanese flag.

Maija scooped as much into her bag as the person divvying out would let her, pulled her hood over her head and walked out.

There was the rest of the world and all of the people who never have to queue and who get to walk by calmly and look askance at the queue like some strange natural phenomenon that marks our neighbourhood in its own piquant way.

Maija felt like every passer-by could see into her bag and through her bag into her soul.

They know what happened to me.

They think that it is my own fault.

They know that my bag is full of meat that expires today.

They think that I am a regular customer.

They know that I have a stupid, black husband.

They think that things are going to hell for us.

They are wrong.

After getting home, Maija took out her copy of *Cooking for Every Home* and opened it to the page for roast beef. Onto the table from between the pages fell a card sent by Salme around the time it happened. Salme hadn't had the energy to write more than one sentence.

It doesn't matter what the birds are singing.

THE CARRIERS

Helena Malmikunnas stood next to the window and was alive.

I am standing next to the window, she said to herself.

I am standing. I have feet. Two of them.

Outside there are blue buses and trees.

Trees, like bones. The bones don't have any leaves. The bones are cracked.

Someone broke the bones.

And stood them up in the yard.

The smell of coffee came from behind her.

Maija had made coffee.

Maija is my sister.

Maija is alive. I can tell from the smell of the coffee.

I can tell there is life from the smell of the coffee.

Pekka is here too.

Pekka came out of the kitchen with Biko. Biko was carrying a serving tray.

He was carrying it carefully, as if he were carrying something precious.

It had Karelian pasties on it.

Helena remembered what Alfred Supinen had said about Karelian pasties.

The pasty came to the Finnish interior with the people fleeing the yard.

By "the people fleeing the yard", Supinen meant the evacuees.

Homes, land and trees had been taken away from the evacuees.

Poor evacuees, Helena thought.

Someone put a pasty in front of Helena. It was Maija.

Helena didn't dare look Maija in the eyes.

Her little sister's eyes scared her.

If she looked into them, everything in them was transferred into her.

Helena hadn't looked in the mirror the whole day.

If you look in the mirror, you see yourself.

It isn't a good idea to look at yourself.

It isn't a good idea to look at what you already know.

The pasty tastes salty, and everyone is here and alive.

Except Salme and Paavo.

They have to be out there in the country.

Someone has to be there too, Helena thought. Otherwise the land wastes away, rotting and disappearing with the wind.

The land wants people and trees on it.

Pekka, Biko and Maija sat on the sofa and tried to be.

They almost couldn't.

Pekka looked at Biko. Biko looked back. Something happened to them.

They had the same thought. Thought is action. At least half way.

Maija poured the coffee.

Pekka looked at it. It was so black that it wasn't any colour anymore.

Sombre isn't a colour.

Before the others came, Helena had collected all of Sini's pictures and put them away.

In hiding.

Somewhere. I don't remember where. Fortunately I don't remember. Maybe I won't ever find them. Good if I don't find them. Bad if I don't find them.

I can't decide, Helena thought. I don't know how to decide. I don't know how to move. I don't know how to live. I don't know how to die. I don't know how to anything. I will never be what I was again. I will never be anything.

Perhaps an image of a person, but not a real person.

Maija put her hand on Helena's shoulder.

No-one can put anything on me anymore, Helena thought, even though she knew it was Maija's hand.

Pekka paced back and forth in the apartment, wanting to be different.

Wanting to be violent.

It was not of this world. Being violent does not fit in this world, even though this world is violent.

It is too big a thing for this world, for this room, for this moment.

Pekka asked Biko out onto the balcony.

There in the wind and the noise Pekka talked to Biko. You name it, he said it.

Maija took her hand from Helena's shoulder, and Helena felt like nothing would ever hold her down again.

She realized Maija's hand had been holding her on the ground.

She grabbed the hand and placed it back on her shoulder.

Maija looked at her husband and her brother.

Maija remembered what Sini had said after the first time she had seen Biko. "Don't worry. We can wash him."

Maija remembered what Sini had said after seeing Pekka with his pan flute. "Play something Russish."

Maija remembered other things as well, but she didn't want to remember.

Maija didn't want to laugh, even though laughter lived inside her and wanted to come out almost every day.

Helena moved beneath Maija's hand and took a pasty from the plate.

The crust crunched, and butter ran onto her fingers.

She felt like rubbing the melted butter into her face, creating a new face.

She didn't have the energy to keep her old face.

Why do they talk about keeping face?

What good is there in keeping something ugly, to keep it for others' sake?

Helena wanted to talk about normal things.

But she didn't know where to start.

Some normal thing – right now – Helena thought.

Everything normal had left her head and been replaced by everything abnormal.

The balcony door squeaked. Pekka and Biko came inside.

Say something normal, Helena wished, but didn't ask.

Helena thought, if we were in the country, I would ask you to chop down some trees or drive the tractor too fast across the fields or kill some animals and roast them in the yard in sight of the women and get raging drunk and sing country songs off key, or I would ask you to do something else loud, common and coarse, because coarse and common keeps us on the ground, but when we're here in this city apartment, I can't do anything but be alive and breathe and put something in my mouth to keep me alive until tomorrow, until the day after tomorrow, and until the day I'm supposed to lower my only child into the ground.

Maija caught Helena as she collapsed, limp.

Helena spilled out of Maija's arms. Pekka and Biko came to her aid.

Together they carried Helena to the bed.

Biko fetched a towel, moistened it a little and put it on Helena's forehead.

Pekka tested her pulse – her wrist throbbed in short thumps like a baby's.

They gave Helena one pill, after which she slept.

They couldn't leave the apartment.

Maija fetched two mattresses from the attic. She took the sofa and curled up in foetal position.

Pekka and Biko promised to watch over Helena and Maija's sleep.

Helena woke up in the middle of the night to the fact that she didn't have anything.

You can't explain it to the men who jump up, ready to do anything for you. You can't say, "Help, I don't have anything." You can say, "Help, my leg is hurt," or, "I can't reach the pot on the top shelf." You can say, "Will you make me food?" but you can't badger people asking for things that are impossible. It has to be enough to know that they want to help. Their desire to carry me, not today, but perhaps a week from now.

Wanting is already an action.

Helena indicated to the men that they could sit down.

She went out onto the balcony.

The night whispered and hummed.

The balcony railing was damp and cold.

She took hold of it with both hands.

And squeezed.

The world depended on that railing. If she let go, the world would disappear.

She sensed that Pekka, Biko and Maija had come to stand behind her.

She knew that they would always stand behind her.

They would say that the railing was only a railing, that the world didn't depend on it.

The world depended on whether there was anyone standing behind in case you fell.

Or decided to fall.

A new night came. There can be many nights in one, Helena thought as they led her to the bed.

I have to stay in this bed now. I have to give them time to breathe.

Time to talk about the things of the world, things that belong to them and keep them there.

I can't wear them out. I can't drag them here with me to this place where nothing has any form or purpose.

This is what people call sorrow.

No-one has been able to give it any other name.

Sorrow is a beautiful name.

Ugly things are given beautiful names to cover up the ugliness.

So the bones and the flesh and the gashes don't show.

I have to let them talk out there in the living room about everyday things, to gather their strength.

I have to sleep now, Helena thought.

That's what the one being carried has to do for the people doing the carrying.

I can't do much.

I can do that.

THE IMMIGRANTS

You can't track time. It goes on its merry way. Time not only passes you by – for good measure it backs up, runs you over and then continues forward indifferently. Anyone who says he can keep up is already adrift like a piece of trash.

So thought Kimmo Hienlahti the day after he was released. He had sat in prison for nine months pressing German licence plates with a machine and painting road signs. He had liked the simple work and the unstimulating surroundings. He could see a bay and the sea from the window of his cell. He had stared out for the first two weeks and seen birds he had never paid any attention to before. He had borrowed a bird book from the prison library and learned to identify dozens of species within a couple of months.

While he was painting road signs, he had thought that it would be nice sometime to drive along the Turku motorway and turn off at the Piikkiö junction to find that he had painted Piikkiö with his own hands, doing his part so that people could find their way to that charming town.

Now he sat at his computer with his eyes open like a newborn. Finland had changed while he had been away. The same birds circled over a different land now. Most of his business partners had disappeared without a trace. Companies had been laid low in the dust. Whole industries had disappeared in the roaring of the wind – only the wings of aircraft still reached for the sky. A heavy silence hung over the land as before a thunderstorm when he was a child.

Everything that had been obvious a year ago was now embarrassing, shameful. Kimmo felt like a citizen of another country, a strange interloper who had returned to his birthplace but no longer knew anyone.

Kimmo turned off the computer, picked up a pair of binoculars and walked to the window. A few birds flew back and forth over the reeds. It was hard to grasp the freedom of birds. Does the eagle understand its freedom? Not likely. Perhaps it sees its life as limited, limited by danger and hunger. Kimmo felt that being deprived of his freedom had been the best thing to happen to him in a long time. Lying on the uncomfortable bed in his cell he had realized that there had been too much freedom, that it had got out of hand. What did you do with everything if you didn't get pleasure from anything?

Kimmo moved the binoculars from the reeds to the other shore. Nine months ago that white, modern office building had housed the Innovation Centre. Now the wall said Invalid Foundation.

The phone rang.

The voice was muted and congested, so much so that Kimmo did not immediately recognize the caller as Nyström, who welcomed Kimmo back to freedom and asked in a timid voice if Kimmo had a moment. Kimmo said he didn't have anything else.

Nyström asked Kimmo to listen for a moment. Kimmo agreed because the haste and arrogance had disappeared from Nyström's voice.

Nyström's speech was slow and stripped-down. He used neither adjectives nor English-language jargon. He spoke in simple independent clauses without seasoning what he said with strident opinions or hyperbole. He reproached neither the labour movement, the inflexibility of bureaucracy, nor the taxman.

He said that the customers no longer wanted talk. At least not our talk. They don't want consultants. Or at least they don't want us. They don't want to advertise. Or they do, but not much. That restaurant where we used to go isn't there anymore. People aren't consuming anymore. Or they are, but not luxury goods. Everyone is talking about necessities now. No-one is talking about luxuries anymore. This is all strange to me, but if I think carefully, it is all logical and comprehensible. Still, it is difficult for me to accept it. Do you understand, Kimmo? Or I do accept it, but in the same way a ship accepts a storm. I don't have any hobbies anymore, because no-one else does. You can't play golf alone. Or you can, but it's boring. My wealth has melted away. Not all of it, but a lot. And it keeps melting away the whole time. I'm not calling because I need money. I'm calling because you're the only person I *can* call. Times are bad if you can only call the person you complain to.

Kimmo listened and listened.

Nyström's speech was good, because evil was speaking it. Evil breaking down makes an interesting sound.

Kimmo put the phone on speaker, picked up the binoculars and focused his eyes on a seagull circling over the reeds. The seagull circled. Nyström spoke. Kimmo watched and listened.

THE TAKERS

They walked to the door of the house and rang the doorbell. The person who opened the door had no time to react before one of them pushed his foot in the door and wrenched it wide open. They recognized the person from his photograph, but the person did not know them and was surprised when he saw them. In his life he had become used to surprising everyone and no-one surprising him. For this reason he was unable to be hospitable and in his confusion asked them to leave. However, they did not leave because they had been forced to leave so many places so many times in their lives. And besides, they had a task to complete.

There were two of them, one dark, one light.

They told the person what the purpose and meaning of their visit was. The person said that there must be some misunderstanding, but they clarified the matter by recounting in detail what the person had done. The punishment he had received from the judicial system was incommensurate with what he had done and so they were forced to come to complete the job that society and the authorities had left unfinished.

The person backed against a black chest of drawers and said he would pay them anything if only they would leave. They said that unfortunately money had lost all significance as a means of payment in this matter.

The dark one sat down on the divan and looked out the window.

The light one ordered the person to sit on the sofa because speeches were in order before the procedure. He said that he might stutter a little at the beginning of his speech. If the person laughed, the dark one would hit him immediately.

The person sat and said he was interested to hear what they had to say. He was lying. He was not interested in anything other than his life.

The light one began.

You kn-kn-know that the ki-ki-ng-dom of heaven belongs to chi-chi-children.

The dark one checked to make sure the person did not laugh. The light one continued.

You know that this is the case, but you still act as if you did not know. When you offer money, you offend even more. In court you played innocent. You imitated an innocent person. I know everything about imitation, and I can say that you imitated poorly. If you imitate well, others believe you. A good imitator becomes the person he is imitating. But you cannot imitate an innocent person, because you don't even believe it. You have to want to be what you imitate. Get me some water.

The dark one rose, went into the kitchen and came back with a water glass in his hand. The light one took a gulp from the glass and cleared his throat. He said that the dark one would take over from here and that the system would be the same: if the person laughed at the dark one's poor Finnish, the light one would hit him immediately.

The dark one began.

The one who went away, not my own. Is in my heart, because blood is in family. There are troubles, small sorrows and big sorrow. Trouble is when sleep too long for work or wallet missing. Then is small sorrow. If own dog and it die, comes small sorrow. What is biggest sorrow, big of all? Do you understand?

The person listened, but was unable to answer. His gaze was fixed on the fish scissors the light one had taken out of his pullover and was turning over in his hand. The person was reminded of gills, bones and fillets and the crackling sound that comes when scissors crunch through a fish's neck.

You no answer. No problem. We know biggest sorrow. It no see, no hear. It is. No matter what do, it is. How on earth make it away? No need answer. Soon you not able.

The person considered his alternatives, which he usually had at least ten of at any one time. Now they had shrunk to two, attack and escape. Both seemed hopeless. He had no weapon, and it was ten metres to the door.

The light one and the dark one sensed the person's thoughts and sat down on either side of him on the sofa. They were quiet. Together with the person they achieved a silence so profound it was almost audible. The light one looked over the person and the dark one nodded.

They ordered the person to stand.

The person felt faint.

He felt like the legs had disappeared from within his trousers and the air from within his lungs.

The person felt a strong urge to defecate and urinate.

The dark one realized this because he had experienced similar urges in a similar situation in his previous life. It was not diarrhoea – it was the language of the organism. The organism took the place of the brain, because in certain situations the brain stopped working. The organism spoke because the person had spoken all he had to say. The organism said: There isn't much material in me because I haven't had breakfast, but I want to eject everything from myself, even if it is just the sputum, the salts, the acids and all that mess that is left circulating in here even after everything has come out of both ends.

The person asked permission to visit the restroom.

The light one said he understood the need, but that it was not possible now, just like everything else. The person had played God, and in that moment lost the world of possibilities.

The person stood, swaying.

The light one asked the person to stand up straight, because the final speech was coming now, after which they would move from words to actions. He said that he had taken the exceptional step of writing this speech down. It was short and had been written by the next of kin.

The person rocked. The dark one took hold of him and lifted him up.

The light one cleared his throat, took the piece of paper out of his breast pocket and began.

"Life is taking and giving. You took my sister's reason to live. You gave a reason to kill. We will not kill. We will take your reason to live. A draw. You sat nine months. We waited nine months. Our gestation period was the same length. It is time to give birth. The prognosis is for a child who is a man of few words. But hopefully he will be otherwise active and optimistic."

The light one folded the paper and put it in his pocket, and then nodded to the dark one. The dark one grabbed the person and led him into the kitchen. In the middle of it was a round, wooden table. The kind they used to have in the back rooms of stores in the days when the store's own butcher carved up pig and cow carcasses fresh.

The person began to scream. He screamed so hard that he lost the very last shred of his humanity and became an animal. He began to bite and kick. The light one hit him once on the cheek and ordered the dark one to give him the thick, silver tape. The light one said that he would now be placing Jesus tape over the person's mouth, tape which had been developed for precisely these situations. The name came from the fact that Jesus succeeded at almost everything he ever tried until his Father intervened. You tried to play Jesus and his Father, God. As your reward and as a memento of a good effort, we will now put this tape over your mouth for a moment. When we get everything ready, we will remove the tape, but I can promise that afterwards the screaming will stop as if it had hit a brick wall.

The dark one held him. The light one bound him.

Then the dark one took two freezer containers and a bottle of spirits out of a bag. One of the containers was empty. The other had some sort of liquid in it. He poured the alcohol into the empty freezer container and sterilized the fish scissors in the container.

The light one held the trembling person in place.

The dark one took a pair of forceps and a drop cloth out of the bag and spread the cloth over the butcher block. He set the container on the edge of the butcher block and nodded to the light one, who kicked the person on the back of his knees, making him collapse into a kneeling position. The light one moved the person against the butcher block so that his whole head was on the block. Then he tore the tape off his mouth. First there was no sound, as if the person had lost his voice, but then one long, shrill sound came out of his mouth. It resembled the scream the light one had heard in his childhood coming from a broken fish trap. A curious seagull had got stuck in the trap and was screaming in such a thin, metallic voice that the distress had infected the light one, and he had run to his father.

The light one took the person by the neck and squeezed, extinguishing the sound.

The dark one nodded, giving the signal. The light one repositioned the person's head and ordered him to open his mouth. The person opened it enough that the light one managed to push his right hand in against the upper teeth. He rammed his left hand against the lower teeth and lifted the mouth open, and lightning-quick the dark one pushed a piece of wood about five centimetres long in as a brace to keep the mouth open. The light one held the person's head in place and warned him not to struggle, which would only result in unnecessary injury. He stressed that the operation would be over soon and that the person would then be able to continue his normal life.

The dark one put thin protective gloves on his hands, took the scissors, shoved his right hand into the mouth and drew the tongue out as far as he could. The person gagged. The dark one took the fish scissors and clipped off the part that the person had used up and no longer needed.

The light one released the thrashing person. The person fell onto the kitchen floor and lost consciousness. The dark one placed the removed part in the freezer container. It would be perfectly preserved in the special liquid for the necessary period of time. The light one cleaned up the mess and called the emergency number. He reported the address and the nature of the emergency. The dark one placed a towel under the unconscious person's head. Blood flowed out of his mouth onto it.

They left the house and walked to the car. The dark one placed the freezer container in a cooler. They looked at each other and knew that they had done both right and wrong. They also knew that the thing they had done would bind them to each other irreversibly. They drove the first kilometres in silence. As they traded residential areas for motorway, the dark one suggested some calming music. The light one flipped through radio stations until he found a classical one. The announcer said that Beethoven's "Piano Sonata Number Eight" is also called the "Sonata *Pathétique*", and that it was now being played for them by a Hungarian pianist, András Schiff, who now lived in England.

The dark one asked the light one what *pathétique* meant. The light one said that if there was a tremendous amount of emotion that included a touch of self-pity and that the whole thing was on the verge of overflowing its banks, then you could call the surge of emotion pathetic. The dark one said that in that case he had been in a pathetic state a couple of times, but that he had never felt self-pity. He said that pathetic situations came along quite often as a bus driver. The light one said that he might not have succeeded in explaining the term properly, because it was French.

They listened to the beautiful, plangent, fast piece of music. The light one felt that at the beginning of the piece something shocking happened that forced someone to run away, and that it was this racing the composer had clearly painted in the piece. Then the running stopped and the fugitive put up his feet under an oak tree and listened to the warbling of the birds. The light one thought it was amazing that someone could play his life that way.

The piece ended, and the car was silent.

Then the dark one said that he wanted to meet this Beethoven. The light one said that he had died a long time ago. The dark one said that he didn't think a person like that could die easily, and if he did die, the notes would force their way out of the grave and float up to the tops of the trees.

The light one said that the person there on the floor of the house was losing blood at a tremendous rate. The dark one ordered the light one not to worry about it – the ambulance would come quickly there in the city. The person would surely survive. The light one said that was precisely what he hoped.

He thought a person should live with his actions in this world. That was every person's duty and lot in life. Even if there weren't friends or family, there were always actions. They followed a person through life. They were faithful. The light one thought that this is sometimes forgotten in all of the rush and bustle of work. This person would come to see this if he survived. The light one hoped that the person would have his actions and their consequences with him every day for the rest of his life.

The dark one said that the light one's actions in the world of work had been somewhat lacking as of late. The light one looked at him sternly and said that he was still searching for his permanent place in the commercial world and reminded the dark one that none of it had been for lack of effort. The dark one asked why the light one had not stayed at the computer company. The light one said that he didn't have the patience to correct simple problems and answer simple authors' questions about whether backup copies should be stored on a memory stick or a separate hard drive. He said that there had been one author in particular who had irritated him by pressing him about the origins of his unique last name. The dark one thought the author had just been doing his job. If they weren't interested in details, they wouldn't be authors at all. He thought that the light one could become an author and in that way make use of all of his recent ex-periences. The light one thought it was not a good idea. He did not believe that the feeling you get when you turn into a Peruvian street musician could be captured on paper. The dark one thought that it would be worth trying, because the perspective of an immigrant is always valuable.

The dark one said that his future was in taxis. In a taxi you can serve people and drive them from place to place and lift their bags and open doors. He thought he had been born to be a servant. It is a natural trait. It doesn't have anything to do with servility, though. I want to serve, to create energy. A taxi driver's job is the best in the world. A small, enclosed space, a couple of people to serve at a time –

you can concentrate on them. You can demonstrate your skill. You get to act a little better than you are. And then as a last resort there were dustman jobs. Even if the end of the world comes, the dustmen will still have two more weeks of work afterwards. Someone has to clean everything up.

The light one said that he still hadn't found his place in the world. He said he had been driven by the wind and carried by cars. And there wasn't necessarily anything wrong with that. Strength of will is overrated. The light one said he was nevertheless hopeful for the future, because entrepreneurship is mostly a way of life. Bumps in the economy would always bring certain things to a head and make everything look hopeless from time to time, but as the son of a small businessman, he believed everything would make a turn for the better in the end.

The dark one agreed. Everything will work out if you can stay on the sun's side, even if everyone is singing about the moon and wanting to admire it, just the two of you. But without the sun there is nothing.

Then they were quiet again and listened to the hum of the road.

THE SHARER

Paavo Malmikunnas stood in the line at the post office looking at his parcel slip. His name and address were written in block letters, and the pen had been pressed against the slip so hard it had almost ripped through. Paavo snorted. The sender's emotional state had been strong and purposeful. Paavo gave the slip to the worker, who disappeared into the back room.

The worker came back and extended a cardboard box to Paavo. On the side of the box was written "Fragile – Handle with Care". Paavo transported the box home carefully, placed it on the floor of the closet and threw a coat over it. Then he walked to the sewing room and made sure it was empty. Salme had gone out walking with her girlfriend. Paavo got the box and carried it to the kitchen table.

The box was filled with paper. At first Paavo thought there wasn't anything else in it, but after moving the crumpled paper out of the way, he found a freezer container on the bottom of the box packed in with pieces of styrofoam. Paavo lifted the container carefully out of the box and set it down next to the sink.

There it floated lifeless in the freezer container's liquid. With it a person could express love, hate, longing and sorrow. It was often taken up just in the nick of time when all other means had been exhausted. There it rested, retired from service, separated from the whole, orphaned. A piece of flesh a few centimetres long, which could be tremendously expressive when need be.

Paavo sat down on a chair and took his time examining the piece. He had not asked them to mail it, but he now felt gratitude towards the senders. Paavo knew that he would not be able to thank them officially for the package for some time, but if the opportunity were to someday come, he would speak eloquently and at length.

Paavo looked at the piece and suddenly felt a strong desire to speak. He did not even remember when he had last spoken. He had either been splitting wood in the shed or looking out the bedroom window. At the birch tree he had planted, the stump that remained of the spruce tree, and the small field he had been digging potatoes out of for fifty years. The birch, the stump, and the potato field had looked foreign, as if someone had moved them there from somewhere. His gaze had not fixed on anything – it had roamed across the landscape like the wind, indifferent and foreign. His eyes had become dry cavities when the water had stopped flowing from them.

When did I last speak to Salme? Paavo thought as he looked at the piece. It has been quite a while, he thought, but how long I can't say. I do not know where my speech went. It disappeared like a bird from a feeder. Or the speech didn't disappear, just the words. I couldn't find them anymore. Or I couldn't find the right ones. I think words are important. They are tools. I learned that as a shopkeeper. Place them carefully if you want to make sales. People didn't just come to buy the yarn and buttons and needles – they also come to chat. If you just stood there silently in front of the balls of yarn, they could easily take you for a capitalist. But if you place your words nicely in a row like stones next to a path, then they even start looking at yarn they didn't originally have any intention of buying. Speech is good, but now it has left me, and I don't know when it will come back.

Paavo was afraid that the unspoken material would sour and soon rot the entire skull. People were made to say something. Not necessarily a lot, but something. Otherwise the connection is broken and all that keeps it hanging on to humanity is breathing. Paavo thought of Salme, who had become used to their shared moments of conversation. Salme is creeping around out there, withering away with every step, and could easily show up lying at the end of the flowerbed at any moment. She did still have the energy to have gone on two outings with her weaving group to another county, even though she did come back quiet.

Paavo walked to the door of the sewing room and was about to say something, but then remembered that Salme was out walking. Paavo went back into the kitchen and crouched in front of the freezer container. The piece, which had turned bluish, floated in the liquid. Paavo felt like saying to it what he couldn't to Salme.

If only you knew how much the secret weighs – at least five kilos. I can't tell Salme that I ordered you. I just can't. I would like to show you to Salme, but instead I have to hide you, or if worst comes to worst, destroy you. I can talk to Salme about the other thing, the thing that caused you to be floating in this liquid. And I should talk about it, because it is my and Salme's common business, the sorrow I mean. They've written and talked about it a lot in the papers, but not once have I heard it talked about in the way I have experienced it. Sorrow is a bad, ugly feeling. Right after the longing comes a violent urge – you feel like breaking and killing. Sorrow is a round, spiky steel ball swinging uncontrollably in the air, and then they talk about working through sorrow, as if you could even think about work like that when the sorrow falls on you and slices everything to ribbons. Sorrow made me so loud that I ended up mute. I didn't dare open my mouth, the things coming out of it the whole time were so inappropriate. Then the steel ball disappeared, and it was replaced with a pillow. Not a normal one, but a huge, shapeless, unnaturally soft one. When I laid my head on it, I didn't feel anything anywhere. The anger disappeared in that softness. And everything else, because I didn't know or feel anything. An unfeeling person, an unknowing person, an unknown person, that's what I was.

But now when I look at you, I feel like at least some kind of person for the first time in a long time. Is this where recovery starts, who knows? but at least I may be able to get a handle on speech again. Everyone should have a part of another person, if not the whole thing. And I wouldn't have wanted the one who you belonged to in my kitchen. A sample specimen is enough.

Paavo heard the front door rattle. He grabbed the freezer container, took a chair, climbed up on it and jammed the container into the top cupboard. Salme came into the hall, sitting down with a sigh and taking off her shoes. Paavo slipped into the bedroom and sat in front of the window. Salme came to the bedroom door to make sure her husband was in his place and then went into the sewing room. Paavo waited a moment and then walked to Salme's door.

Salme was sitting hunched over next to her sewing machine. Paavo tried to find appropriate words, but all that came to mind were inappropriate ones – those Paavo returned to his throat. The sewing machine knocked a seam together. Salme didn't hear Paavo come in.

"Is that the table cloth?"

"Yes."

"For Helena?"

"Yes. You're talking."

"Yeah. I thought I had to. That it was time."

"No more chopping?"

"No. It's full."

"What?"

"The shed."

"Are you going to talk all the time now or just this once?"

"I don't know. If I start talking, anything might come out."

"That's not a problem. What was the parcel slip about?"

"Hobby Hall sent the shawl."

"You got it for me?"

"Yes, for you."

"Show me."

"There will be time enough for that later. How is Ritva?"

"She booked a trip. To the Canaries. She wants to see the volcano. I don't remember the name."

"Teide. That's the name. It hasn't been active for years, but you can at least get the smell of it there, the sulphur or whatever," Paavo explained, noticing that he had got hold of speech and fearing that he would lose it if he didn't continue immediately. The feeling was the same as when as a child he had tried to pull a worm out of thick, muddy soil with his thumb and forefinger. If you gave the worm even a millimetre of slack, it retreated into its hole and disappeared into the darkness.

"Listen, Salme. I've been thinking lately what if we went on a trip? We've never been anywhere other than twice in the capital. Let's go and see what the world is like. And I also meant to say I'm sorry. Sorry that I've been like this, or rather like I have been. We have enough wood for five winters now. Being in my own head for months on end it occurred to me that a lot has been taken from us. Without permission. We've been robbed. Do you remember that word from the old world, 'robber baron'? They had the nerve to call button merchants names like that, even though with all the work we did our hourly wages weren't even as much as the men at the paper mill were getting. I've been thinking about how much has to be taken away for nothing to be left. And what is that nothing? We've been shown life and death – at least those experiences can't be taken away from us. But have we seen too much? That was what kept me thinking out there in the shed. This is that relativity stuff we talked about once. What is enough for a person? What was enough for us is too little for many entrepreneurs these days. What we understood as affluence is just scraping by for someone else. Did they build a new kind of human without us noticing? Did they secretly develop a completely new creature? I almost went crazy a couple of weeks ago when I started thinking about the children and you and everyone we know. I got a strange sort of feeling that everything was disappearing. You were off travelling with the weaving group then. I had to run over to Kallio's house. I knocked on the door, and Kallio answered, and when I had made sure he was alive and still in this world, I turned away and ran to make sure the Esso station was still in the same place as before and hadn't been borne away on the wind. If I could see Kallio, that that meant I wasn't crazy. Because I'm not. But that day I visited the place that Alfred Supinen talked about once. Do you remember? He said that humans had been fixed up with such big heads that you could get lost in them – inside the head, I mean. No other living thing has an imagination like this, one that can spread life out in so many directions sometimes that everything gets blurry. This is partially why I never cared about travelling, since my thoughts took me wherever I wanted to go for nothing. I meant to ask where Helena got the money for her therapy. I hear she's getting the full treatment with all the best listeners in the country with her around the clock. At least we don't have money like that. Maybe Pekka or Maija loaned it to her, although I doubt it was Pekka. Has Helena said anything to you about it? I just mean I hope there isn't any monkey business going on. Malmikunnases have never gone in for that sort of thing. We've never been in so much trouble that we haven't been able to take care of our taxes and bills ourselves. Isn't that right, Salme?"

Paavo went silent. Salme looked at her husband and wondered if anything more was going to come out or if she could say something now. Paavo was out of breath, waiting for Salme's reaction.

"Yes. Well. There you have it. Was I supposed to answer something?"

"About where Helena got money like that."

"Maybe she sold her car."

"She doesn't have a car."

"Perhaps she sold her sofa set."

"You can't get money like that selling furniture."

"A grown woman can always come up with something. Since you haven't been talking, let me ask, do you know what Pekka has been up to?"

"A general manager doesn't have time to call home."

"But a service man would."

"What do you mean by that, Salme?"

"Nothing. Would you like some juice? Your throat must be dry after talking so much."

Salme went into the kitchen and then yelled back, "Why is the chair dragged over here? Have you been in the top cupboard?"

Paavo rushed after Salme into the kitchen.

"I was just organizing things a bit . . . the parts for the juicer and . . . then the dustpans and . . ."

"What are you putting those up there for? They belong in the cleaning closet. I'll get them down."

"You don't need to go rummaging around up there. I'll put them away later," Paavo said and moved the chair over to the table. "Let's have that juice. I feel dizzy."

"Sit down for goodness sake."

Paavo sat, and Salme gave him a glass of sea-buckthorn berry juice. Paavo drank it in two gulps and sighed. Then they sank into their own thoughts.

Salme thought that Paavo was now Paavo again. Or at least almost.

Something in him had been knocked into a new position, but that wasn't any wonder. We don't end up at the finish line the same as we were when we left. Once when we drove the Simca over a pothole, afterwards all of the things in the boot were in a completely different order from before we hit the hole. How is that for a metaphor? But the truth is that life doesn't spare anyone, not even the ones that think it does and use plastic surgery to try to add on more years. The reaper man doesn't show you your wrinkles in a mirror – he cuts us all down like grass with his long, curved knife. But what am I going on about? It is clearly a sign of recovery that Paavo has started asking about things that aren't his business. Isn't the main thing that Helena gets treatment? It's all the same where the money came from for it. We've been like sheep before the law and the taxman and everything for decades. It isn't anyone's business how I send my daughter to that place by the seashore to get patched up.

Paavo was thinking that Salme was beautiful, even though she did try to get into the top cupboard. We're private people here, even though we live together. I have always given Salme space to do her own things, and she has always given me the same bit of freedom. So for the moment, the top cupboard will stay shut. I took this part of him, because he took everything from my daughter. And I will go to the grave with this, and if God shows up on the scene unexpectedly and actually exists, I'll tell him just how things are. And if he sees fit to stone me and throw me over on the hot steam side, I'll say to him that I had worse times down there on Earth than you could ever create here in Hell! And if God turns out to be a reasonable type, he will overlook the whole thing and let me take the freezer container along with me as a memento.

Then Paavo and Salme looked at each other and smiled a little.

THE CONSUMER

My name is Salme Sinikka Malmikunnas, and everything I have said has been twisted. It doesn't go word for word the way I told it, just in the same general direction. This was clear to me from the moment I talked with the author the first time.

I have now read this whole stack of paper the author sent the week before last. I had to explain to Paavo that a woman from the *raanu* group had sent a little larger pile of patterns all at once.

I had to set the papers aside when *that* part came.

I guessed that he wouldn't keep his word not to write about it.

I sold him life, not death.

I couldn't stand to read it with these eyes.

But now that it has been a while since I read it, I don't think of the author with anger. I can't afford feelings that big anymore – I don't have the energy for them. Everyone does his work as well as he can and sells it on. The consumer is the one who makes the final decision with his wallet, whether he will pay for the truth or contortions of it.

That's the trick if he wants to get a book out of these papers and then get the book sold. If a book does come out of all this, he will have to go to the book fair. We did make an agreement that he won't tell the idea behind the book or the story of where it came from, but instead just say like all the others that it all came from his own head and it is all a lie from start to finish.

I don't envy this profession either. We poor humans have to try to sell everything. Helena has said some ugly words about this now that she's in better shape. She said that people have to submit to everything here in this world. That you have to sell the work of your hands, your arse, your speech, your knowledge and your skills. And Finns have even learned how to sell silence. We won't be running out of that anytime soon. The soughing forests will sooner disappear. She said that somewhere between Kuopio and Iisalmi there was a sort of silence centre where you can pay to sit on a bed with your mouth closed. As a former shopkeeper I didn't comment or start poking fun at the silence entrepreneurs, especially since I've paid at least the recommended retail price for muteness here in my very own home.

Given the circumstances, things are going well for us. Especially if you compare it to the state we were in at the beginning when I first met the author. "It pays to compare," Alfred Supinen always said. If Alfred's finances were in a slump, he said, "What's this compared to the position of the Romanian Gypsies?"

Evil has now received its reward, as we read in the paper, but in my opinion it was paid to that man in an unreasonably large lump sum. Just reading about it was hard enough, at least for me. Paavo was just in a good mood and said that everyone had to start by learning his letters. In the paper it said that if they had recovered the tongue immediately and the surgeons had connected it back up to the stump, the man would have been able to speak to the end of his days almost flawlessly. But since the part wasn't returned, his speech will remain a sort of gurgling forever, even though you will be able to make out some of it. I will say that it must have taken rough men to be able to go and do a job like that.

I was able to use the seven thousand euros to buy Helena such good treatment that a completely different person walked out of the doors of the hospital than went in. I didn't get my whole first-born back, but my first-born nonetheless. The money went to a good cause. And hopefully everything I told the author did too.